THE MAN ON THE TRAIN

THE MAN ON THE TRAIN

W. J. Chaput

St. Martin's Press
New York

But for the simple fact that Winston Churchill did travel through Vermont during the night of December 28/29, 1941, all events, characters, and settings in this novel are products entirely of the author's imagination.

Design by Jessica Winer

Library of Congress Cataloging in Publication Data

Chaput, W. J.
    The man on the train.

    1. World War, 1939-1945—Fiction. I. Title.
PS3553.H314M3   1986   813'.54   86-13702
ISBN 0-312-51112-4

10 9 8 7 6 5 4 3 2

*This first one is for
Nana*

An author's note of gratitude:

to Martin H. Wennar, M.D., surgeon and frustrated expedi-
tionist to Kilimanjaro and Peru, for his medical advice;
to Edward Menkens, who niftily avoided conscription into
the Union Army, for his early years in Addison County;
to Paul G. Ford, who believes he figures in this novel;
to Jon B. Haynes, who is a good friend and nothing short of
Turbo 5;
to Walter H. Tappan, who was with me in the beginning
and for whom incredulity has become virtue;
and to Mary G. Young for her generosity, constancy, and
love.

—April 16, 1986
Vermont

A letter to President Franklin D. Roosevelt from Prime Minister Winston S. Churchill

Former Naval Person to President Roosevelt   *9 Dec. 41*

I am grateful for your telegram of December 8. Now that we are, as you say, "in the same boat," would it not be wise for us to have another conference? We could review the whole war plan in the light of reality and new facts, as well as the problems of production and distribution. I feel that all these matters, some of which are causing me concern, can best be settled on the highest executive level. It would also be a very great pleasure to me to meet you again, and the sooner the better.

2. I could, if desired, start from here in a day or two, and come by warship to Baltimore or Annapolis. Voyage would take about eight days, and I would arrange to stay a week, so that everything important could be settled between us. I would bring Pound, Portal, Dill, and Beaverbrook, with necessary staffs.

3. Please let me know at earliest what you feel about this.

ONE

THERE ARE THOSE WINTER NIGHTS in Vermont when the dark is as dark as death—and as sullen.

On one of those nights, a night of deepest dark in 1941, a night little more than a week after the melding fears of the Japanese excursion into Pearl Harbor, most of Vermont huddled in distrust and early winter gloom. From the highest mountains above the town, Richmond must have seemed a pitiful sight at eleven o'clock, with the pulsing of its few lights like lost galaxies in a distant frozen void. But the lights were there to establish human enterprise and guard the sleepers beneath the shoulders of the black hills. A river, a trench of slush and sluggard brown water called the Winooski, wandered westward down the valley like a ribbon of wet rubber on the move.

The bridge across the Winooski River was an impermanent scaffolding of wires and rusted steel beams. Hours before on this night, people who lived across the river had listened to the war news from New York with foreboding. The kids had been stashed, and the beds of the old people rattled and shook through the darkened houses on dreams of crazed yellow faces and rape.

A rail line, the silvery threads of the Central Vermont Railroad, cut the town in two with a grade crossing at

1

Melon's Feed Store. And beyond the tracks, very near the river and tucked away behind the crumbling brick blocks that housed the retail hopes of Richmond's Chamber of Commerce, the railroad station was alight and awake for the Washingtonian, the overnight express train from Montreal to Washington, D.C.

The Washingtonian never stopped at Richmond, but Whitley Raymond, the station master, had a fire in the stove and a tuft of smoke over his chimney as he waited beneath the yellow lights on the platform for the roaring headlight to appear out of the dark.

Whitley Raymond plugged one nostril with his thumb and blew his nose between the rails at his feet. He looked up at Janice Brill's windows across the way. She'd gone to bed, he thought. Her house and the few others seemed so empty, as though the town had been evacuated. Whitley Raymond cleared out his other nostril and decided to go in and telegraph Lucien Beebe, the clerk in Essex Junction, to find out if the train had left there yet.

Whitley Raymond went through his empty waiting room and into his office, where his desk was built into the bay windows. Lucien Beebe answered quickly with his practiced hand: Train Number 20 was still in Essex Junction. Beebe said the mail was on board the Washingtonian, and he thought Jaeger would have the train moving any second.

"Shit," Whitley whispered. He knew that no conductor on the railroad ran as late as Alex Jaeger, the Central Vermont conductor this night until White River Junction.

The train had left Montreal's Bonaventure Station at 8:40 P.M., hoping to cover the 671 miles to Washington in a tad under seventeen hours. After the flat emptiness of southern Quebec, the express had crossed the Canadian–U.S. border at Highgate Springs to race along the shore of Lake Champlain before it turned eastward and buried itself in the black interior of Vermont.

2

Whitley Raymond went out to spit from the platform onto the oil-soaked ballast of crushed granite. Parker, the engineer, would have to make up the lost minutes in the miles between Essex Junction and Montpelier; he'll be going like thunder when he passes here, Whitley thought.

In Essex Junction, Lucien Beebe also waited. The hissing bulk of the Washingtonian, with its eleven cars in a livery of green, almost sable, stood on the tracks under his train shed. They were late.

Beebe left his telegraph key and went out onto the platform. There was no sign of the conductor. Beebe strolled along toward the locomotive. The baggage car door growled and thumped as Beebe passed. The engineer, Parker, stood at the top of the ladder between the locomotive and its tender. "Where the hell's Jaeger?" he shouted. "We're two minutes out and I've got steam."

Beebe knew how engineers hated to let off valuable steam while they waited. And with time to make up, Parker would want a full steam chest to make the next stop, Montpelier, on time. Too much steam and the locomotive would blow itself up. That delicate imperative haunted some engineers, and Parker was more haunted than most. He launched a gob of tobacco juice over Beebe's head.

"Dark night," Beebe said.

"Damn him," Parker said, turning for his whistle cord. The locomotive's whistle yelped.

"Everything's on," Beebe called up.

Parker was a tall man, his face a round moon against the black night above the telegraph clerk. Beebe looked back into the train shed, and as he did, a man ran from the waiting room to the train.

The conductor jumped down from a middle coach to meet the man. The passenger got on quickly. Jaeger raised his arm.

3

"Romeo!" Parker bawled to his fireman. "Hit the stoker. We're gonna move. Adios, Lucien. How's your boy?" Parker leaned out of his window high above the platform and Lucien Beebe to watch for Jaeger's signal.

"He's better," Lucien shouted. The locomotive stirred. There was a rumble as though molten rock were about to seep up between the ties under the rails. Lucien backed away from the train.

"Babies can get awful sick," Parker shouted quickly.

The conductor lowered his arm and Beebe thought he'd heard Jaeger's yell.

"You take care." Parker grinned at him. The conductor was just reaching for a railing on one of the cars.

"Romeo!" Parker shouted behind him into the cab. "Wake up, goddamn it." He lifted his fingers to Lucien in the callousness of a man with the weight of purpose on him.

The locomotive's drivers turned slowly, its two hundred tons gathering energy. The couplings ground tight; the Washingtonian moved with a tractive force of 46,300 pounds, the 4-8-2 Mountain-type locomotive dragging its cars easily; with its high drivers, automatic stoker, and superheated steam, the engine had frightening power.

Parker looked back once more to be certain he was clear. He twitched his fingertips again to Lucien Beebe—an oddly aesthetic gesture from Parker.

Lucien Beebe thought he heard Parker shout again over the roar of steam in the cylinders. And as the cars went by, he looked for the conductor. But Jaeger had everything locked up and tight.

Whitley Raymond stood on his platform, his bare hands in his back pockets.

The night was indeed quiet, he thought. He yanked his watch out. Eleven-fifteen. And the town was sleeping. Whitley looked to check that the switches were set to guard the siding into the freight shed. He'd hear Parker's whistle any second now. Almost Christmas, he thought. With the war, there were few decorations, few lights, as though Pearl Harbor had banished all thoughts of tenderness. There wasn't time, Whitley thought. Roosevelt's squawky radio voice had canceled all the good things.

Whitley saw the slow swing of Gus Dragon's lantern down near the far crossing. Dragon, the crossing guard, was outside his shack, poised with his crank to lower the crossing gates when the Washingtonian went through.

Whitley took out his watch again.

On board the Washingtonian, Alex Jaeger, the conductor, had everyone settled. He'd made his rounds of the other cars and gently eased the door shut as he entered the last car, the crowded parlor car. Baskins was in his usual seat near the middle of the car.

Jaeger didn't look at Baskins, but paused beside the paint salesman's feet.

"Snowin' yet?" Baskins called up to him.

"Not yet," the conductor answered.

There were two card games in the car and a thick gray pall of smoke and whiskey. Baskins had interrupted his conversation with two other salesmen to speak to Jaeger.

"Gentlemen, we're in good hands with this guy," Baskins said to the two men, pointing his glass of whiskey at Jaeger. "Good man. How's the wife?"

"Haven't got one," Jaeger answered. He pushed his train roster into his coat pocket.

"You haven't?" Baskins laughed. "Hell, I thought you was married."

Jaeger smiled and turned to leave the car slowly. He could hear Baskins yammering away to the men who'd had the misfortune to sit near him. Leonard Baskins coughed a lot, shouted the punch lines to his hardware-store jokes, and an-

5

noyed almost everyone on every train ride. His weedy voice rasped over the seats, even above the laughter and talk of the other men in the car. Baskins had an alcoholic's thinness, a caved-in chest, and a face of narrow flat cheeks. His eyes dulled to the dark stare of a rodent whenever he stopped talking.

Jaeger left the car.

Parker had the train booming through the rock cuts and fields before Williston, as Romeo fed the monster a noxious meal of crushed coal and steam. From the black summits of the mountains above Richmond, the locomotive headlight glimmered like a shooting star trailed by a bright orange flare whenever Romeo cracked the doors on the firebox to bathe the cab in hot flame and smoke. Parker kept his feet planted against a water feed pipe, his eyes—like hot nickels—reflecting the roaring glare beside him.

In the parlor car, Baskins saw the man walk down the aisle. He was a blond stranger with his hands stuffed into his hunting coat, obviously able to balance easily against the motion of the train. Leonard Baskins went back to his two cronies, who were grinning to each other. "So—here's where it gets good. I says to this fella, 'You've got girls here?' This was a hardware show, right? We always stay in the Copley Hotel across the street, you see. Whenever we're in Boston. All of us. Anyways, this fella says, 'You follow me.' And do you know—upstairs they had cots—honest to god—they had cots with bitty curtains around 'em. And each cot had a girl in it!"

The blond man had stopped next to Baskins.

"Here we were at a hardware show an' they had girls right upstairs! Took me ten minutes to make up my mind which one I wanted. They was all young. Bazooms out to here."

The blond man bent over.

"You want somethin', pal?" Baskins asked. "Just a minute," he said to the other two.

The blond man whispered something. Baskins winked to his friends: he was listening.

"Now?" Baskins said.

The blond man stood away from Baskins. His light hair softly covered a bald spot. He wore hard canvas logger's pants and a black woolen sweater up around his neck. He was early thirties, his skin soft and pink, as though he'd been in the cold. But his eyes were hard and quiet like beads of blue glass glued into a china doll's sockets.

"Are you kiddin'?" Baskins asked. "I always leave my stuff in the cubbyhole up there. Why's he want it moved now?" And then to his cronies: "Damn conductor says my sample case is in the way. This conductor's a prick anyhow." And to the blond man: "Tell him I'll be there presently." And to his cronies again: "I'll be there when I damn well feel like it." He pushed a strap of hair off his face and patted it back into place over his ear.

The blond man left the car.

"Damn railroad. Ya' pay to get some comfort and they give ya' nothin' but trouble. Not like the Pennsy, I tell ya'. There's a railroad. These hicks want to be like the big boys. Ha!"

He dumped the last of his whiskey into his mouth and left the glass on the round table between them. "I'll be right back," he said to the two men. "I wanna tell ya' about the girls. Gorgeous! They were gorgeous. Ever been to a hardware show? No? Wait—I'll be back soon's I find out what this bullshit's all about."

He struggled to stand up. "Whoa!" he shouted. The others laughed, including the card game across the aisle.

Baskins went from chair to chair, greeting everyone as he tottered up the aisle. He had trouble with the door. A rush of air sucked the handle out of his hand—an outside door between the cars had been left open.

He gave the handle another lurching tug and wedged his shoe in the crack, then his shoulder. The air hit him with a

7

blast of rigid cold. Finally between the cars, on the shifting grate over the couplings, Baskins gripped the raw steel edges around him to steady his lunge for the next car across the plate. Black air spilled through the open door to his right. He had the drunk's fear of the commonplace, as though he couldn't figure all the odds neatly.

The blond man stepped out of the shadows on the other side of the grate. Baskins's ears tickled with the cold. He focused as best he could. "Watch it, fella. This ain't easy," he said, the fear coming into his tiny eyes. "You go by," he said. "Come on, you go by—I'll wait for you."

The blond man blocked the door into the next car. His solidness in the heave of the train angered Baskins.

"Come on, for chrissakes," Baskins yelled. "Goddam hicks. Hurry up—go on by!"

Baskins looked quickly out the open door next to him. He was very cold suddenly, and he shuddered. He thought the blond man didn't understand. He decided to make his move. One leap, clutching the folds of rubber curtain, would get him there.

The blond man stepped onto the grate. He smiled, reaching for Baskins. "I'll help you," he said.

Baskins felt the man take his arm, both hands to his upper arm. Baskins almost fell over, his knees buckling. "Whoa!" he yelled. The man lifted him. Baskins clung to the curtain—he was on the grate, the couplings below, but at least he wasn't near that door. "Thanks, brother. This ain't easy," he said, gauging the short distance to the next car's platform. "Okay, I'm ready. Here I go."

Baskins reached out with his free hand, expecting the blond man to release his other arm. "Let go!" he shouted. "Let go!" The man held on. "I've got it—thanks, pal. Let go, will ya'?"

The blond man's smile had gone.

"Come on, let go!" Baskins whined.

Baskins watched the blond man's coat move. He had something in his hand. Baskins tried to focus. He couldn't. One of the man's hands came up against his forehead and pinned his head against the curtain. ". . . the hell's the matter with you?" Baskins sputtered. He opened his tiny eyes wide to look at the blond man. Then Baskins was afraid— more frightened than he'd ever been in his life.

The blond man hit him hard on his neck. It felt like a hornet's sting. "Oh, shit!" he whimpered. "Don't. Don't do that!" His neck was on fire. Piss soaked his pants like warm cream. "Don't do that," he cried.

His eyes inflated like little white balloons. His breathing stopped.

The blond man released his forehead. Baskins lurched, he was sliding, his feet useless. He tried to throw his hands out, but the blond man grabbed one of his arms.

The roar shook his brains and shattered his vision. "Don't do that," he rattled. But he knew no one could hear him. "Don't do that," he said inside what was left of his consciousness. "Don't do that . . ."

"Parker, you sonofabitch, you're almost on time," Whitley said to himself when he saw the locomotive's headlights sweep around the curve a quarter-mile away. He put his watch away. Gus Dragon had the gates coming down. The town slept and this train would rip through Richmond like a rocket. He stood back from the edge of the platform. "Must be doin' seventy," Whitley said quietly. A railroad man to his bones, Whitley Raymond loved the shudder in the rails. Parker had a monstrous plume of grey smoke spewing from his stack over the bright beam of the headlight.

Whitley jumped when Parker let the whistle go for the crossing. Gus had the gates down; Whitley saw him with his lantern in the road. There were no cars.

9

The platform trembled. Whitley got ready to wave. He raised his arm. Parker always watched for him. Here it comes, Whitley thought. He could see Parker's hand stuck out into the fierce night wind as the train shook the platform, its whistle blasting high up into the dark mountains. Then the thing came at him. Whitley screamed and leapt out of the way. There was a gigantic crash of splintered wood and glass. He hit his head on the platform, but stayed flat on his belly as the deafening blast died away.

The lights of the train passed the crossing.

"What the hell?" Whitley said, scrambling to his feet. His platform had become a junkyard. Where his bay windows had been, there was a hole and the white office walls. Papers fluttered in the air.

Something had come off the train.

"Holy shit," Whitley said when he saw the baggage cart. He spun around. The train was gone, the night silence coming back. Something crashed again inside the station—the clock on his office wall bounced and tipped off his ticket desk. "Holy shit!"

The baggage cart was flat—its plank end-frames were gone. There had been two crates of plumbing fixtures on the cart, waiting for the kid in the morning.

Whitley staggered toward the cart. Bits of sink and piping were strewn the length of the platform. "Holy shit," he whispered.

The thing had completely cleaned off the cart, including the crates, and gone straight through his office windows. If he'd been in there on the key, he'd be dead, he thought.

"Holy shit," he said as he gingerly stepped over bits of torn wood and part of a white toilet bowl.

Whitley peered inside through the hole into his office. "Holy shit," he whispered. Glass and plaster and torn wood. His chair upside down.

And then he saw the face.

10

Whitley wrapped his arms around his chest—he felt as though his heart would burst.

There was a human face with eyes open, teeth smiling. It had hair. And it was peeking out from inside his flag cabinet. "Holy shit." The blood shined in the bright overhead lights, shined on the desktop—the telegraph key was gone. Blood was spattered across the floor, and it leaked from the face in the flag cabinet.

"Holy shit," Whitley said.

TWO

KEMPER FELT THE FREIGHT ELEVATOR SHUDDER after the third floor. He reached for the greasy wooden wall to steady himself and knew what it was to be fifty-eight and prematurely spent.

When the door slid open he saw boxes piled to a whitewashed ceiling and a worn path on the concrete floor ahead of him. He didn't like this. The warehouse was littered with tattered bits of cloth and heaps of hats. He saw some overcoats hung on an iron pipe.

He was here to meet with the FBI on a dingy December morning in 1941.

He let himself into the outer room of the office. Lit by a single bare bulb, it had once been some sort of foreman's office, but now its glass walls were whitewashed. "I'm Frank Kemper," he said to the college kid at the desk as he continued into the next room.

"Just a minute!" the kid shouted. "Moffet is on the telephone."

Moffet was a chunky forty with red hair and an acne-scarred face. Kemper shook Moffet's hand and sat heavily into a chair. The windows in this room were round, like church windows, and if Kemper had kept his bearings, looked out high over Fifth Avenue. A white room with a long table for a desk. Moffet hung up the telephone and opened a drawer. Kemper knew this was not going to be pleasant.

12

"I've heard about you—heard your name," Moffet said into the drawer. "How are you feeling?"

"I'm all right," Kemper said. He's done more than hear about me, Kemper thought.

On the table there was a plaster cat's skull with long delicate incisors. To one side of the piles of paper was a relic of a National cash register with a red NO SALE rung up in its window.

Moffet was waiting for him, pausing over an open file, watching him. "This dump is a bankrupt exporter's setup. Guy shot himself in the gents' out back. We're just using it. You ready?"

Kemper tried to smile, but drew in his breath slowly.

"There's a guy—" Moffet said, "There *was* a guy. Name was Baskins—Leonard Baskins. He was a German courier who carried their mail and money all over the Northeast. Regular Abwehr type. This Baskins was a zero. We turned him two months after he went into business and sent him on his way because he was harmless. He helped bring some of their agents in over the Canadian border—mostly New England, New York State once in a while. This guy's dead. He killed himself two days ago. And we need an ID. He's in—" Moffet checked the papers in the file, "—Richmond, Vermont. In a funeral home or something. He worked as a paint salesman. The coroner's office in Vermont called the paint company telephone number—that's us—to say he'd jumped off a train. Guy was finished, anyway. He was an alcoholic and weak. Too far from home and no smarts. You with me, Mr. Kemper?"

"Every word," Kemper said.

Moffet made a sucking noise in his teeth. "These Germans are so thin on top, know what I mean?"

"Not all of them," Kemper said.

"You'd know that, wouldn't you?" Moffet said. "Well, the creeps Canaris sends us are thin all right. Not a pro in

13

the bunch. All amateurs and all very dim. You know this Baskins, don't you? Or, knew him?"

"I've seen him. You keep thinking like that," Kemper said, "and they'll have the FBI by its balls in no time."

Moffet grinned. "Not likely. We just got through that Brooklyn mess."

Moffet meant the spy trials of nineteen German agents in Brooklyn. The FBI had finally acted with resolution, after years of tripping over themselves, and had cleaned out a raft of enemy agents along the East Coast.

"Don't pat yourselves on the back yet," Kemper said. "The war is well and truly on now and you'll meet a few Germans you won't like."

"Don't think so, Mr. Kemper. We're tight."

"You're too tight, Moffet. You only work with what you know."

"Isn't that why we have you Naval Intelligence people with us? Why the hostility, Frank?"

"Don't call me Frank."

"We're too cocky, is that it?"

Kemper flipped his hand, as if pushing Moffet away absently.

Moffet grew agitated. He closed the file, reached into his vest pocket, and took out a cigarette lighter.

"Whom do I see?" Kemper asked, gathering his coat.

"See the superintendent of the railroad up there. His name is Cody. Baskins's body is in the Ball Funeral Parlor in Richmond. Can you beat it? A funeral parlor. Wait a minute, please. I'm not quite finished."

Kemper had moved to leave.

"There's a Montreal cop named Quenneville. Marcel Quenneville. You should check in with him. Your office has asked that we relay orders to you. They need you in Ottawa right after Christmas, and . . . You can't wait to get out of here, can you?"

Kemper sagged so suddenly he knew Moffet saw it.

14

"Churchill's coming for another chat with old Franklin. It's very likely he'll go up to Ottawa while he's here to see Mackenzie King. Naval Intelligence wants you in Ottawa by the twenty-seventh of December. So do we. You can run up to Vermont, be back here in the city for Christmas, and get a train to Ottawa after the holiday.

"We've got cash for you!" Moffet tossed an envelope across the table. "Unlike the ONI, we need accurate travel vouchers at the end of each trip. That shouldn't be too hard for you."

Kemper got out of the chair a tired man. His overcoat felt like chain mail. "That it?" he asked.

"Just be sure Baskins is Baskins. When we get your ID, we'll probably ask you to either bury the bum there or ship him back here. Depends on the coroner's office in Vermont. They're running tests on what's left of him. Other than that, it's a free ride for you."

Kemper had seen too many Moffets, too many shabby offices, and had bumped through too many free rides.

"See you in a few days," Moffet said, standing at last. "Vermont's pretty dull this time of year, Frank."

But Kemper had gone out into the first office and out into the cold warehouse to walk through the stacked cardboard remnants of some poor bastard's business. A man had shot himself in the gents' over this trash heap, Kemper thought. "Not worth the moment it takes to die," he said to himself as the freight elevator thumped down to the lobby.

Kemper was on the sidewalk before he realized Sheridan was behind him.

"Hold on, hold on," Sheridan had said, like a Cockney cabbie. And when Kemper turned to face this man holding his arm, Sheridan smiled. "You don't look well, Frank."

Sheridan was the director of British Intelligence, or MI6., in the United States. The British had been in New York for a long time. A cold rain fell on them as Kemper walked on

15

with Sheridan at his side. "I'd like some coffee," Kemper said.

"Did you see Moffet?" Sheridan asked.

"I saw him," Kemper said, quickly veering off the sidewalk and into the street. There was an automat across Fifth Avenue. The rain fell harder now.

"Did he tell you about Arcadia?" Sheridan said as they waited for three trucks to grind by from the intersection.

"He told me about Churchill," Kemper said, ducking behind the last truck and onto the curb.

"Same thing. Awfully good to have you Americans finally with us, Frank."

"Some of us have always been with you," Kemper said. The air in the automat was warm and sticky with grease.

"Not like this," Sheridan said. "I love the apple pie in these places."

Kemper got coffee while Sheridan got a wedge of apple pie from one of the windows. They took a table at the window away from the other patrons.

"You look thin, Frank."

Kemper smiled and dumped sugar into his coffee.

"You going to pack it in after this?"

"I have packed it in, Edward," Kemper said. "It was packed in for me."

"Just as well. You've done your part. You deserve a rest. How awful was it?"

"Don't have one," Kemper said. "I've never felt anything like it. When your heart stops, Edward, everything stops."

"I knew you were going to see Moffet this morning. I wanted to see you too. But not him. Moffet doesn't always understand these things, Frank. These FBI people are a queer lot—they're all policemen. How's your coffee?"

Kemper snapped a match and touched the end of his cigar with it. "Coffee's fine, Edward. I'm glad to see you."

"We're all terribly glad you're alive."

"I'm happy for that, too," Kemper said.

16

"Sylvie's well—and David?"

Kemper grinned. The cigar smoke nudged the window and hung there in midair. "They're fine, at last report. Haven't seen either of them for months. David was in Amsterdam. But he'll be in London now. And your son?"

"Royal Engineers in Dulwich. He saved a man's life, I'll have you know. He jumped into a heavy sea off the South Coast after a naval cadet of some sort—the boy had fallen from a buoy tender. Martin went in after him."

Kemper patted Sheridan's sleeve. A Yellow Cab had pulled up outside. A woman was getting out. Long legs and packages. The day was very dark. Kemper wondered where she'd come from. "He's a good boy, Edward. I'm not surprised. Sheila would have been very proud of him," he said.

Sheridan's features drooped slightly at the mention of his dead wife's name. Kemper saw him regain his strength. Sheridan cleared his throat and batted away some of the cigar smoke hovering between them. "I saw your Janet not long ago," Sheridan said. "She's changed. She looks eager now. I wish I'd known you two were having trouble."

"*We* weren't," Kemper said. "I was."

"What happened?"

"I don't know. We were going to meet for tea at Guptill's one afternoon, and I watched her from the window before I went in . . . and realized I didn't want to open that door. I didn't want to go inside."

Sheridan tilted his head slightly; Kemper recognized that the man's deafness had increased.

"That was the last time we did anything together. She and Sylvie left London for home. We wrote two letters each—the lawyers wrote the rest."

"And the cellist?"

"I don't know," Kemper said. "I haven't seen her for years."

"She was a beauty."

Kemper took a long, slow breath. "I had a chance with

her. I actually drove away from her in Leeds. I watched in the mirror. She had her hands in her coat pockets . . . never waved, never moved. And I drove away. As simple as that." Kemper paused, flicked his cigar ash on the floor. "I was a fool to drive away from that woman. Had I to do it all again . . . lost chances."

"And you couldn't open the door to Guptill's afterwards."

"You were always such a decent man," Kemper said. "Too damned decent."

"Wish I could reciprocate," the Englishman smiled. His white, white teeth had always surprised Kemper with their perfection.

"I have to go to Vermont for a few days," Kemper said. "An Abwehr courier named Baskins—I don't remember his real name—killed himself."

"We'd like you in Ottawa with us. Churchill is at sea now, but he'll have Christmas with the President, and if the War Cabinet is willing—and they may not be—the plan is for Churchill to keep the Canadians coming. This conference, Arcadia, should mean the beginning for us all, Frank. Churchill wants to leave here this time with a signed agreement that the Americans are with us. We wanted another meeting like Placentia Bay. Bermuda, I think. But Roosevelt is too ill. They'll do it this time, Frank. With war declared, everything can come out into the open. Everything aboveboard. We really are terribly pleased to have you with us. It was dicey for us with all the America First talk—your Father Coughlins and the German-American Bund."

Much of what Sheridan referred to was alien to Kemper. Before Pearl Harbor, and before the declaration of war by Congress on December 8, Kemper knew that many Americans had fought hard for the United States to either remain isolated from the European conflict or to go with the Axis side. But with the Japanese visit to Pearl Harbor only days behind them, most Americans now gathered to the cause

18

and shut their mouths. The rabid Father Coughlin, a Catholic priest, was an anti-Semite who had broadcast his virulence for years to American audiences.

America was still new to Kemper after his eighteen years in England with the Office of Naval Intelligence. He'd been back in the United States for only ten months and had spent most of that time listening to his stuttering heart in one hospital after another.

"You should see your people yourself," Sheridan said. "But we've already got permission to have you with us in Ottawa."

"Why me?"

"We were hoping you'd help us out from time to time over here."

Kemper drew on his cigar. He remembered Berlin. The uniforms and flags. The Brown Shirts beating that woman on a fine spring day in 1938 in front of Gestapo headquarters on Prinz Albrechtstrasse.

"Besides," said Sheridan, "you know Churchill."

Kemper sipped his coffee and looked away from this earnest, gentle man. Fifth Avenue seemed strangely empty in the midmorning rain. So many intelligence people were gentle.

"Lots of people know Churchill," Kemper finally said.

"I do not," Sheridan said grimly.

Kemper had worked for them all: for the Americans as an officer in Naval Intelligence; as a liaison with the French for a time; and with the British in the end because only the British understood the German bitterness. Many of them were kind. Many of them were also dead.

"I'd like to see him," Kemper said slowly. "With this war, I may never again. I'm very tired, Edward."

"We're all tired."

"Don't be quick with me," Kemper said. "I mean *tired*. I'm fifty-eight years old—I've got hair that's white. Look at it!"

19

Sheridan dropped his eyes.

Kemper whispered: "This may be inconvenient for you people, but I'm not up to these cat-and-mouse games anymore. The Germans won't win . . . but they'll make everyone bleed. And I don't give a goddam."

Sheridan finished his coffee quietly. He refused to say anything more engaging than how greasy his pie had been. But as he got up to leave, his felt hat held at his chest, his regimental tie askew, he spoke softly: "I'd like to understand, Frank. Believe me, I would. These horrors in a man's life can drain away all his best. Remember me after Sheila died?" He touched Kemper's shoulder. "You've done your share for us and I wouldn't blame you for sitting on your arse forever."

"I may do that, Edward. I may just sit on my arse forever."

THREE

COMING HURRIEDLY INTO THE ROOM, Dr. Beam pulled his green braces off his shoulders and sighed loudly. Beam had white hair cut short. He hiked up his trousers before he sat down on the leather sofa.

"They're all out for lunch," he said loudly. "This lunch hour is my only rest. Funny how women love to run an office—point of pride with 'em. God, I could tell you stories about nurses that would give you another heart attack."

Kemper finished tying his bow tie and sat on the edge of Beam's polished desk, unwrapping a cigar.

"Stoke some nymphet with her mother's dreams, put a starched white dress on her, throw a cape on her so she looks like an extra in *Das Rheingold,* and send her flouncing out into the world to do real damage."

The naval hospital in Virginia wanted Kemper to see Beam periodically until he was completely recovered. "Completely recovered!" Beam had snorted. "They're dangerous. Who told you you'd ever be completely recovered? Damn fools. You can't recover completely from what happened to you."

That was October. This was Kemper's third physical with the old bird.

"Sit down," Beam sputtered. "You got another cigar you'd give an old man? Sit down! Jesus, you're as nervous as a whore on her wedding night."

Kemper handed the doctor a cigar and sat next to him on

the sofa. Beam had his shoes off now, his feet on a glass table. There was a wooden duck on the table with "I saw the Grand Canyon" carved into its back.

Beam got the cigar going and relaxed deliberately; Kemper saw a good deal of theater in this man. Beam shouted and screeched, laughed like a cannon shot, wore high-buttoned boots made from glove leather, and gave the most abbreviated medical exam Kemper had ever had.

"Very fine," Beam said. "Very fine cigar. Where do you get 'em?"

Kemper told him about the cigar shop on Thirty-eighth Street and the Argentine clerk who knew where the best thin cigars in the world were made.

"Panama?" Beam asked.

"Just the outer leaves. The inside is Cuban."

"Damn fine. Thirty-eighth Street between Second and Third. Funny about cigars, isn't it? Only the worst people smoke the best cigars."

Kemper let out a plume of smoke through his nose.

"Let's get this over with," Beam said. "You're as healthy as can be hoped for right now. Heart's healing nicely, thank you. I think you'll live for a bit. 'Course you won't live long eating those goddam chocolate bars."

"A filthy habit I picked up in Belgium," Kemper said. He felt frightened, but in a subtle way, as though his central nervous system knew something he did not.

"You'll kill yourself eating those damn things. Your heart is fine—for the present. Blood pressure's where it should be for a man who eats chocolate the way you do. You follow that diet those quacks gave you in Norfolk?"

Kemper said he didn't.

"I don't know anyone who could. Damn fools. I'll bet the place was filled with women."

"Nope," Kemper said. "Just nurses."

"I'm worried about your leg. Could have something to do with your heart. Could be arthritis—you're old

22

enough—but I doubt it. You limp more than you usually do?"

"Nope," Kemper said, drawing on the cigar.

"I thought you did when I walked in here with you. If you lost that lower leg in France in the Great War, you shouldn't be having much trouble with it now. God knows that was a long time ago. Did they shape the bone when they cut your stump?"

Kemper said they had. A field hospital in France had had a row of saws on the wall, and a British surgeon in a London military hospital had stitched it up.

"Still, you're getting old," Beam said. "Could be you'll get a twinge now and again from the stump. You are a wreck."

"I've been better," Kemper said.

"Somehow I doubt that. I wrote to the Navy and told them to throw you out—pronto."

"I'm obliged to you."

"Nothin' to it. Damn fools would believe anything. You mind that leg."

Kemper tapped his cigar ash into the saucer at his elbow. Dr. Beam drank coffee; Kemper realized there were cups and saucers all over the man's office and a stack of plates on the windowsill behind his desk. The window ran with the cold rain.

"Actually, I'm more concerned about your mind." Beam was staring toward his bookshelves across the room. "You've got to do something about your self-pity. Pity is very unhealthy for us. Grand for others, but self-pity will eat you alive. Nothing has happened to you that hasn't happened to many men. You said you loved to fish, so fish. Make fishing your life. You've had some trouble—lost your wife and marriage, had a whale of a heart attack—but you're alive. That's good. You *are* alive. Act like it."

Kemper bristled. "You needn't go on," he said.

23

Beam grunted. The office grew silent; the driven rain pattered on the window like buckshot.

"Many things in my life are not as they once were," Kemper said.

"I'll wager most things are the same with you," Beam said softly. "You've come off the course all right. I can't understand why you want to get back on. Change is good for us—all of us, including you."

Kemper looked for his suit jacket. The crease in his pants had been doubled by the cleaners. His shoes needed a shine. But Beam kept his silence intact once more; waiting, Kemper thought.

Beam lifted a smoke ring out over the Grand Canyon duck. "I'll grant you," he said, "that you nearly died. But there's a large distinction between nearly dead and being dead. And I'm sure that divorce business wasn't easy and isn't over yet. No one married and in harness for thirty-three years can chuck it all off in a year and a half. And your work has been important to you—is to all of us, I'd say. But there's something inert about you. Something in reverse, as if you never expose yourself to anyone. I suppose you've learned a bit of that in your job. Just seems dangerous to me."

"I've lived this long," Kemper said bitterly.

"Have you?" Beam shot back. "You've come up against a pretty mess at the age of fifty-eight. Our hearts don't just stop without provocation, you realize."

"I've had more than a few moments over the years when I thought I might be breathing my last," Kemper said slowly. "But I have never felt the cold breath I felt when my only heart stopped. I feel it now." Kemper realized he had told Beam a secret.

Beam waved his cigar in the air, as if he were whacking flies on a summer porch. "Sounds about right," he said. "You had a peek over the edge."

Kemper stood up.

"You need something to get your eye out of the gutter," Beam said.

Kemper got his coat from the table in the corner. "Go on," he said, adjusting his watch chain across his vest.

"I don't think so," Beam said. "I haven't the heart myself anymore. One of the profound hazards of my trade is having to watch people killing themselves. Mind your stump—you're not young."

Kemper wanted to get out as easily as he could. "I'm going up to Vermont tomorrow," he said. "I'll be back before Christmas."

"How pleasant for you," Beam said sarcastically. "Why are you going?"

"I'm still a cog in the Navy. Until they read your letter."

"Forget the Navy—find a place to fish in the spring. But you won't do that, will you? They'll start the music, and you'll dance again, you damn fool."

Kemper left Beam in his office and went quickly to the street to find a taxi, all the while mumbling to himself. And when the cabbie asked him "Where to, bub?" Kemper thought he'd tear the man's head off. Instead, he swallowed his bile and said, "The Plaza," and enjoyed the gray rain in the trees along the edge of Central Park.

FOUR

KEMPER WAS AGAIN REMINDED of the war gloom when he spotted the watchful faces peering from under the awning of the Plaza Hotel. They laughed too quickly. They clutched at bags and swaddled themselves with scarfs; the women wore winter wraps. All of the clothes were in hues of black and brown, as though the Japanese might scream out of Central Park through mortar bursts. The American faces had the vigilance of the great forests when the stick snaps at night and the stag hangs on its indecision about whether to fight or run. Kemper guessed they'd run.

His smugness was real. He did feel superior to these huddled masses aghast that they were in for a fight. He'd been there for Naval Intelligence when Hitler and his crowd had moved into the old Chancellory Building in Berlin; he'd been there eavesdropping in a telephone booth with the American correspondent from the *Chicago Tribune* as Hitler and Chamberlain talked by themselves in a Munich corridor. Chamberlain had kept one hand on Hitler's shoulder, as if to connect with him.

Kemper knew the Germans; had lived and eaten with them. And liked them for their terrible ability to move men.

He turned away from the Plaza, walked around the fountain, and went down Fifth Avenue until he reached a shoe store beyond Fifty-seventh Street. He'd not have his old shoes polished; he'd buy a new pair. Americans didn't know, as the British were beginning to understand, that war brings rationing, and that good shoes are priceless in war.

The clerk went clucking into the back for a brown pair of boots—not unlike Dr. Beam's, Kemper mused. He kept his eye on the faces pressed to the shop windows. The hard, swallowing murk of a December afternoon in New York. These people will have to learn for themselves, he thought.

Sheridan had needed help with something this morning. Kemper didn't know what, but he was curious. Churchill would be in Ottawa. He would like to see him again. He liked the man. Liked his anvillike resolve to wage war with the worst of them.

On a day something like this one in 1938, Kemper had driven away from London to meet Churchill alone in a country inn near Colchester. Churchill was delighted, almost exasperated, with the bulky files Kemper had carried from Berlin in a diplomatic pouch. Here were Luftwaffe estimates for German bomber and fighter strength. Kemper had their current fuel stocks and production figures. Churchill pushed his plate and cutlery to one side. "Good god!" he said, over and over, as Kemper gave him the documents one by one. "I have a man in Berlin," Churchill said, as if reminding himself, "and we've known for years these men were low and liars, but never . . . I've never had figures like these."

Churchill gathered the papers into a neat stack and stuffed them into his satchel on the floor. The fireplace warmed their feet and the tiny dark room.

The clerk had the boots. Kemper paid for them and left the store to join the faces on the sidewalk. There had been many more diplomatic pouches after that one, more indications that the Germans were, to the last man, mendacious. Kemper had last seen Churchill in London in August of 1939 in a St. James flat. "You've taken great risks," Churchill had said then. Churchill, so long out of politics and

27

building brick walls at Chartwell, his country house, was back in the Admiralty as First Sea Lord. He was only weeks away from Downing Street as the King's first minister with his Coalition War Cabinet. And only weeks away from war.

"Great risks," Churchill said, his eyes bright. "We navy men do cling to each other, don't we? But then, who else is there? I daresay your people will be hard on you if they discover you've been sharing their secrets with me. I am in your debt. England is in your debt. We'll not forget what you've done, Frank."

Kemper had puffed on his cigar.

They finished that last brief evening together with monologues on the dangers and duties of marriage. Kemper's Janet had sailed months before for New York with Sylvie. David was in school in Paris. Although nothing final had been mentioned or decreed, Kemper was feeling his family dissolve. "I think I have played some part in this disturbance to your family," Churchill had said. Kemper said he had not, but then realized that he didn't know who had. For years Janet and the children had enjoyed London, and Berlin in '34 and '35, but near the end, Kemper found himself left out of their plans for birthday celebrations—after he'd missed too many.

The gaping crowd at the Plaza Hotel was gone. Kemper went inside to the Oak Bar and asked for a table in the corner. The park was there in the gloom, out the window at his elbow, across Central Park South. The cabbies' orange roof lights shined. The rain had turned to snow.

Kemper ordered a roast beef sandwich and coffee. His boots were brown and perfectly snug. The nearly black walls of the Oak Bar, the dull yellow lamps, and the hushed voices of men at the bar allowed him to feel safe, quiet, at rest, and very tired.

His life had collapsed in a heap in 1940. Janet divorced him in April. Late in the fall the London embassy dis-

28

covered that someone had been tossing the British lion sensitive chunks of American intelligence—and that the special someone was probably Frank Kemper. They proved nothing, although Kemper remembered the joy and consternation in that bastard Manning's face when, as chargé d'affaires, he'd complained of official incredulity in the matter. "We were at Yale together, Frank." As though being at Yale were a guarantee of anything.

Kemper was ordered back to the United States in February of 1941. His heart stopped in March.

Kemper bought a paper at the bar and went back to his table by the window. He wished someone would speak to him.

FIVE

THE DARK, WAXY SMELL of washed stone flooring greeted Kemper as he stepped into the lobby of her apartment building. Her maiden name, Janet Neary, had been near the bottom of the row of buzzer buttons; she'd answered quickly. Kemper hoped the meeting would be civil, or at least brief. He had the money with him; she'd be pleased with the unexpected cash in hand. She always was. "Her hand," Kemper said under his breath as the elevator opened high in the building. There was a thready green rug in the corridor, lights with pink shell shades along the walls to her door.

The click came as Kemper raised his hand to knock. The door opened. "Oh god," she said. The gleam in her face went out instantly, like a candle snuffed out by an east wind. "Come in. I have friends coming. I thought you were they. Come in."

Kemper went beyond her to wait in the narrow, cavelike hallway. Her perfume was fresh and too strong in the enclosed space. Kemper fished out the envelope. "I've sold the stocks—I've brought you exactly half."

"How are you?"

"Just over seventeen hundred dollars to you." He held out the Chase Manhattan manila envelope. "It's in cash. That's the last of it."

"I'm surprised to see you," she said. She hadn't closed the door completely, but waited with her back to the knob; she was confused.

"I'd like to have Sylvie with me this Christmas—for a

30

day or two. I'll call to set it up. When is she getting in?" Kemper asked.

"Sylvie left Chicago yesterday morning. She's here—not here—she'll be here in the morning. She's with Adele. They're shopping."

Adele was Janet's mentor in all things salacious. The woman ran a dress business somewhere on Manhattan. Kemper had never wanted to know where because Adele had left her claw scratches on their lives for years now. "Sounds very unpleasant," he said slowly. The expectant motion of this woman—once his wife—had been cut in midflight. Her coat and gloves were in a grey chair in the living room. Kemper looked back at her. "I'll call," he said.

The door buzzer frightened him when it went off. She pressed to let them in. "They're here," she said, trying to gauge how she was going to do all this. Kemper knew he had insinuated himself directly into her rather rigid privacy. How was she to do friends and the ex-husband in one exacting stroke? He'd help her.

He handed the envelope to Janet, this Janet Neary who now looked faintly familiar to him, yet not his, not his to know. "There isn't any more," he said.

"How are you?" she asked again.

Kemper moved to leave. He could hear the elevator begin to whine in the corridor. "I'm all right," he said.

She softened and blushed suddenly when she heard him lie. "It took you a long time—the recovery. You look fit."

"Fit for what?"

The elevator bumped open. "Sylvie and I have decided to go to Winter Park for Christmas—through New Year's actually. We've only just decided."

There were voices in the corridor—a woman laughing. Kemper stopped. "She won't be here?"

"She'd like to get away from all this dreary rain. This war has frightened her. Winter Park was her idea for Christmas."

"When do you leave?" he asked quietly.

31

"Tomorrow evening. We have a sleeper."

"I've got to go to Vermont tomorrow. I was going to come straight back." Kemper felt the resignation stiffen his bones. His daughter was only twenty. And this woman knew just what to say to make him yield. What was he, as the lost parent, to say to a child's wish to be where he wasn't?

Two men and a woman were at the door, the woman gently poking her head through to see what was inside. Her hair looked powdery and sun-beaten. The men waited outside. "Hi, hon," said the woman, her eyes taking Kemper in with a practiced glance. "Ready?"

Janet grinned and kissed her. "Hi, Bob. Hi, Bob."

"I'm Esther Randolph." The woman held her hand out to Kemper.

"I'm Janet's ex-husband." He thought the woman would know his name. And she must have, because she knew instantly how tentative this little event was to be. "I'll wait in the living room," she said, sliding between Kemper and Janet Neary.

Janet had the men coming through the door. Which one was hers? Kemper wondered. "Two Bobs," Janet said to him. "Makes it simple."

The men—both angular, with fresh haircuts and white scarves—smiled at Kemper. They said their names, but Kemper closed his coat and nodded to his ex-wife. "Enjoy Florida."

"Please call her, Frank. We'll be at the Coral."

He said he would, nodded again, and turned to walk to the elevator.

"Merry Christmas?" she called after him.

He wished her a Merry Christmas and listened to hear her door close as he waited for the elevator. He was nearly away when she shouted—not the words, but that familiar sound of her voice after him.

"Oh good," she said as he held the door. "This came

from David. I thought you'd like to have it. He's very worried about you."

Kemper took the letter—an Amsterdam postmark.

"He should worry about himself," Kemper said. "I wrote to him and told him to get off the Continent."

"He'll do that, won't he? I told him to go to Jessie's flat."

"Jessie's flat may not be there!" Kemper shrugged. "Parts of London are a wasteland."

The bright rain-soaked leaves in the oval garden behind their flat near the Thames came to him as a gauzy vision. It disturbed him. Memories of nightmares are frequently more frightening than the thing itself.

"David will be fine. So long as he leaves. He said he would," she said. "I thought you'd like to see his last."

Kemper hoped the leaves were there, hoped the bombs hadn't split their velvety skins in the garden that Jessie, a London friend, had shared with them.

"Thank you," he said. He pushed the button to drop out of her life. The remaining stocks had been their last piece of marital business. Finished.

As he rode down, he folded David's envelope in half and pushed it deep into his coat pocket. He'd not read this one. Not for a while, at least.

Many serious reasons required my presence in London at this moment when so much was molten. I never had any doubt that a complete understanding between Britain and the United States outweighed all else, and that I must go to Washington at once with the strongest team of expert advisers who could be spared. It was thought too risky for us to go by air at this season in an unfavourable direction . . . The Prince of Wales was no more. The King George V was watching the Tirpitz. The newborn Duke of York could carry us, and work herself up to full efficiency at the same time. The principals of our party were Lord Beaverbrook, a member of the War Cabinet; Admiral Pound, First Sea Lord; Air-Marshal Portal, Chief of the Air Staff; and Field-Marshal Dill . . . With me also came Sir Charles Wilson, who had during 1941 become my constant medical adviser.

SIX

KEMPER'S ONLY DIFFICULTY when he left the city early in
the morning concerned his resolve—he didn't want to go.
Beam had been right: strained music was in the air with an
invitation to the dance.

The city of St. Albans was at the end of an attenuated
tether. He drove for hours over wretched roads laced with
ice, through Middlebury in the afternoon where he thought
he couldn't drive any longer, through Burlington, and on
into the north where the darkness and distance seemed complete.

This isn't anywhere, he thought when he circled the park
in the center of St. Albans. There was one large hotel—the
Jesse Welden House. The stores and bank were shut up for
the night, the town's main street deserted.

Kemper left his car at the curb and climbed the wooden
stairs to the hotel's wide porch. Inside, the lobby smelled of
dust and wet wool. There was a dining room off the lobby,
a carpeted flight of stairs, and a desk of gleaming oak.
Strangely enough, Kemper felt pleasantly expectant as he
clanged the bell at the desk. The desk clerk said he had
room. "But you've missed supper."

Kemper signed the register.

"'Course there's a diner down the way if you're hungry."

Kemper wanted to wait for a bit. One of the tallest clocks
he'd ever seen slowly sliced the minutes with a pendulum
larger than a dinner plate.

34

"Top of the stairs, turn left. End of the hall on your right, Mr. Baskins. How long you think you'll be with us?"

"Long enough."

"The bar's open," the desk clerk said. He held out a key tied with string to a wooden stick.

This is small-town living, Kemper thought as he got the lights on in his room. The park maples were tall and close from up here. The tar paper on the porch roof at his window had a crust of old snow. Floral wallpaper that must have been forty years old gave the room a homely feeling. The single bed was brass, its bedspread white and clean, and the room was miserably cold.

"Not bad," he said to himself. Kemper's lost leg ached with the tension of the long drive. "Just what the doctor ordered."

He filled the bathtub quickly and lay in the rancid heat of the faintly sulfurous water. He wondered where he was. Canada was nearby. New York City was not. And this was not the Plaza Hotel. Still, the water was hot and he was very tired. "They'll start the music, and you'll dance again," he whispered.

SEVEN

HANNAH DOLL WAS HUNGRY. Mr. Burgoyne, the old sheep farmer, was the last customer of the day. He seemed not to know where he was.

Hannah crossed from her desk to the shelves next to the shop window to remind him that she closed at eight o'clock.

"I know," he said. Burgoyne had a beard like white Brillo and a blind eye. "I know," he said, raising his head to Hannah. "Seems a shame to leave this Huxley here just because I haven't the money."

Hannah knew what he wanted. The old man had been in days before reading portions of *Eyeless in Gaza*.

"Take it with you," she said and patted his hand.

He shook his head. "No, I'll not do that to you," he said, tipping the book back into its slot. "Times are hard."

"You can pay me after your spring sales."

"No. I thank you, though." He laughed a bit, then looked round the shop. Her desk, the lamps and overstuffed chairs, the books—he's confused again, she thought. "Books should be free," he said, almost under his breath. "Isn't right for people to make money from words."

"How would they live?" She pressed her hand against the books at her shoulder.

"Who?"

"The authors—the people who write?"

"Pay them a living wage and free their spirits. They free ours."

36

Mr. Burgoyne twisted around at the footfall in the hall-way, his good eye held aloft for clear sight. "Who's that?" he asked.

Hannah had heard him in the kitchen. "Paul?" she said softly. "This is Mr. Burgoyne. The sheep man? That's Paul Streicher, Mr. Burgoyne."

The blond man in the shadows said, "How do you do."

Burgoyne turned to Hannah and raised his hand to cover his mouth. "Where is he?"

"In the hallway," she answered. "Come. I'm closing, Mr. Burgoyne."

"You know him?" Burgoyne said as she guided him to the double glass doors of the shop, the dim hallway, and the front door.

"Of course I know him," she said. "I do wish you'd take the Huxley. Your last chance."

"Not on your life," he said. "Where is he?"

"Here." Hannah turned the old farmer to face the blond man who leaned against the wall. She put the light on.

Mr. Burgoyne studied him closely, his good eye wandering patiently, even to Streicher's canvas pants. "Don't marry him," he said to Hannah.

"Good night, good night," she laughed. "There'll be no marriage here." She had Burgoyne aimed for the door and released him in the same way kids release clockwork soldiers that, with great purpose and single-mindedness, strut into midair off upper landings.

Hannah threw the bolt after the old man slammed the storm door. She hesitated, her face at the glass, her finger on the light switch, until the old man's head had vanished along the sidewalk. "Where have you been, Blue?"

"New York," he said. "Plattsburgh."

"You said you'd be over this morning." She turned to greet him.

"I tried. I couldn't."

"But you didn't call—why didn't you call?"

"I didn't know when I would be here."

37

Hannah crossed her arms and pushed the rug into place with her foot. "I wish you didn't live so far away. I was worried. I was very worried."

"You shouldn't be," he said. He'd stood straight from the wall and turned to go back into the kitchen.

Hannah shut off the shop lights and walked after him. His coat was over the back of a chair.

"Where's the new bottle of whiskey?" he said. He was asking, but he didn't like it that he had to ask.

"In the cellar way—on the shelf," she said. Hannah had stew on the stove, bread cooling on the table. Two places had been set.

He went down the cellar stairs and then came up again quickly, bouncing into the kitchen, bottle in hand. She gave him a glass from the table. "I went to St. Albans," she said, as though that were a vital point.

He poured the glass full of whiskey and sat down. He hadn't looked at her yet. When he was gone, she did very little other than watch the hours pass. When he was here, he brought something with him, something from out there. She looked over the sink and out to where the clothesline hung in the dark. He carried some bit of the awful out there in with him; that was the part of him that frightened her. "Did you hear me?" she asked. The house was quiet, expectant.

"And what did he want?"

"He," she said emphatically, "is dead. He wasn't there." Streicher lowered his glass slowly.

"He took his own life." The words seemed hard for her, like crumbs on her tongue. "I knew it! I've known it for months."

Streicher said, "He was a troubled man."

She reached for the stew. "I never liked him. I've said that for months as well. I just wish he hadn't done this." She put the stew pot on the table. He still hadn't looked at her. "Life can be so damn hard."

"You could not have helped him," he said quietly.

She stood over him, pushed his hair to cover his bald spot, and then let her hand slide to his neck.

He turned her slowly and pulled her onto his lap. "Don't think so much," he said, playfully kneading her breasts. "You know you think too much about these things."

"That Menard snake said he wants to see Leonard. I didn't tell him that Leonard is dead, but I think he knew already. They're all liars!"

"Who is Menard?" Streicher asked. He reached for his glass when Hannah put her head on his shoulder.

"That oily-haired banker. He wants more money. He wants at least one hundred a month—and he wants it now! He said Leonard is to call him immediately! *Or else*."

Streicher finished his whiskey and held her.

She raised her face to him. "Can you imagine? Or else! My god, the man is dead! Menard will hold the corpse in escrow waiting for Leonard to wake up."

Streicher kissed her, covering her face with his, his hand to her cheek, softly.

Hannah had reason to fear the awful out there, as she called it. She was the remaining half of one of those curious partnerships that some women have. Her partner, Margaret—the name so rarely said now without a catch in her throat, and more rarely said for that—her partner of almost five years had shriveled with cancer and died a penurious death in a Cowansville, Quebec, hospital. They had been partners in this house, one of the oldest houses in Sutton, Quebec, partners in the bookstore, and partners in a sheep farm in the hills south of Sutton near the border with Vermont. And for all that, which wasn't much, they were partners in poverty.

Both women knew for a long time that Margaret was being destroyed by something more serious than a nervous disorder, which was what these country doctors had promised them. And when the hospital charges and lying doctors' fees and the dreadful, battering trips to Montreal to save Margaret mounted the costs of "nervous disorders," the miserably small sheep farm had to be sold to enable Hannah to bury Margaret in April, 1940, pay off the medical fools, and keep this house and store for herself.

Streicher was right. He'd learned at least that much about Hannah in the last nine weeks. She did ponder the awful out there. But Streicher knew nothing of her life alone here in a land of borrowed dreams. And he knew nothing of Brussels and the baby.

"I was very worried," she said after they'd eaten and gone up into the chill of her bedroom. Hannah stood quietly nude, the cold of her room tingling her skin. She held her dressing gown at her side like a furled flag of reluctance.

"I am all right," he said from the chair.

Her room under the roof, its dormer windows and white paint—Hannah and Margaret had painted everything in this room white to battle the always-imminent dusk of the isolated northern town—her room was, she imagined, something like living inside a summer cloud of white cumulus. The bed and the paintings went to shades of red, with pinks in the curtains.

Streicher's pipe smoke seemed to stuff the room with his presence.

Hannah stood facing him. His long legs were crossed in obscurity. After nine weeks, she wanted to know who he was. She hadn't ever wanted to worry about another soul again.

"I'm not going on," she said.

He stirred slightly.

"I know Margaret had her feelings and she worked for your people. I'll miss having the extra money, but I'll not miss it enough to deal with people who kill themselves."

He waved his pipe stem. "That's all you need to say. I've told you. I can make other arrangements."

"It's not as simple as making arrangements. It's the differences between us that bother me," she said. "I don't believe politics matter. And I don't give a damn for this war."

40

"I know that."

"I'd like to feel safe for once. I took those men to St. Albans because I needed the money, and it was easy to do. But no more . . . not after Leonard." She flipped her gown, pulling it along the floor at her feet. Her hair had flashes of deep red amid the browns. She was once very beautiful, she knew. There had been men who stared at her on Zurich sidewalks when she was a schoolgirl; her large breasts and her uniform were a lure for their fantasies of white stockings and candy-sucking intimacies. "I think I feel what made Leonard do what he did. Although I never liked him, I think I know what killed him. He was a sad little man. I once saw a rabbit that lived for a while after a man shot its back legs off. Leonard had the same look in his eyes—that rabbit's disbelief."

Streicher had become very still. There were these moments when she stood unconsciously naked with him, as though she hadn't the slightest concern for his dreams. But then, how was she to know she was all that he'd ever imagined a woman would be? He was thirty-one and committed still to his imagination.

"Margaret believed in your new Germany," she said. "I don't."

Streicher sighed and closed his eyes.

Her voice was like a sleeper's soft moan. "I don't want anymore, Blue. I don't want the worry. I want to know where you are—what you're doing." Then: "Do you hear me?"

Streicher nodded. "I hear you. I'll get you out of this. We'll go back to Europe—both of us."

"How? With a war on?"

"After the war."

"How do you know there is an after the war at all?"

"We will not lose this one," he said. "I'll get you out. Besides, there are parts of this world where there is no war."

Hannah looked hard at him. "Where?"

"South America."

"Don't be bizarre. South America is all corruption and hot sun."

"Take your bath," he said. Hannah was bringing everything in the universe to her feet again, he thought. She does that. She's captivated with herself. She'd done it to him again—he worked well when he was alone, his task made sense. But here, with Hannah, his purposes always changed: he wanted to please her, comfort her, care for her, and forget the icy demands of who he was.

She was soaking in the tub. Streicher caught the lavender luxury of her steaming water. He was weary; the drive from New York State had been mind-numbing. But this bedroom was here like a silken white beacon at the end of black, twisting roads.

Streicher was an SS officer, and unique to the experience of the North Americans. The German intelligence service under Admiral Canaris, the Abwehr, had for a decade been milking the American continent of its best secrets. Abwehr agents, despite the bravado of men like Moffet in the FBI, had already sent to Berlin thousands of American aircraft designs, bombsight diagrams, and troop levels. The Abwehr had been silently at large in the Americas and hugely productive. The new Germany knew more about American and Canadian intentions than anyone could have guessed in December, 1941.

With the declaration of war imminent in 1939, the private designs of Reinhard Heydrich and his SS intelligence service—the *Sicherheitsdienst,* the intelligence service of the National Socialist Party itself and a desperate rival of the more benign Abwehr—these designs brought men like Paul Streicher to North America, men who were not the affable, somewhat gentlemanly amateurs of the Abwehr. The Paul Streichers were professionals trained to accomplish the Nazi dream. With a lust for brilliant black uniforms and silver braid, their first task was to squash the Abwehr, to reduce Canaris and his service to a collection of file clerks; but more, their task was to provide Nazi leaders themselves, through the Blond Beast, Heydrich, with the private means to destroy anyone . . . anyone, anywhere in the world. And they did have the means.

Despite their shared socialist convictions, Hannah's partner, Margaret, had acted alone to help the young Abwehr men cross into the United States. The money Margaret actually got from the new Germans was little enough, but because her parents had been German immigrants to Alberta when Margaret was very young, and because Margaret believed capitalism was founded on the greed of the powerful few, she had said yes when she was asked. There was no war in 1937. Sutton, Quebec, was isolated and cold for the two women, who had lived a deliberately cloistered life.

But then Margaret brought the awful out there into this home. The few dollars were needed and Hannah continued after Margaret's death, as much for the money as for something of Margaret left alive.

And Paul Streicher? His mission was to twist and destroy the North American Abwehr network of couriers and observers. With great care. Heydrich had made their assignments very clear to the few men chosen to serve in the *Sicherheitsdienst*: Canaris and his Abwehr must not know that the SS was engineering its primacy in the filthy world of crossed loyalties and human disasters.

Paul Streicher had been on the continent for less than six months. There were other men like him here. They numbered fewer than six, but were far deadlier than anyone imagined in the innocent days of 1941 when the world had not yet awakened to the curdling screams after midnight.

He left his pipe in the ashtray and went into the bathroom. Her eyes were closed. He paddled water over her chest and shoulders. "I don't want to lose you," she murmured. "If I ever lost you, I'd give myself over to the convent. I may anyway."

"You? A nun?"

"Don't laugh."

"Things will be well," he said, rubbing her breasts. "You and I will be all right."

Paul Streicher had come to know the painful tug of crossed loyalties himself: he was here with Hannah, fastened to her as he had been to nothing else in his life. He was a man bending under living flesh that cared for him as he had never been cared for before.

He was born in Cologne in 1910. His father had been a chemist with the immense chemical firm, I. G. Farban. His parents were divorced when his father retired prematurely into the perpetual self-absorption of mental illness. Streicher's mother had remarried quickly and still lived in Cologne with her cabaret-owner husband, tending bar until the early morning hours.

Paul, as the frightened son of bitterness, retired with his father to an uncle's house in Augsburg, where Streicher's father locked himself into a makeshift chemical laboratory in a chicken shed under the linden trees. His uncle gave Paul the iron slap of discipline, and as a minor Nazi official, dressed the boy in bright uniforms for the first time. Streicher was wounded in a riot in Ulm in 1933 and briefly jailed afterwards, until his uncle and the party saved him from the horrors of rats and piss-soaked bricks. He never finished medical school, although he desperately wanted the safety and certainty of a physician's confidence among other men.

After joining the Hitler Youth as a cadre instructor in 1934, Streicher felt the promise of power. He was hauled into the *Sicherheitsdienst* in 1937 and sent almost immediately to England in the guise of a chemist from I. G. Farban, where he consulted with British brew masters on the fermentation of malt. He became a budding alcoholic while in England, and was so buoyed by his later recall to Germany into the bosom of the SS that he once danced on Heydrich's table during a drunken celebration. Streicher was reprimanded for his lapse in severity. His father, he knew, was by then completely submerged in madness. On his last visit to Cologne, Streicher's mother had reviled his attacks on "Jewish vermin," laughed at his uniform, and had him chucked out of the cabaret.

Hannah soaked for a long time, at last lifting herself out of the tub and into the chilliness of her house. He'd be downstairs by the fireplace on the couch and drunk by now. Her bed was inviting, an island of stillness, as she wrapped her gown around her waist. She could leave him down there with his bottle, or she could take the chance once more and retrieve him. She went down after him and first saw the lights as a new wash of yellow on the stairs.

There was a Christmas tree. A short one alive with strands of yellow lights. He had moved the couch and the table and had the tree on the rug in the middle of the room. He was on his knees, gathering tinsel threads on the floor.

She wanted to speak, she wanted to shout and to clap her hands, but found she couldn't. He hadn't seen her yet. She stood at the bottom of the stairs and cried so quickly she was embarrassed. She had wondered if she would ever cry again, but now reached her clasped hands to her chin and blinked. She wiped her cheeks.

He tossed the tinsel into the fire—she caught his eye as he stood up.

"Where did you. . . ?" she said softly.

"Christmas is here," he said.

A few glass ornaments had been hung on the inside boughs of the tree. There were two wrapped presents in the lower branches. She smelled the pitch on him as she hugged him. "You don't know what you've done," she whispered into his ear.

"I think I do," he said, lightly.

Hannah touched the boughs, the brush of spikey rows against her hand.

She sat on the couch to stare at the tree. He was busy and frequently out of the room, taking ornament boxes into the kitchen. Hannah had only the vaguest sense of where he was. She concentrated on the glittering tree. He'd made up the fire.

He came back into the room with two glasses she had never seen before. Warm to touch, they had the aroma of heated cinnamon and rum. "What is this?" she smiled.

"It's English," he said. "I hope you'll like it. I've got a pan of the stuff on the stove."

She sipped her drink and tasted the hot rum; it flooded her middle with warmth. He'd gone out of the room again. She had nothing for him—she hadn't thought of Christmas in any personal way at all. She sold books to be given as gifts, but the holiday hadn't touched her in years. He had packages in the tree for her. She wiped her cheek again. The rum was wonderfully gentle.

He dropped the quilts on the floor by the tree and, giving her his drink, spread them out for her to sit with him. He was pleased with himself, she knew. He had reason to be.

She shook her head when he reached the smallest package out of the tree. Folds of pale pink tissue inside a pink box held a crystal pendant on a gold chain. A point of ruby scarlet was imbedded in a polished oval. She whispered to him as she lowered her head and he fastened the clasp under her hair.

"I've never had anything as beautiful." She knew she was alive at last. The fire and rum warmed her skin. The weight of the crystal on her chest. "I've got to see it," she said.

"One more," he said, pulling her back down onto the quilt beside him.

"I haven't got anything for you," she said. "I didn't know. I feel awful."

"Don't," he said. "You are my gift. And I am being very serious. You are to have nothing but good feelings tonight. And this is for you," he said, handing her the other package.

This box was larger, flatter, and very heavy. Hannah tugged at the ribbons and opened it. A mirror. Very old. A hand mirror of porcelain and gold with a polished oval

46

glass. Oval like the pendant, she thought. He's got it all right. The shapes and colors were right. The man had an eye for completeness and beauty.

He took the mirror and held it up. She opened her gown, the pendant there between her breasts—transparent quartz with its ruby center. "I feel very beautiful," she whispered.

"You are," he said, touching the pendant. He turned it over; she saw that "1941" had been etched into its reverse side above the name "Blue." She covered his hand and the pendant with her hand. "You don't know—you couldn't," she said. "You have made me feel beautiful—that's what you've given me."

They lay together quietly for a while, rolling in the heat of the rum and fire. And when they made love, he pulled out of her and opened her legs to lie on his side. He held the mirror so that she could watch; she saw her thighs, her wet auburn hair between her legs, and the creases and folds of skin as he opened her. She watched him go into her again and slowly rock her until she bit her lip and muffled a moan.

The fire was there, the tree with its yellow points, and Hannah saw the light shatter and run with her tears before she closed her eyes. His head came to rest on her breasts. "You don't know what you've done," she whispered. He was quiet. "You can't know," she said, releasing herself to float on ripples of yellow light out into the darkness.

EIGHT

*IT WAS HOPED TO MAKE THE PASSAGE at an average of twenty knots
in seven days, having regard to zigzags and détours to avoid the plotted
U-boats. The Admiralty turned us down the Irish Channel into the Bay
of Biscay. The weather was disagreeable. There was a heavy gale and a
rough sea. The sky was covered with patchy clouds. We had to cross the
out-and-home U-boat stream from the Western French ports to their
Atlantic hunting grounds. There were so many of them about that our
captain was ordered by the Admiralty not to leave our flotilla behind us;
but the flotilla could not make more than six knots in the heavy seas, and
we paddled along at this pace round the South of Ireland for forty-eight
hours. We passed within four hundred miles of Brest, and I could not help
remembering how the* Prince of Wales *and the* Repulse *had been
destroyed by shore-based torpedo-aircraft attack the week before. The
clouds had prevented all but an occasional plane of our air escort from
joining us, but when I went on the bridge I saw a lot of unwelcome blue
sky appearing. However, nothing happened, so all was well. The great
ship with her attendant destroyers plodded on. But we became impatient
with her slow speed . . . The night was pitch-black. So we cast off our
destroyers and ran through alone at the best speed possible in the
continuing rough weather. We were battened down and great seas beat
upon the decks . . .*

*. . . When fresh escorts joined us from the Azores they could take in
by daylight Morse signals from us in code, and then, dropping off a
hundred miles or so, could transmit them without revealing our position.
Still, there was a sense of radio claustrophobia—and we were in the
midst of world war.*

Kemper awoke to a raw morning drizzle. The tiny city of St. Albans couldn't house more than ten thousand, he thought. With four days remaining until Christmas, some of the storekeepers had framed their display windows with borders of cardboard holly. The automobiles were battered, undoubtedly a product of local gravel roads that could shatter the fenders off a Buick.

In the park opposite the Jesse Welden House, as a centerpiece of sorts, was a Victorian fountain of four nubile sprites with a crust of snow on their young breasts, and over their heads a fluted tray on a column. A man hurried past the fountain, his collar up, his hat mushed over his ears, his arms swinging. Walks like a lawyer, Kemper thought.

His first impulse was to conjure images of London and to spit on this derelict collection of rural squalor. But no, there was a composure about what he saw. The buildings were shabby Civil War remnants. Two jewelry stores. A drugstore next to a blue front with *Quality Female Wear* in gravelly, ornate lettering overhead. On the opposite long leg of the rectangular park, there were churches—at least four, he thought—and a courthouse where a man with loose earflaps was jerking a blue flag down a pole.

Kemper's second impulse was to like the place. He dressed quickly and hurried down to a dining room filled with more than hotel guests at breakfast. The brightly lighted room seemed to be a meeting place. Kemper heard bits of everything that made up a small American town on Sunday morning. Lawyers and judges sat uncomfortably with their wives. The women were heavy and many wore furs; one in particular in a veiled blue hat wore a fox pelt on her shoulders with the black nose and eyes of the beast's head glumly slumped over her left breast. Traveling salesmen at a middle table passed around catalogues and maps. The waitress placed a plate of eggs, potatoes, hash, and rolls in front of him. Kemper realized, as he picked up his fork, that these people knew each other. And they did not know him.

St. Albans was the port of entry for the railroad into the surrounding countryside of dairies and lumber mills. The railroad had built this city and continued to control its thin northern prosperity. The landowners and powerful built houses to the east of the city on a leisurely hill, while the workers, or blockers as they were called, punched their short-stepped houses into a crowded checkerboard of streets west of the dividing rail yards.

Kemper walked through the rain to the train station. Cigar in hand, he went to the agent's window and asked for a timetable. There was a passenger train halted inside the black spiderwork of the soaring train shed. Kemper stood with some of the passengers while the train was loaded and then watched as its blast of coal smoke and steam shot into the arches overhead and out into the cold morning air. The train was headed for New York.

Kemper stepped from the platform into the railroad headquarters building. Vacant walls of gleaming wainscoting hushed the sounds of the offices. The superintendent's office was on the second floor. While Cody was found Kemper idly stood at the windows. From here the rail yards occupied acres of cinder-black ground. The car barns and machine shops were red brick and exhaled oily smoke. Steam burst the ground here and there in thin dancing geysers. Dozens of rail strands were woven through the yards into two main line tracks to the south. On a street below him, delivery trucks and rusted sedans crashed over the rails.

Cody was a huge man. Nearly bald, the superintendent had a wide smile and hands like bear paws. A heavy gold watch chain reached across his vest. Kemper guessed Cody weighed two hundred and fifty pounds.

"The Central Vermont is a small railroad, although we connect with all the big ones," Cody said. He obviously enjoyed being Cody. Kemper brightened immediately. "I was in New London when this guy killed himself," Cody said.

Kemper asked him what a superintendent did for a railroad. "I am the railroad, Mr. Kemper. I run the thing. Everything."

"I have to go to Richmond to identify him."

"Not much to look at," Cody said, "from what I hear. He must not have known or cared that the Richmond station was there. If it hadn't been for the baggage cart he smashed, he might be alive. Most of our suicides go off the bridges—we had a man jump into a rock cut two years ago. This Baskins fellow was a queer bird, I guess."

"Someone you knew?" Kemper asked.

Cody and Kemper occupied two leather chairs under a map of the United States that had the rail lines in brilliant red ink.

"Knew of him," Cody answered. Kemper liked the way Cody sprawled. There was something of the western desert in his speech. "I didn't know what he was doing. Can't imagine it—but they say he was a German spy. Everyone here thought he was a paint salesman. He was around the station a lot. He and the other salesmen. You want coffee?"

A trembling, elderly man in a rumpled suit had careened into the office with a tray of white mugs and a coffee pot. "Help yourself," Cody said. "Need my morning coffee."

Cody said he thought Kemper and he were about the same age. He wanted to know what Kemper did, but dropped the sugar spoon and raised his hands, saying he'd worked with government people before in Texas and knew they had their damned secrets.

"Nothing secret about it." Kemper answered. "I work for Naval Intelligence."

"And this guy was a spy?"

Kemper relaxed in the thick warmth of the chair. "Not a spy. He was a courier—a delivery boy for the spies."

Cody shook his head. "This war is a terrible thing. The

51

railroads aren't going to sleep a wink. What was he doing here?"

"The Germans have brought men through here for years."

"They have? On this railroad? From Canada?"

The coffee was like hot varnish.

Cody relaxed. "Gossip is he had a girlfriend here—some teacher—Dorcas something. Helluva name, isn't it? Dorcas? All those salesmen are tanks. My guess is he was drunk and fell out a door. He left the parlor car that night . . . just never came back. Dorcas Baldwin—that's her name. She's a schoolteacher in the high school here. Things just got to be too much for him."

"Most of these people are in over their heads," Kemper said, thinking immediately of himself—Moffet, Sheridan, and the misery of his last months in England when the embassy made his life brittle.

"He's in Ball's funeral parlor in Richmond," Cody said. "You might want to talk to the sheriff here as well. His name is Bernard Sykes. He's got questions, he says. Came to me, but I knew you were coming—or someone from the FBI—I gave him damn little. Can't tolerate the man. He hasn't got a goddam thing to do but serve court orders—and he pounds in here! I didn't say a word about you coming. On second thought, don't talk to him. He'd ruin any good morning!"

"I'm in the Welden House, registered as Baskins's brother."

Kemper saw Cody's forehead crease.

"I'd like to skip in and out of this town without leaving a wake," Kemper answered. "And . . . if anyone does ask about Baskins, I'd like to hear a little straight talk. People aren't always as forthcoming with us as they might be."

"Who invited you to a wake?" Cody smiled.

"You don't need another superintendent, do you?"

"There's only one, friend. You wouldn't be my first choice if I did."

"Too old?" Kemper asked, grinning.

"Shit, I was eighteen when I started with the Sante Fe in New Mexico in 1901. I spiked rail and shot Indians. We're both too old. And I'd say by the looks of you you've shot a few Indians yourself."

"A few," Kemper said. He asked to use the railroad telegrapher if he needed to. Cody rubbed his eyes and said he'd tell the dispatcher to give him time. Kemper downed the last of the varnish and left Cody sitting alone in his office. Cody yelled and offered him a railroad pass to Richmond and back, but Kemper needed to keep this business once removed, and waving, shook his head. Dr. Beam has the answer, he thought, as he walked out to the platform. He'd never thought of himself as retired, never as anything other than what he was. But living in this godforsaken state and fishing through the syrupy green summer evenings had some appeal to him.

He'd surprised himself and found he was comfortable here. The emptiness of the land must have room for one more. The place had cause for few pretensions in anything, but on the other hand, Kemper felt more fit. Were the days actually more manageable here? he wondered as he got another cigar going in the empty train shed. Not bad, he thought. I haven't fished for years.

Hannah held him on her back steps. His departures were becoming more difficult and, she thought, more dangerous every time he went: so much of something she loved went with him. His black-and-white Cushman's bakery truck was parked behind the grape arbor.

"Safe home," she said.

"I'll see you day after tomorrow," he said. "After lunch

sometime. Say nothing to Menard. Just talk to him. I'll deal with all of them after this. You have done enough."

"Be careful with Mouton," Hannah said. "He's not to be trusted. I still don't understand why you need to see him at all."

"I haven't met him," he said. "I have to know if he's safe for us."

"I've told you—he isn't. Look at that truck! Can't you find something less obvious than that?"

"I don't mind being obvious," he said, smiling.

"I'll miss you."

"Not as much as I'll miss you."

She could feel the pendant between her breasts. "You are something, you know. You truly are."

He backed the truck into the road, waved to her, and turned onto the main road, heading for Quebec City.

NINE

KEMPER FOUND THE FUNERAL HOME on the eastern edge
of Richmond. A large yellow house, possibly once a farm-
house, connected at the back to a newer addition with a
small barn behind that. Gaunt maples crowded the funeral
home. The fields were open and lightly bleached with old
snow. As he left his car in the drive, Kemper stopped to
search the mounded grey mountains above him for signs of
the human touch. He walked on, feeling the weight of
something indescribable, he thought, but very near claustrophobia.

"Where's your gun?" Ball said to him inside. Kemper had
come into an anteroom painted entirely in pewter blue.
There were pins of light, like stars, in the ceiling. Kemper
looked again at Ball, a broken elm of a man in striped trousers and a vest. Ball had to be seven feet tall. He had his
hands behind his back.

"I don't carry one," Kemper said.

"Thought all you G-men carried big pistols. Like to see
it, if you've got one."

"No gun. I'm here to identify a Leonard Baskins. Have
you got him?"

"Damn right, I've got him. You want him?"

"No thanks," Kemper said. "But I need to see him."

"You really from the FBI?"

"What are the plates for?" Kemper pointed to the wall,

55

where place settings of china and glass goblets were displayed. "You sell dinnerware, do you?"

"'Course I don't sell it. I give it away to my patrons. One of the best ideas my brother ever had."

"And the lights?" Kemper pointed at the ceiling with his cigar.

"I love 'em, too. Another of Randall's ideas—not so good as the plates, but helps to set the tone, I think. Most of my patrons are consumed with thoughts of celestial justice when they drop in here. The lights help to settle 'em down."

Kemper had stopped listening so he could watch this apparition. As thin as any man could be and continue to breathe, the funeral director, Ball, had a bright red face as narrow as a wind vane. His arms were like hydraulic levers with wire baskets for hands.

"Of course, they're hoping for celestial peace against the odds. They know damn well they don't deserve any peace. You hungry? I'm having my lunch. Got an egg or two to spare. And I've got my brew."

Ball's waiting room, if that's what it was, was devoutly peaceful—the blue paint did the trick. The rug was a darker blue, and thick. "Why do you give plates away?" Kemper asked.

"You have no idea," Ball said, leaning forward, "how people like a good deal. Just business. But, oh my, don't these plates bring in the business. My brother Randall was a genius on the business side."

"Is he here?"

"Not any longer. He's been dead almost three years. Anyone who buries a loved one out of the Ball Brothers' Memorial Funeral Parlor and Crematory gets a sixty-four-piece dinner set, according to how big a deal they sign up for. Death is a bigger deal for some than others. Hell, there are folks who won't pay to bury their mothers. Then, there are others—there's a woman, Mrs. Castle in Barre, who

56

pays top dollar to bury her cats. She's got so many plates she could sell 'em wholesale. I'd like to eat."

Kemper followed Ball into a white room with pews. There was an open coffin up front on a trestle draped with folds of cerulean blue velvet. As Kemper hurried after Ball, he saw an old woman's powdered face was just visible above the edge of the casket.

"This is my office," Ball said. He kicked the door shut. There was a fireplace, and windows that looked out onto fields and the grey scud of cloud that had drifted into the valley. Ball had his lunch spread on his desk. The office had an ancient untidiness to it; Kemper thought most of the calendars and papers were probably where they'd landed years ago. The room appeared disturbed, but not recently. "Where is he?" Kemper asked.

"Let's eat first—he's out back."

Kemper said he was in a hurry.

"Have a bite with me. It's Sunday, no day to be in a hurry." Ball ran to a cabinet near the fireplace, bent over, and ran back with a canning jar of clear liquid. "Have a brew—you must have time for a brew." Ball checked the regulator on the wall. "Cocktail time, anyway." It was ten minutes to one.

Kemper relented and pulled up an office chair. Ball had glasses from another cabinet. They were goblets, Kemper saw when Ball filled them both with brew. "See if that doesn't put you away," Ball said.

The brew was the hardest cider Kemper had ever tasted. He said so.

"Hundred-forty proof." Ball smiled with satisfaction. "I use the stuff to start the hearse in February. Make it myself. Like it? Have a pickle."

Ball began cutting slices from a cheese wheel on a Bible stand near the window. "You help yourself to the ham," he said, carrying the cheese in a linen napkin to the desk. "Isn't that the finest cider?"

"Not the smoothest," Kemper said.

"It does have a bite, doesn't it? Baskins is out back. We'll eat first—sandwiches okay? I had to do the Specklers this morning. You don't know the Specklers, do you? You haven't missed a thing. And Willa Carboni's crowd will be here in two hours."

"That's Willa, is it—" Kemper pointed his cigar "—the woman in the casket out there?"

"That enough cheese?" Ball asked, holding up a sandwich. He was reaching for a plate from a wooden crate next to the desk. "That's Willa," he said. "Had a hell of a time with her hair. Hate hair . . . I just hate hair. My brother Randall always curled hair. One of those touches Randall was famous for. That and teeth. Randall had a smiling option for a while. We thought it was kinda' thoughtful. Randall knew how to make 'em smile so they didn't look so overwhelmed. But, people being what they are, they didn't care to have their old aunts grinning like pumpkins when they came for services. I'll have to admit, our smiling option gave us trouble. Randall was a man before his time. Have an egg. Can't tell ya' how much I miss my brother."

"I can see that," Kemper said. "Those eggs are pickled!"

"You betcha. Good, aren't they? Where you from?"

Kemper had a mouthful of ham. "New York," he mumbled.

"You really work for the FBI?"

"Not really."

"That why you haven't got a gun?" Ball said, swinging back in his chair, his feet on an opened desk drawer.

"I work for the government. We don't carry guns."

"Randall and I went to New York every Christmas—did it for years. We slept at the Algonquin—do you know it?"

Kemper said he did and reached for another egg. Ball's round brown eyes darted over his desk to the window and the fields. Kemper expected to see something move out there when he looked. "Randall and I used to love to sit in

58

the Algonquin lobby and drink dark rum and coffee. They had these little sandwiches."

Kemper said he'd been there.

"Every Christmas we went. People seem to hold off dying during the holidays. 'Course they make up for it right afterwards. Christmas can put an awful lot of people in my Poughkeepsie."

Kemper asked him if he was married.

"What for?" Ball answered.

Kemper couldn't quickly think of a reason to be married. He'd get to it, he thought. The brew was working its magic. "What's a Poughkeepsie?" Kemper asked.

"My refrigerator," Ball said. "Out back. Baskins is in it."

"You do have a crematory here?"

"Out back. Only one in the state. Every Christmas we went to New York." Ball tapped the jar with his foot, but Kemper said he'd had enough.

"How's the ham?"

"Couldn't be better," Kemper smiled.

"Smoke it myself," Ball added.

Kemper hesitated—the thought hung there in his head like a lead plumb bob. "You smoke this ham in the crematory?" he asked, hoping the lead weight would be lifted.

"That's right," Ball said. "It's maple cured. Takes days to do it right."

Kemper felt the weight drop. And the buzzing began in his spine. He shifted and crossed his legs. He was far from any home at all, and far from three dusty rooms on the eighth floor above West Seventy-ninth Street. His spirit of recovery had been an illusion. For years he'd had family trappings and children who trusted him. "I'd like to see him now," he said.

Ball stared at him as though Ball were party to ominous secrets, as if Ball knew too well why men unraveled and flew into pieces.

Kemper felt the soft pulse of fear enter his chest. He had

nowhere to go. He'd die here. "I've got to get back," he said, scrambling nervously to his feet. A sharp vision of gray sheets and exquisite pain shot out of his imagination. The pain was back, his heart seizing again.

Ball slowly pushed the brew jar away from the edge of the desk. "He's in the Poughkeepsie."

"Now!"

"Right away," Ball said. He reached for the keys.

Kemper wanted the man to move silently and quickly. He'd shoved Ball's hospitality away. Oh god, he thought, my heart's going again.

Without saying a word, Ball took him into the next room, the one with the cement floor. A shining steel table with sluice lines and a drain into the floor. The back wall was a solid construction of grey drawers—six oversized file drawers. Kemper waited while Ball excitedly unlocked the lower middle drawer. Ball glanced at Kemper and then, resolved to something, he yanked Baskins into the bright light. "No one gets away from my Poughkeepsie," he said.

Kemper thought he'd drop. He clenched his hands. Sweat ran down his backbone. Ball unwrapped a shroud of white coarse cotton to reveal the smashed remains of a man. Baskins's eyes were open—like golf balls. Ball pulled the cotton away from the man's chest and abdomen. Baskins was a bag of splintered bones with nothing but the soft ripple of Jell-O-filled skin.

Kemper felt his breathing stutter. "Close it," he choked. "Close it, damn it."

Puzzled, Ball flipped the cotton over the body and slid the drawer into the wall. The room was inundated with the acrid hum of machinery. There was a brass plate near the top of the refrigerator machine that said MEREDITH-POUGHKEEPSIE, INC., 1921, POUGHKEEPSIE, NEW YORK.

"Don't touch me!" he said when Ball's hand took his arm. But Ball hung on.

"You shouldn't drive."

Kemper glanced at him and then at the car. "I have to—
I've got to get back. Just a touch of your brew."

"Hold on," Ball said softly. "Brew, my ass. Brew
doesn't scare a man the way you're scared."

He has seen it, Kemper thought.

"Come and sit a minute . . . in here."

The first real jolt—just like the first time—gripped his
chest. Kemper closed his eyes. He knew he was trembling
. . . that Ball could feel his arms shaking.

Ball left him under the pins of light. Kemper studied the
dishes on display, the pewter blue, and the sparkle of the
glass goblets in narrow boxes of blue light.

He was alone and bent over when Ball got back to him.
"I need some water," Kemper whispered.

"I've called a doctor," Ball said. "He lives up the road.
He'll be right here. You'll be all right, you know."

Kemper held his breath when the new pain fluttered in his
ribs. "It's my heart," he said through his teeth.

"It's not brew, I know that. You're damn scared, but
you'll be all right."

Ball lifted Kemper's feet and Kemper lay on the sofa, his
head hard against the wooden arm. Kemper kept his eyes
closed to quiet his fear. He was going. And he was miles
from any safety.

He wondered if he'd fainted, because another man was
suddenly above him when he opened his eyes. Kemper let
himself be poked and pushed. The doctor had a stethoscope
cold on his skin. Kemper lay listening to the thudding in his
body.

"I'm Doctor Wally," the man said. Kemper told him
about Norfolk and the first blinding rush of pain months
before, and now this. Dr. Wally smelled of cloves and flour.
Kemper was amazed as Ball described him and their visit
with uncanny accuracy of human detail.

"I think you're okay," Dr. Wally said.

"I'm not," Kemper said.

"You've had one helluva scare, but I think your heart is okay. This isn't a heart attack. Tell me what you're doin' here." Dr. Wally was small: small hands and a leathery face with a manicured mustache like a Cuban casino manager.

They talked for a while. Ball vanished to answer a telephone somewhere in the house. "So why are you here?" Dr. Wally asked again.

"I told you," Kemper said, letting his eyelids close.

"Haven't got any sense at all, have they? You're not in danger now, Mr. Kemper. Least, I don't think you are. But you have no business being anywhere but home and quiet. Christ, you've already had one heart attack. They trying to kill you?"

Kemper said he'd go back to New York.

"I think your nerves are shot."

"Have been for years," Kemper said.

"Is there anyone who can come and get you?"

Kemper thought of Moffet and the college kid. "No," he answered. "There's no one."

Ball was back, rocking on his heels. And when Kemper said he'd drive back to St. Albans and his hotel room, Ball shook his head no. "He'll stay here the night," Ball said. Kemper thought of the Poughkeepsie and the white cotton out back.

"If he does, Farley," Dr. Wally said, "you don't give him any more of that brew. Hear?"

"Randall went out with a bad heart," Ball said. "He couldn't touch the stuff. I didn't know," he said to Kemper.

"Not yours to know," Kemper said. "I don't drink much anyway. Seemed harmless enough."

Dr. Wally laughed. "Nothing Farley eats or drinks is harmless. I'll have my son bring you a little light supper if you want. You can call for it later on. Stay the night and go back in the morning. You're exhausted. This anxiety will kill you, if you don't get quiet and stay quiet."

Kemper did feel better. Quieter. This country doctor

seemed to know the difference, and the difference was everything to Kemper. He could deal with collapsed nerves and anxiety—he'd done it for years—but not with another heart attack. He'd panicked. The Poughkeepsie. And Baskins. The sight of that man. And the brew. He'd get quiet and he'd stay quiet. He'd watch himself much more closely from now on, he thought.

"Is that right?" Moffet said sarcastically.

Kemper held the earpiece tightly.

"He was drunk and either fell off the train—or jumped?"

Kemper said he believed so. He'd slept for more than an hour on a couch in Ball's house. Ball had a service going out back, and the driveway was full of trucks and cars.

"Well, which is it, dammit? I'll tell you something, Frank. You better look again because Quenneville in Montreal called us a second time. Says there's something damned strange going on up there, and he doesn't know what it is. You go and see him tomorrow. I told him you'd be there if I could find you."

Moffet's telephone voice sounded like sandpaper on tin.

"Where the hell are you, Frank?"

Kemper said he was in Richmond, but was staying in the Jesse Welden.

"I called there," Moffet snapped. "They never heard of you."

"I'm there," Kemper said.

"I talked to that railroad superintendent, Cody." Moffet was all business. "He said he saw you this morning. The coroner's office up there is slow as shit, so you wait till I tell you to leave. And talk to that Frenchman in Montreal. I want to hear from you tomorrow night. Seven o'clock, Frank. Have you actually seen the body?"

Kemper said he had.

"In the coroner's office?"

"No," Kemper said. "Here . . . The Ball Brothers' Memorial Funeral Parlor and Crematory. In Richmond."

"What the hell are they doing? For chrissakes, how can a coroner do the tests if he's in one place and Baskins is in another?"

Kemper said he didn't know. Moffet grunted and clicked the telephone line dead except for the hollow crackling.

TEN

*IT HAD BEEN INTENDED that we should steam up the Potomac and
motor to the White House, but we were all impatient after nearly ten
days at sea to end our journey. We therefore arranged to fly from
Hampton Roads, and landed after dark on December 22 at the
Washington airport. There was the President waiting in his car. I clasped
his strong hand with comfort and pleasure. We soon reached the White
House, which was to be in every sense our home for the next three
weeks. Here we were welcomed by Mrs. Roosevelt, who thought of
everything that could make our stay agreeable.*

Kemper got away early in the morning. The pale sun rising
high in the east rode with him through empty fields and
past steaming herds standing outside barns.

Ball had become as thoughtful and fussy as a man could
be without being an old wife. After supper Kemper had
been shown into a warm, flowery bedroom upstairs with a
voluminous soft bed of down covered with quilts and flannel sheets. Ball protested that he'd been more than a little
responsible for Kemper's collapse; the old man spoke of his
brother and how Randall had needed weeks of darkened
rooms and warmth only to die just before eight o'clock in a
night of deep cold over new snow. "God knows, I tuck 'em
all in when they're dead," he said when Kemper had

breathed the heavy sigh of relief. "Haven't had anyone with me since Randall went. I'm glad for your company."

And there had been that odd bit of news this morning while Kemper got his coat on: "I suppose you know your business," Ball had said. "I guess I've just seen too many country policemen to know how these things are done. You just don't seem all that interested in our friend back there. Hell, the sheriff from St. Albans was more curious than you are."

Quenneville was in the dining room when Kemper asked for his key in the Jesse Welden House. Kemper hadn't seen him for years.

The corpulent Montreal cop of three hundred pounds or so was at table as Kemper crossed the room. Quenneville leapt up and pumped Kemper's hand. "When that FBI ass-hole told me it was you, I couldn't wait," Quenneville said. "Have breakfast—coffee—sit, sit, my friend." Kemper thought Quenneville was not only more stout, but more of his hair had gone, his jowls shook, and his grin had become, if anything, more his dominant quality. Quenneville was, despite the years, one of the world's most affable human beings. And one of its largest.

"Ah," he shouted, smacking Kemper's shoulder, "my kids! You should see them. I've had four more. I was thinking as I drove here this morning that we last saw each other—you and I—you remember? Paris? Do you? Four I've had. Four darlings. They are so small . . ." He held his huge hand at about table-level as Kemper eased his leg and moved a coffee cup. "That makes eleven!" Quenneville laughed. "Can you imagine? Eleven kids. The church is so happy with me. I have missed you, my friend."

Quenneville carried with him the disturbing aftertaste of forgotten years, when he and Kemper had met in Paris and traveled for months through Alsace as agents of North American vigilance against the German horde. Quenneville

66

was one of the few men Kemper had met who was at home anywhere in the world. Quenneville regarded any other man as one of his many Québécois cousins, and therefore reasonable. Every woman, other than his wife, was to Quenneville a niece close to his heart. Kemper had long ago known that few men had greater kindness and forbearance than this man. Quenneville's chatter about kids was a playful foil this morning to Kemper's well-known hostility for anyone under the age of thirty.

"I didn't want to see you," Kemper said. "That FBI asshole, Moffet—your word—" he said when Quenneville peered up from his oatmeal, "I never expected to see you again," he added. "Moffet said your name and I felt very sad."

"Sad?" Quenneville asked, his fingers fluttering.

"That you were still mixed up in all this. I've always thought you deserved more."

"You are not alone, my friend. For years I've been telling those guys who are my bosses that I am wasted in this business. I should be a grand civil servant by now. But do they listen?"

Women near the window stared at the voluble Quenneville. He dove back into his oatmeal.

Here was safety of a sort, Kemper thought.

"I am a cop," Quenneville said. "Just a cop. But you should see my kids. Frank, they are wonderful. And my youngest, Gizelle, she's only seven months and so tiny she sleeps in my hand." The Montreal cop held his palm up for Kemper to examine, a hand the size of a baseball glove. "This is good cereal, Frank. Nice place. How come you used the name Baskins? I found you," Quenneville said, pointing with his knife.

"That old business—honey for the bears."

They had used a variety of names in Alsace when they hunted as a pair. "I remember," Quenneville said. "You are playing the game."

A waitress brought Quenneville a plate of eggs and bacon. Kemper waved away the fat cop's insistence that Kemper eat something.

"I rejoice to see you again, but you have changed for dumps. You are not the same."

"And you're not the first to notice it," Kemper said. "As a matter of fact, everyone notices it—even people I've never met before."

Quenneville had sent telegrams to the Norfolk hospital. He stopped eating, searching, his jowls moving slowly.

"This is my final trip for them," Kemper went on. "I had to identify a suicide. I've done that . . . I'm going back tomorrow."

Quenneville shrugged.

"They don't understand fatigue. If I died right here, they'd be pissed off. I've told ONI to count up my years and retire me. This FBI bullshit is something extra they've tacked on—an afterthought to be certain I mean it."

Quenneville carefully buttered his toast. "Mean what?" he asked.

"I'm finished."

"Are you?"

"Seems the decent thing to do."

"This stuff is never decent—you know that. You are hanging on, my friend. You haven't stopped anything. How is your wife? Sorry," Quenneville smiled, "your ex-wife? I always liked her."

"Everyone does."

"And your children?"

"David is in Europe. God knows where. Sylvie and her mother have gone to Florida for Christmas."

Quenneville nodded, having understood that Kemper was a man who had lost. He wiped his mouth. "Just as well you are going back, my friend. We are in some shit here."

They were alone now in the dining room. Snow fell through the grey maples in the park. Quenneville said,

"This Leonard Baskins—he might have killed himself. Maybe not. There are people living in this place who have helped the Abwehr for years. One of those German-American Bund groups. Small potatoes all of them. They use a house on the lake here to hide Abwehr agents. They get the agents onto the right trains. They make a few bucks—they hurt no one. But now—" Quenneville sipped his coffee. "My guess—I know you don't want my guess, but I did get up in the dark this morning to see you. My guess is that with the United States no longer neutral, these guys want out. Their feet must be very cold. You know yourself how the Abwehr has used this border and Montreal. Especially Montreal. But we knew most of them . . . or thought we did."

"Baskins was only a courier," Kemper said.

Quenneville cut into another egg. "I know that," he said. "Everyone knows that. But for these local nuts he was Canaris himself, I think."

"He was a drunk."

"So? We are all drunks, are we not? If it isn't booze, it's money. If it isn't money or booze, it's power. Everybody walks with a crutch."

"He had a girlfriend here, yes?"

Quenneville shrugged.

"A teacher in the high school?"

"So what?" Quenneville smiled.

Kemper poured himself more coffee and looked out to the falling snow again. The framed dreariness.

"There is more," Quenneville said deliberately. His head was actually larger than Kemper remembered. His eyes were dark and complacent. "The Abwehr has had only three radios in North America to call home with. There is the big transmitter in their Mexico City legation; there are two more in New York."

"There are? Does the FBI know there are three radios? Should I tell Moffet?"

"You decide," Quenneville smiled. "Your FBI is a pain in the ass, Frank. They are babies, they are so new at this spy stuff. Babies. They are very willing to accept information—not so willing to be grateful for it. They think the rest of us are nobodies."

"Three radios," Kemper said.

"Now four. There is a fourth. Some of your Naval Intelligence guys who love radios are listening. There is suddenly a fourth. And where do you think it is?"

"Now you are playing the game."

"Ah. We know. No, we don't know—there may be more than one. Signals came from Nova Scotia for a few weeks, then nothing for a while. Now—can you guess?"

"Montreal?"

"Maybe. Quebec, we think. In the Townships somewhere. But the transmissions are short—too short. No pattern for their transmission times, but most are made at night. Another book code, possibly. But different."

"There are four radios . . . maybe five."

"Curious, isn't it?" Quenneville asked.

"No, it isn't. Not at all."

"Hear this," Quenneville said, raising his eyebrows. "The transmissions don't sound like Abwehr. We have all heard Abwehr chitchat. These are not Abwehr."

"Don't ask me to guess."

"You should," Quenneville smiled. "They are using powerful transmitters—only very short messages from Germany. At very high speed."

"The SS?" Kemper sighed, letting his chin rest on his hand.

"You do remember. I have been alone with that thought until now. I knew you would know."

"I remember it all," Kemper said.

"Lyons—that farm where that woman shot her dogs? The high speed stuff from there?"

"The *Sicherheitsdienst*. They're more likely to stab each other in the back."

"Maybe," Quenneville said. "But if those guys are in Canada, we are in some shit, my friend."

"Not for long, you're not. They're fanatics. They couldn't keep blood off their hands—they'd show themselves as soon as they landed."

"Maybe they have." Quenneville stopped eating. He rubbed his nose. Three men in suits and carrying leather sample cases stood in the dining room door. Kemper watched them decide to leave. Quenneville overpowered any room he was in.

"Baskins?" Kemper asked suddenly.

"Possible?"

"Anything's possible, Marcel."

"Interesting, yes?"

"No," Kemper said, pouring more coffee in both their cups. "Baskins fell off a train."

"Did you see where he fell?"

"Nope." Kemper dumped sugar into his coffee.

"I hear from this guy Cody that Baskins landed inside a station. Many feet from the railroad tracks."

"He bounced well," Kemper said. The vision of Baskins in the drawer sliced into his imagination.

"Maybe," Quenneville said acidly. "The train was going very fast."

"You're stretching yourself, Marcel."

"Maybe," Quenneville said again. "There is a woman named Hannah Doll. She owns a bookstore in Sutton, in Quebec. She is also a courier. I don't want her hurt. I have let her play the game, but she is an innocent. She knew Baskins well."

"Have them jailed, Marcel. Stop the game."

"Not yet, my friend."

"Who are they here?"

71

"A banker—Menard, I know. And the mayor. And I think the sheriff, but I'm not sure about him."

"Wonderful," Kemper said. "Merry Christmas, Marcel. They all deserve each other. And they don't deserve us."

They will start the music, Kemper thought, and you will begin the dance. "I'm leaving tomorrow morning. If I could, I'd leave now," he said to the great round Montreal cop. "All of you will have to go on without me. Please listen to me, Marcel: I'm not going to make it if I don't stop now. I'd like to find a place to fish for the summer. I'd like to read, and I'd like to make my own fishing rods. I'll make you one, if you like."

Quenneville flipped his hands in mock disbelief. "So be it," he said. "I don't blame you at all. I'd like to stop myself, but this is a bad time. The war will not go away. I'd like it to. I wish everyone could be happy and peaceful.

"There are not many of us, my friend. We are the old guys, we have seen these Nazi creeps up close. They are murderers—you know they are. If the old guys don't help now, there is no one to stop them. My RCMP is young like your FBI. People are going to die and be hurt. And no one should be hurt—ever. There is too much pain in this world as it is."

Kemper knew he was hearing the litany according to vows of duty and self-sacrifice. "No." He shook his head.

"So be it," Quenneville said. "I will not bother you."

"After you've had your heart stop—feel that, Marcel. Then we can talk again."

Quenneville frowned and looked for a waitress. "You have changed much, friend. It's now all 'I—I—I' with you. You have become another victim."

"I have every intention of not becoming a victim."

"You are the victim if you think you are. You are right. You should leave. Merry Christmas, my friend. Fish well."

72

ELEVEN

DECEMBER 22, 1941, and northwestern Vermont tried to regain its slim confidence with tepid Christmas touches while the war darkened its future. Quenneville left Kemper on the sidewalk and sank heavily into his Pontiac at the curb. Kemper went to listen to a confection of amateur choruses rehearse the *Messiah* in the Methodist Church across the park. Their director was a nervous preacher, who flashed with anger and threatened to abandon the event when they failed. But their hearts weren't in it. This was another effort to comfort their best fears; their fears were stronger than the music, more savage; the music seemed almost childishly frivolous.

Kemper poked through the shops while the early northern darkness nuzzled the park maples. Snow fell silently. Men wearing black barn boots shifted their cowshit feet as their perfume gift boxes were wrapped in a department store. There was a mannequin on a glass shelf above a display of ladies' underwear; someone had nibbled her elbow and eaten a chunk from her thigh, leaving flat white scars.

Kemper went into the hardware store, but their fishing tackle had been boxed away for the winter. A short dark man with a boneless bulb of a nose jabbered at his customers and finally at Kemper. He went away quickly enough, after telling Kemper he didn't want to see any salesmen—he was too busy. Kemper told him he was not a salesman and

73

searched a knife display for a tiny pocketknife to replace the beautiful knife stolen from him in the Norfolk hospital.

He found one: thin, of polished bone with brass rivets and good steel in the blades. Kemper hauled out one of his cigars and shaped its ends with the knife as he waited to pay behind a farmer who was buying rat poison. Kemper was next up. The short dark man held out his hand to take the knife.

"Thanks, Mayor," the farmer said over his shoulder as he was leaving.

Kemper raised his eyes. His cigar curled a circle of blue smoke over the counter. "You the mayor?" he asked.

"I am," the man said. "That's a good knife."

They were alone at the counter. Kemper felt the tug of duty. He'd take the knife and leave quietly after the man finished wrapping it in Christmas foil. "You visitin'?" the man asked as he reached for the hanging string from a ball on the ceiling.

"Visiting," Kemper said.

"You got folks here?"

"No," Kemper said. He reached for his package and felt the presence of the fat Montreal cop and a weight of years on his tongue. "My name is Baskins." And then slowly: "I'm leaving tomorrow morning."

The man's hands held over his cash register drawer, motionless. "You staying locally, are you?"

Kemper could actually feel the venom transit the smoky air over the counter. "Across the way," Kemper said, pointing. "Place is an awful dump."

"Is it?" the man asked, deliberately spilling Kemper's change on the counter. "Most folks like the Jesse Welden— been here for years. Very famous. Best food for miles. Sorry you aren't comfortable."

"Doesn't matter," Kemper said.

Kemper turned and left, slipping his precious new knife into his coat pocket. I'll be damned, he thought. Given the

74

choice—and that brief transaction did contain a choice—given the choice, he'd gone with the weight of years. He'd tweaked the man's bulb of a nose. And strangely, Kemper felt content and quiet as he crossed the park to the hotel.

Had Kemper walked to the end of the sidewalk, past the appliance store, and ducked around the corner, he'd have seen the tearoom run by Mrs. Willis and her cousin. A narrow presumption of a business, the tearoom gave the women of the town somewhere to rest while their husbands bought feed or sold cars.

Had Kemper passed the tearoom, he'd have seen Morison Menard at a table with Hannah Doll. Menard, with his glossy black hair glued to his skull, hunched in a businesslike way over the table, his shoulders forward as if he wanted to confine his conversation with Hannah to the area between them. "I've waited longer than I wanted to," he said.

Hannah hadn't touched her coffee.

"I think I've been fair in this. I'm a patient man, but patience is no reward. We have a deal between us. You krauts pay us money to get your people on trains, we provide the security and the beds. You said Leonard would always pay us from down south. Leonard was a fool, but I'm sorry he's dead. Takes a hard head to stay in business these days."

"And a hard heart," Hannah said. She disliked Menard so much she had to hold herself in place.

"Well, as I say, matters have been allowed to sort of lapse . . . what with Leonard's tragedy. We haven't had any money to speak of for months. Leonard drank a lot, and I think his vices got the best of him in the end. He had our money, all right. And what he didn't drink he took with him off that train. I hate to have things get like this—you're right about a hard heart, I guess—anyway, we need to do something about arrearages and we've got to do something about future installments. You said you'd contact some of your people. Have you?"

Hannah said she had.

"What does it look like?" Menard asked.

"I'm not certain," she said. Menard wore sweet cologne that always made her want to retch.

"Well, we have to do something, don't we? As I say, we've waited a goodly long time. I'd hate to have to take any action, but if we don't arrive at some mutually satisfactory agreement, I'll be forced into a box. You see that, don't you?"

"What will you do?" She watched her fingers shake. She couldn't hold herself much longer.

"Well, we don't want to go into that now. But we—my associates and I, especially Sykes—we'd be forced to protect ourselves."

"What does that mean?"

Menard smiled his oily banker's smile. Hannah wondered what his wife felt when he arrived home for the evening. How could she feel anything but repulsion?

"Tell you what," he said, brightening suddenly. "I'll meet you at the boathouse on Christmas Eve at seven o'clock. Give you a few more days."

"Christmas Eve? Are you joking?"

"Business before pleasure."

"Won't your family miss you? I thought you had children?"

"They understand," he said.

I'll bet they don't, she thought.

"I'll be there," she said.

"Hope that doesn't put you out," he smiled.

"It doesn't," she said, pushing away from the table. "Meeting you will give me something to do on Christmas Eve."

She left him hunched there, smiling his oily banker's smile.

Kemper was reading in bed, listening to the radio for the eight o'clock news from New York. His isolation was nearly complete, he realized. The Jesse Welden study had yielded a book called *The Dangerous River,* by a displaced Englishman named Patterson. Kemper had quickly read the first fifty pages; it was the tale of a man's year in the frozen fearsomeness on the Nahanni River in the Northwest Territories. When he heard the news announced from New York, Kemper tried to balance the relative obscurity of a place like St. Albans with the staggering loneliness of Patterson's battle with wolves. The Jesse Welden was, in comparison, a bright anvil of civility.

The war news was the same, he thought. He lifted Patterson's book again. The United States was firing its industrial boiler coast to coast. Edward R. Murrow, calling from London, described the plight of refugees adrift in the North Sea. Then Kemper heard the name Churchill. He'd landed in Virginia this afternoon, the news reader said, and was hurried to the White House, where he planned to have his Christmas holiday with the President. Churchill's naval uniform was described. The Prime Minister and the President were weaving the integrity of the Grand Alliance, as it was called, to encounter the ravages of fascism around the globe. Nothing was said about Ottawa.

Kemper had been told to be in Ottawa on Saturday, December 27. Should he go back to New York or stay over here until Saturday? Or should he drive on now to Ottawa and wait for Churchill there? He'd be closer to Patterson, the Nahanni River, and the wolves; in fact, he could peer into the vast emptiness from Ottawa's Parliament Hill.

The knock at the door came like a shot in the night. Kemper got out of bed and found the sheriff smiling in the hallway.

"Mr. Baskins?" the sheriff asked. He wanted to come in. Kemper hesitated for a moment, but then let the man

77

squeeze by. "Think we could have the door closed, Mr. Baskins? Ben Sykes—Franklin County Sheriff."

Kemper shook his hand.

Sykes was thick in the shoulders, with light brown hair mixed with grey when he took his hat off. His uniform was ornately dressy with lighter blue patches along his shoulders. The epaulets were dark blue. A long .44 Colt was strapped to his hip with a bulging cartridge belt. The sheriff had a head cold and a kindly face, except for the thin set of his lips, which seemed somehow cruel.

"Sorry to bother you like this," he said after he'd gazed around Kemper's bedroom. Kemper shut off the radio.

"Go ahead," Kemper said.

Sykes had no coat with him. Kemper wondered where he'd come from to be without a coat. Or Sykes could have left the thing downstairs to get the full mileage out of his uniform. Kemper went for something nearer the uniform show and was convinced of it when he saw Sykes pose with his thumbs hooked into his cartridge belt.

"Leonard Baskins your brother?"

Kemper nodded—honey for the bears, he thought.

"Unfortunate, that was. Sorry to hear the news. You clearing up some of his business?"

"Why do you want to know?" Kemper thought he'd go for innocent belligerency.

"An unaccompanied death. We have to do this every time anyone dies alone."

"My brother wasn't alone. He stepped off a train at the wrong station."

"I expect he did, didn't he. Well, there was no one to see how it happened. I hope you don't mind—this is just to get things straight. Do you live near your brother in Hartford?"

God knows what Baskins had said, Kemper thought. "I live in New York City," he said. "My brother didn't live in Hartford." Kemper had no idea where Baskins actually had lived.

"Thought he did," Sykes smiled. "Where did he live?"

"He lived in hotels like this one, sheriff. He was a salesman. Always on the road."

"He drank a lot."

"He did," Kemper said.

"Drunk when he went off that train."

"I suppose so."

"You wouldn't mind my seeing some identification, would you?"

"Why?" Kemper asked.

"Just like to know who I'm talking to."

"You know as much as you're going to know. Why are you pestering me?"

"No reason to be hot about this. I like to be careful."

"I expect you've made a career out of sticking your nose into a lot of things that don't concern you."

Sykes was fundamentally a bull, one of those stereotypic small-town behemoths who, once elected, separated the human race into cowboys and Indians, bad guys and good guys, harmless ass-kissers and potential enemies to be watched: the only good guys, his own back-slapping cronies. True to his calling, Sykes puffed out his chest and rattled the cluster of keys at his belt. He started to speak, but Kemper cut him off. "What'd you say your name is?"

"Wait a second, bud."

"You wait a second, you yahoo. How is it you're asking questions about a death that didn't happen in your county?"

"Here! I suggest you settle down. Ain't none of your business what I do."

"You made it my business when you knocked on my door!"

"Now, you listen here—" Sykes moved ominously. His thin lips almost vanished in sourness. "You've no call to get hot about this thing."

"And you have no reason to be asking me for identification."

79

"I'm the law officer in this county."

"In the county. But that's their problem. I'll wager the city police chief would have something to say about your right to be here." Kemper hadn't any idea what he was talking about.

"We can find out," Sykes said coolly.

"Forget it," Kemper said. "You're only doing your job. My brother's death has really upset me." Kemper smiled and Sykes seemed to be shifting gears, looking for reverse. "You must see a lot of folks disturbed by some pretty nasty deeds—and this is so near to Christmas."

"I do," Sykes answered.

"My brother was a deeply troubled man. I understand there was a woman in town he was close to."

"I don't know. He was a salesman. He was in and out of here a lot."

"Leonard was in and out of a lot of spots," Kemper said. "He wrote to me often—said he had money in a bank here, but I can't find it."

"How much?" Sykes asked too quickly.

"I don't know. That's why I'm here."

Kemper couldn't figure out what Sykes wanted. He said, "How did you find out my brother died?"

"Common knowledge," Sykes answered in a practiced response.

"Is it? And what things are you trying to straighten out?"

"Official curiosity," Sykes answered. "Lots of people knew your brother."

"Official curiosity, my ass," Kemper said. "Why did you drive all the way to Richmond to see his body?"

"I didn't drive anywhere," Sykes spat.

"Cody says you were in his office looking for answers. What are you doing, Sykes?"

"Hold on here! You just hold on!" Sykes shouted. The color had risen in his cheeks.

"That loon—Ball—in Richmond says you came to see

80

my brother's body. Why? My brother didn't die in your county, Sheriff."

"I did not go to Richmond."

Kemper knew he had Sykes in something. When the sheriff lies, when the cop or the border guard shades the truth, the truth is not something he wants anyone looking at. "If you weren't there," Kemper said, "then your twin brother was." Kemper took another shot into the dark cave. "Ball says you were. If you're not lying, then someone is."

"I'll be back, Mr. Baskins," Sykes suddenly said.

"I'm leaving in the morning."

"When you've cooled off a touch, we'll talk. I'll see you in the morning." He sounded disturbed—his tongue in overdrive. Kemper didn't want him to go. He thought that Sykes had experience in talking to people—that it was most unlikely he'd bluster like this unless he found himself in deeper waters than he'd expected. Something in the past few minutes had thrown Sykes. Kemper could only wonder, because the sheriff was gone; it was like reeling in a beast of a bass on light line and having the fish suddenly dive for the bottom.

"I hear the music," Kemper said aloud. The room seemed strangely vacant.

Laughter came from somewhere upstairs. He felt scattered. His heart seemed intact, or at least regularly content for the moment. Did Baskins fall off the train? Or was he pushed? Kemper was here to identify a body. He'd done that in spades. Quenneville and his sheriffs and mayors were on another level of the game. Kemper didn't want to play.

Had the mayor with the clown's nose triggered the sheriff? And why would Sykes show up at all to question Leonard Baskins's brother?

Honey for the bears, he thought. Only I'm the honey.

Later, as Kemper strolled onto the concrete platforms in the empty train shed, he saw a child standing near the far brick wall across the rails. They were alone, each watching the other. Kemper crossed to the kid, slowly. The boy's head was covered with a cloth hat tied under his chin, and a scarf had been knotted around his neck. His pants and boots were white with snow.

Kemper nodded to the kid. "Kinda' late to be out, isn't it?" he said.

"Waiting for my father," the little boy said, wiping his nose with his sleeve and tugging on the rope to his sled. A wooden box had been tied to the sled. "He's the conductor," the boy said proudly.

"How old are you?"

"Ten."

"How far did you walk?"

"From my house."

Kemper turned to see up the tracks into the dark. "What's your name, son?"

"Walter."

"Your father on the train from Montreal?"

The boy's face was red with the cold. "He buys us food in Montreal. I wait for him and take it home. He can't get off the train until tomorrow."

Kemper wanted to hug this child who waited late at night with his sled. "You're a good boy," Kemper said.

The tiny face brightened. "I know I am," the kid said. "Are you lost, mister?"

"I think so," Kemper said.

TWELVE

THE EASTERN TOWNSHIPS OF QUEBEC look like Dorothy's Kansas after the tornado. The flood plain of the St. Lawrence River is wide and unrumpled except for the occasional towering tumulus of granite here and there. The farms are small, the buildings weathered grey, the barnyards mires of mud and diligence. South of Quebec City, among the hazardous lives of the not-so-prosperous towns, there is a lake, Black Lake, that was once a lure to fishermen scrambling away from their wives and children for a weekend of giant pike and whiskey.

Black Lake was open this night, with only a skirt of crackling ice along its shoreline, truly black and abandoned to the boreal cold that lurked just over the curves of the northern horizon. Men mark the year with numbers and names like January: as one of thousands of Canadian lakes, Black Lake measured the year from one gelid paralysis to another.

Streicher had telephoned straight into the National Assembly building in Quebec City to Jean Mouton's private secretary. A bachelor, the minister was a man of lonely habit and had fled as he always did on the worst weekends to his house on Black Lake. Mouton would return after New Year's.

Don't count on it, Streicher had thought. He got the location of Mouton's cottage from two boys cutting wood along the gravel road that circled the lake. Then he waited until dark.

Mouton was a man of greed. He controlled a variety of work projects in the province and collected his tribute, including a monthly stipend from the Abwehr, under the table from all of them. As a minister without portfolio, Mouton was something of an unofficial bagman for his colleagues in the cabinet.

Narrow in the chest with a delicately chirping voice, Mouton maintained his reticence about what he did. He was a man of confidence, nonetheless, and worried only when he imagined the newspaper howls if they ever discovered his fondness for tight thirteen-year-old flesh. Jean Mouton collected pubescent girls and had had, this afternoon, his last romp on a bed with two of them before he left for Black Lake.

He might have worried about his willingness to share some of his espionage secrets with the RCMP; however, Abwehr people were clumsy and deserved their fate and he was in no danger, he thought. In fact, the RCMP telephoned him regularly to inquire after Abwehr plans; Jean Mouton was always happy to speak knowingly to his police friends in Ottawa. He might have worried about his exposed position; he didn't, though. Once he had the cottage warmed by the stove and the lamps low and homey, he padded out onto his porch and stared at the gentle night on Black Lake. Had he known what was coming, he wouldn't have been on the porch. Had he the means to raise the sun, Jean Mouton would have been able to see across Black Lake to the trees where Streicher was turning the rowboat over.

Streicher heaved the boat to the icy edge of the lake and went back for the oars. His bakery truck was parked between two fishing cabins near the main road away from the water.

The boat rattled across the ice effortlessly and slid into the black water softly. Sleet on a gentle breath of arctic hush hit his shoulders and smacked into the water as he pulled on the oars and turned the boat for the only lights on the far shore. He didn't want his tire marks anywhere near Mouton's house; he planned to row back, replace the boat, and drive immediately onto the highway pavement.

He pulled silently; the boat went easily. Streicher thought about the fish below him and wondered if they'd think the boat in any way a peculiar occurrence in their slowly breathing suspense before the ice.

Jean Mouton extinguished all his lamps but one, and that one he turned down until his shadow grew against the wall. The stove gave off a pulsing crackle of heat and a faint smokiness in the cottage. He got into bed and reached his canvas bag of photographs onto the blankets. Mouton had hundreds of snapshots of young nipples and vulvas; his favorites were those with no pubic hair between their sprawled legs.

He felt warm. Black Lake had always been a pleasing release for him in its quiet—away from the catcalls of the National Assembly. His penis grew as he sorted through his photographs until he felt tired and stashed them all away onto the floor. He blew out his last lamp. Relaxed and alone, he rubbed his balls into a spurt of delicious release, and closed his eyes.

Streicher had seen the lights go down and stopped rowing. Black Lake was indeed black. There wasn't a star or even the faintest glimmer of light anywhere. He shuddered with cold and took off his gloves to get his hands inside his coat and under his arms.

Germany is more than miles from this place, he thought. Somewhere out there a war went on without him. But not for long without him. His years in England had taught him to speak fluent English; those years had also taught him life on the fringes. He'd felt alone and forgotten, cut off from the men who had taken the course of the world's affairs as their own. But now—he shuddered again—here on this si-

85

lent Canadian lake on another continent, he was one of the chosen, one of their emissaries into the bright future of a thousand years of light. He'd tell about this one someday, and they'd listen with delight and consternation that bravery came so easily to some of them, to this man, who now dipped an oar and swung the boat around for the shore.

Mouton was in that nether world of half-sleep before the dreams, and had he thought anything of it, he might have raised his head to listen as Streicher scratched the boat onto firm ice.

The boat balanced finally on the edge, and Streicher listened. There was nothing. He went quickly to the cottage and climbed the stairs to the porch. It had to be Mouton, and it had to look like natural death.

Streicher reached into his pocket for the injector. Shaped like a round, slightly bulbous radio tuning knob, Streicher's injector was a product of his English years alone. With a spring wound by a thumbscrew on the top, the injector had a tiny hole on its flat bottom through which, when the thumbscrew was flicked, a hypodermic stinger shot out to release the contents of a glass vial within. The vial contained a small quantity of concentrated solution of hydrogen sulphide. Hydrogen sulphide in its gaseous form has the familiar stink of rotten eggs, and one part of the gas in two hundred parts of air is more than fatal. Streicher could concentrate the loathesome stuff by the gallon with ferous sulphide, almost any acid, and a few simple chemistry procedures.

He wound the spring. The man within slept with his back to Streicher. The eisenglas in the stove door glowed orange. Streicher tried the knob—the door latch released. He went in quickly, holding the edge of the door tightly, expectantly. Mouton seemed to be alone in the one-room cottage.

There were chairs in the dull gloom of the stove, a rug over to the man's bed. Streicher, his heels coming down firmly and quietly, stepped slowly to Mouton. And it was

Mouton—or enough like the newspaper photographs for Streicher to take a breath.

Streicher got the edge of the blanket in his fingers, his right thumb on the injector's thumbscrew. Mouton sighed and exhaled like a child asleep after a storm.

Slowly, he lifted the blanket. There was Mouton's neck above his pajama top, below his ear. Streicher reached—he snapped the thumbscrew as soon as the injector touched Mouton's skin. The injector fired, Mouton twitched, then opened his eyes, his mouth trying to scream. His eyeballs bulged until Streicher thought they'd begin to ooze. Streicher held the man down until the convulsions ceased, then stood up. Mouton moaned and was silent.

Streicher replaced the blanket against Mouton's face and quickly turned for the porch. He listened for anyone else in the cottage before he shut the door, and then went down the steps to the ground. He knew he'd leave prints, but there was nothing he could do about that. With the holidays coming and the promise of snow, Streicher hoped enough time would pass to cover his entry. The hydrogen sulphide would give Mouton's death the general appearance of a heart seizure while he slept, and all but the best forensic pathologists would miss the tiny swelling on Mouton's neck.

Streicher rowed leisurely back across Black Lake to the trees, where he dragged the boat over the ice and replaced it on the logs. Mouton's side of Black Lake was dark and quiet. Streicher was cold; the bakery truck would have to run for miles before its heater warmed him.

He turned quickly onto the highway and ran up through the gears. He'd drive through Sutton and roll quietly past Hannah's—she'd be asleep in her bed under the eaves—and then he'd cross the border and get to Jaeger's cottage before morning. Berlin wanted him on the air at 7:12 A.M. He'd make it.

THIRTEEN

TUESDAY
DECEMBER
2 3
1 9 4 1

KEMPER PACKED IN THE MORNING before he went down for breakfast. His spirits had flagged once more, and confusion had come to roost on the horns of his decision. There were choices: he could leave now for New York, or he could drive to Ottawa. Either way, he would leave Baskins in Ball's Poughkeepsie, a plump memento of a man's decision to save himself.

Or, he might stay on, with Quenneville's voice picking in his ear, and at least make some determination, as the FBI liked to say, as to why Leonard Baskins was in Ball's Poughkeepsie in the first place.

The Jesse Welden House might be a humane holiday replacement for his dusty rooms on Seventy-nineth Street. He needed quiet. If he stayed here, there was pride to consider, his pride in his work—and Kemper could not easily abandon this last job, a job even Moffet's college kid could do. He hadn't called Moffet last night at seven. There will be consequences for that indiscretion, he thought.

He gazed at the diners eating their breakfasts, as if they had the answer. And he decided to take short steps.

Kemper paid for his coffee, and, puffing on a cigar, hiked down to the railroad station. Cody was somewhere in the yards. The dispatcher said he'd find him. Kemper pointed over the dispatcher's telegraph keys to the windows. Where was the train, the cars that Baskins had left in Richmond?

"Better than that," the dispatcher said. He tipped up his

green eyeshade, leaned, and said, "The whole thing, minus the engine and mail car, is on the far side—near the fence. We don't ever cut that one up."

Soft bullets of rain fell as Kemper slowly crossed the rails. He climbed the steps and strolled the length of the empty train. Like an abandoned house, he thought. Kemper dropped into a parlor-car chair at the end and waited for Cody, massaging the morning stiffness in his stump.

"*I* called it a suicide," Cody answered when he finally arrived. Cody appeared exhausted, irritated. "I came back from New London the next day. Not to be cruel, but suicide doesn't exactly stop any railroad. Why do you want to know?"

"How did you decide?"

"My crews—their reports are clear enough—you can read them yourself."

"If Baskins fell off this train—"

Cody took off his Stetson and sprawled. "This may not be the train. I'd have to check the roster."

"Doesn't matter," Kemper said. "If Baskins fell out a door—those doors are sometimes open, aren't they?"

"Sometimes," Cody said. "If they aren't slammed shut, they'll generally vibrate open."

"If he fell out, he'd have fallen almost straight down. This guy didn't. How far did he travel?"

"Twelve feet, maybe fifteen in all."

"He'd have momentum—the speed of the train. I suppose he could have smashed a baggage cart and station. Seems unlikely, though." Kemper flashed a match and touched off a new cigar. "Seems crazy to kill yourself by jumping at a station. You said they used bridges, yes?"

Cody nodded and drew in a labored breath.

"Even if you're drunk. Maybe Baskins thought Richmond was his stop?" Kemper grinned. "Still, he did a lot of damage. Who closed the door after Baskins jumped?"

Cody opened his eyes. "One of the crew, I guess."

"Was there an open door?"

"I don't know. I guess there had to be—these things won't close on their own."

"And someone jumping has no way to slam the door behind him, because there are no outside handles on these doors."

"There are on some cars," Cody said, smiling.

"Who closed the door?" Kemper asked.

Cody shrugged and slapped his Stetson against his leg. He said the conductor that night was coming in this morning from a run to Boston. "His name is Alex Jaeger." Cody had vinegar in his voice.

Kemper wondered how many conductors worked for the railroad, and how it was that Cody knew Jaeger's schedule? Small railroad? Good superintendent? Or something else?

The train crews had a waiting room at the north end of the station platform. Kemper went in behind Cody. Jaeger was at an open grey locker. Early forties, black clipped hair, and a face smooth and polished. Jaeger looked like a conductor even without his hat and uniform tunic.

"I closed the door," Jaeger said, his eyes darting to Kemper. Cody had asked the question and Kemper caught a whiff of animosity between these two men.

"Which one?" Kemper asked.

"Head end of the parlor car on the right."

"When?" Kemper asked.

"When what?" Jaeger shot back.

"When did you close the door?"

"Montpelier—the police had us stopped there for an hour and thirty-seven minutes."

Kemper understood clearly that Jaeger wanted to know who Kemper was. Conductors were fearsome men at times.

Kemper left Cody on the platform, went back up to the

dispatcher's tower, and telephoned Farley Ball in Richmond.

"How you are?" Ball bellowed.

"Better," Kemper said. "Have you got Baskins in your Poughkeepsie?"

"You want him?"

Kemper slowed Ball down and asked him to roll Baskins into the bright lights once more. "You've got a good eye," Kemper suggested.

"Not as good as Randall's," Ball answered.

"You're too modest. Get him out and take a long look at what you see. Will you do that?"

Ball wanted to know where Kemper was. "You going to be around for Christmas?" Ball asked. "What am I looking for?"

"I don't know," Kemper said. "But if anyone could see something queer, you could."

"If you're around day after tomorrow, drop by. That's Christmas, you know?"

"I might."

Kemper hung up and rifled through the St. Albans telephone directory.

Dorcas Baldwin lived on Messenger Street. The dispatcher told him how to get there. "You can walk it," he said, with an errant eye for Kemper's ability to walk anywhere. Dr. Beam had been right about his leg as well: Kemper knew he was limping. "A bit of stiffness," he said to himself as he clumped down the tower stairs outside. The thought came to him, once again, that bodies do wear out.

Dorcas Baldwin's house had a wide front porch and a bell knob in the center of the door that Kemper spun once.

"This isn't convenient," she said when she answered. Dorcas Baldwin blushed with fear, as red splotches erupted on her throat when Kemper said he was Frank Baskins.

A piano thumped somewhere in the house. "I'm teaching just now," she said.

"Leonard's death was inconvenient for me, Miss Baldwin."

She was a woman older than her age. She could have been a very pretty twenty-five, but Dorcas Baldwin was overweight and wearing a formless polka-dot dress. "Couldn't you come back?"

She relented quickly and showed Kemper down a hallway. There was a child playing an upright piano in the front room. Dorcas Baldwin pulled a handkerchief from her dress sleeve, took an artificial swipe at her nose, and said she'd be finished in ten minutes.

Kemper could smell lamb cooking. The wallpaper was dark and lifeless in the sitting room where she left him. Her books were Reader's Digest Condensed over another shelf of religious volumes. Kemper opened something called *The Darwinian Heresy* and found it to be one of those swollen nineteenth-century religious tracts supporting Christian bigotry and opprobrium. He put it back. The people in her photographs wore high white collars and did not smile.

The piano noise stopped.

Kemper took a quick look at her desk. Piles of lined composition paper, adolescent scrawls in the ornate handwriting of the young females where all is show and no go.

Kemper heard her solid shoes pounding over the hallway rug. "Would you come in?" she said, showing him into the music room. There were two pianos. Shelves of sheet music. The child had gone. Her hands were shaking. Kemper wanted a cigar.

"I have to tell you," she said. "Your brother was an extremely jealous man." Her hair had been so tightly curled it didn't flutter at all when she turned. "We saw each other, off and on. Nothing serious—or at least it wasn't to me. A little more to him. Much more to Leonard. I said I didn't think we had a future—he had asked me to marry him. I

92

said we weren't compatible enough for serious undertakings. He became very argumentative and left."

"He's dead, you know?"

"I know that. Your brother, Mr. Baskins—and I must say this so that you understand—your brother had an alcohol problem. He did. He refused to give it up, even when I begged him to."

Why would she beg Baskins to do anything? he wondered.

"How often did he stay here with you?" Kemper asked.

"I beg your pardon! I'm sorry—" the woman positively whirred with venom—"you have no call to come into my house and accuse me of anything like that. That was a very ugly question. I don't know where you come from, but I saw that same streak in Leonard. I'd like you to leave, Mr. Baskins." Dorcas Baldwin swept her arm into the air as though she were the Bathsheba of St. Albans, and pointed a chunky finger toward the hallway. "This minute, Mr. Baskins."

Kemper remembered another woman who years ago had told him to stand in a wastebasket beside her desk.

"I will not be blamed for that man's death," she said, drawing her shoulders up. "Not by you. Not by anyone. He was an unfortunate, and I am in no way responsible for any of his stupid messes. We were not serious in any way! Now, please leave."

Kemper relished the outside air as he walked back to the hotel. He was passing the desk when the desk clerk crooked a finger at him and whispered conspiratorily, "The sheriff wants to see you, Mr. Baskins. He's in the dining room."

Hannah had last spoken to Quenneville on Remembrance Day. At the start of their conversations in the spring, when Quenneville had first come to see her and was unaware that Hannah was not as committed as Margaret, Hannah had taken some solace from the detective's peculiar familiarity with strangers. She understood he had taken sides against the Abwehr and that she was indecently exposed. Once she began—as with her activities for the Germans—she would be drawn into the center and quartered at the crossroads unless she made it clear that her primary motive in contacting him was survival. He said he understood. Quenneville was always gentle with her, forgiving, and would talk with her as a great-uncle might, even on the weekends and at night when she telephoned his home.

But this morning he was concerned when he telephoned her. "Why didn't you tell this Menard fella there was no money? Leonard was only the moneybags—and he brought it up from New York. You haven't got any money."

"I listened to Menard. That's all I did."

"I know, my girl. But without Leonard there is nothing more to do, unless your Abwehr friends send someone to take his place. With the Americans in the war, I doubt your friends will do anything until they thoroughly sniff the air."

Quenneville was right, as usual: Blue was here, had been here, and he was sniffing the air.

"This is your moment to finish with these guys. You've told me how much you want to stop. Tell Menard. He said the boathouse tomorrow night—Christmas Eve?"

"That's right," Hannah said.

"They are very greedy men," he said. "Tell him you have nothing to offer. You are not American. They will have to cross the border to get to you. Tell him the network is closed, that Leonard was the key man, that you have no further responsibilities to them. Kiss them good-bye. In fact, do not go to the boathouse. That is no spot for a woman on Christmas Eve or any other eve, I think."

Instead of relief, Hannah felt a compulsion to talk. Quenneville knew nothing of Blue. Blue would be ruined as an Abwehr intelligence agent, but he would be with her, and Quenneville might be able to shut out the madness long enough for them to love each other. If Hannah did tell Quenneville about Blue, she wondered what Quenneville would do. And if Blue knew about Quenneville, would he vanish as suddenly as he had appeared?

"And if any Germans contact you, you must telephone to me immediately. Will you do that?"

"I'll try," she answered.

"Do not go to the boathouse. Listen to me please—are you listening? You are quiet."

She said she was listening. She always listened to him.

"You should," he said. His voice sounded like a goose's honk from the far shore of a lake. "You must be very, very careful. After you talk to Menard, call me if you like. But you must melt away like a snowball on a sidewalk after that. You are well?"

She said she was.

"Joyeaux Noël," he said. "Are you going to church?"

Hannah said she would go to mass at the convent in Farnham on Christmas morning.

"Remember me in your prayers, Hannah. You are in mine."

She hung up the telephone with a mixture of consolation and fear. Blue would be furious with her if he knew. And Quenneville might take Blue away if he knew. Better she remained at the crossroads awhile longer. She remembered Heine: "Follow the good path or the evil one. To stand at the crossroads requires more strength than you possess."

The days passed, counted in hours. Quite soon I realised that immediately after Christmas I must address the Congress of the United States, and a few days later the Canadian Parliament in Ottawa. These great occasions imposed heavy demands on my life and strength, and were additional to all the daily consultations and mass of current business. In fact, I do not know how I got through it all.

★   ★   ★

95

Streicher kept his eye on the car following him. He had crossed into Canada at Highgate Springs; the grey Chevrolet had been parked in an auto parts store just across the border and for the last six miles or so had stayed with him even when he slowed for the guy to pass him.

"Not now, you bastards," he said as he turned into a grocery store parking lot. He dropped out of the bakery truck. The car went by, hissing in the rain. Streicher kept his eye on it as he went up the stairs onto the porch of the store. The driver hadn't touched his brakes.

He bought pipe tobacco and talked to the storekeeper to give the car time enough to come back.

Nothing, he thought, starting his truck. He searched the driveways and a church parking area as he drove away. "Not now," he muttered, catching high gear.

He was exhausted but exhilarated. Churchill was coming! The revelation had gone off in his head like a grenade. Berlin had been abrupt: CHURCHILL TO TRAVEL OTTAWA 28. CANCEL ACTIVITIES. TRAVEL OTTAWA 27. NEXT TRANSMISSION 24 PLUS ONE.

Streicher had asked for a confirmation signal. But Berlin wasn't taking any chances with excessive transmissions and simply repeated his code name, KATZ, before they shut down.

He'd nervously unscrewed his antenna lead and crammed his headphones and the key into the radio compartment built into a bread shelf in the bakery truck. Jaeger hadn't been at the house; Streicher left a message under the shingle saying he'd be back in the morning.

He was alone now. The grey Chevrolet wasn't there as he rumbled down Sutton's main street.

Hannah had people in the shop. Streicher retrieved his whiskey from the cellar stairs and drank a double at the sink.

"I saw you drive past," she said, coming up behind him to wrap her arms around his chest. And once in the night, he thought.

She kissed him, then tucked her head under his chin.

He told Hannah he could stay the night but had to be off early the next morning. "That's all right," she said. "We have time enough. You look frayed around the edges. Did you see Mouton?"

He said he had and that she was accurate. "Mouton is a liability," he said. "But we won't worry about him for now."

She seemed lighter, more agile, almost happy as she filled the teakettle and turned on the stove. "Menard says I have to do something about arrearages. Leonard drank some of their money."

"How much does he want?"

"I don't know—a thousand? He wants me to meet him at the boathouse tomorrow night at ten."

"Don't go. Forget him," Streicher said.

She protested and said Menard would be looking for her.

"Don't worry," he said. "I will speak to him. And then I must go away for a while. New York, then Philadelphia. I may not be back until after the New Year."

"When?"

"In the morning."

"Dear god," she said. "This never stops. You won't be here tomorrow night?"

Her disappointment was palpable. He shook his head no and poured himself another double. Hannah stood staring out at the clothesline and the rain.

Streicher had the name Churchill emblazoned in neon letters inside his head. "I will try to get back as soon as I can," he said. He had no idea if he'd ever get back. Alone and on the prowl, he was so certain of what he did, but when she was with him, next to him, his concentration evaporated quickly. He might never get back—he couldn't let that happen.

She was stern, resolved to her uncertainty. "I have customers," she said. "Drink yourself into a stupor. It's all so hopeless. Menard, who I think has a family, wants to meet me on Christmas Eve. And you—" she hesitated "—I'm so sick of being alone. Always alone. I hate it. You'll be god knows where and I'll be here. That's another Christmas to remember."

His dilemma was acute. The rules were so precisely against his situation. There had been clear warnings during his training against any personal involvement. And he had glibly assumed, then, that women had never meant anything to him. They hadn't. Until now.

He had to leave her. He had to give her up.

"You said you were leaving this morning," the sheriff said to Kemper in the dining room. "This is the Reverend Stagg."

The sheriff's companion was a watery-eyed man in his sixties dressed in a dog collar and blue shirt under a ratty-looking suit.

"I've been to see Dorcas Baldwin," Kemper said.

The Reverend Stagg nodded his grey head knowingly, but deferred to Sykes. "She's very upset by your brother's death," the sheriff said.

"Aren't we all," Kemper said. "Good of you to come, Reverend. You knew my brother as well, did you?"

"Ah . . . no. No, I didn't, I'm afraid. But Miss Baldwin is one of my congregation."

"How pleasant for you," Kemper said. "And you're right about her being upset," he said to the sheriff. "She seems absolutely stricken, I'd say."

"Your brother was a nuisance for her. They had . . . well, they had difficulties. I guess he was pretty serious about her." Sykes twirled a spoon in his fingers. "Mr. Baskins? I guess I'd like to know what brought you here. The Reverend Stagg is a friend of mine."

These people are thick as jackals, Kemper thought. The gloomy little man with eyes like taillights—the Reverend

Stagg—waited for the answer as though he were on another wavelength completely and couldn't care a whit what Sykes did. And Sykes didn't remember well enough to lie successfully: last night the sheriff hadn't known anything about a girlfriend; today, he knew Dorcas was upset.

Kemper let their discomfort build, then finally said, "I don't believe my brother is a suicide. Nor do I believe his death was accidental."

Reverend Stagg flickered—just a touch of apoplexy.

"Go on," the sheriff said.

"I believe Leonard was killed."

"Do you?"

"I further believe he was thrown from that train."

"But, Mr. Baskins, your brother was hitting the booze."

Kemper kept his eyes on Stagg. "That's true, Sheriff. But he didn't fall off that train. And he didn't jump."

"Care to tell us how you know this?"

"No, I don't care to tell you how I know anything," Kemper growled.

"Do you see?" the sheriff said to Stagg, who had set his gaze wandering toward one of the waitresses. Kemper noticed a fuzz of white powder on Stagg's hands, and more above the collar on his scrofulous neck. Kemper wouldn't order lunch; the sheriff will bear down now, he thought.

"Well, Mr. Baskins, I think it's fair to say we are having those same thoughts ourselves."

"We? The Reverend Stagg one of your deputies, is he?"

"I am an interested party," Stagg said bitterly.

"My brother was an organizer for a German-American Bund. Some of those people screaming about America first—that sort of claptrap." Kemper let them churn that for a minute and then said, "If he ran true to form, Leonard would have tried to organize something like that here. He was vitriolic against our involvement in a European war."

"Was he?" Stagg answered.

"Any of that foolishness here?" Kemper asked.

99

"Some talk," the sheriff said. "But now with the war on—"

"They've scurried back into the woodwork, have they?"

"There isn't any talk like that anymore. People here are patriots. Way back to the Revolution we've been patriotic."

"I'll let you know," Kemper said, getting up from the table.

"Are you leaving or not, Mr. Baskins?"

"I'm not sure," Kemper said. He heard the name Baskins shouted at him. The desk clerk was waving.

Kemper took the telephone at the desk. Cody was upset. "Look, I don't give a damn what you guys do, but that Moffet jackass from New York just gave me an earful. He's looking for you."

"Did you tell him to call here?"

"I didn't tell him anything. Now, I'll go a long way with a fella when he asks for help, but I'm not a messenger service and I don't want my dispatchers chasing you down when they've got train orders to type. I've got a railroad to run!"

Kemper went upstairs to rest, a man of diminished capacities. These people, he knew, had their concisely circumscribed tableaux in progress, and he wanted nothing so much as to have no part in any of it.

He was exhausted.

The President punctiliously made the preliminary cocktails himself, and I wheeled him in his chair from the drawingroom to the lift as a mark of respect, and thinking also of Sir Walter Raleigh spreading his cloak before Queen Elizabeth. I formed a very strong affection, which grew with our years of comradeship, for this formidable politician who had imposed his will for nearly ten years upon the American scene, and whose heart seemed to respond to many of the impulses that stirred my own. As we both, by need or habit, were forced to do much of our work in bed, he visited me in my room whenever he felt inclined, and encouraged me to do the same to him. Hopkins was just across the passage from my bedroom, and next door to him my travelling map room was soon installed. The President was much interested in this institution . . . He liked to come and study attentively the large maps of all the theatres of war which soon covered the walls, and on which the movement of fleets and armies was so accurately and swiftly recorded. It was not long before he established a map room of his own of the highest efficiency.

Kemper had to stop reading.

There is a passage in *The Dangerous River* that describes Patterson's effort to stay alive during one calamitous night when, walking the hundred miles in bone-crushing cold to an outpost on Great Slave Lake, he crashed through the frozen Nahanni and climbed out barely alive. The lone Englishman, a tenderfoot in appearance, a chunk of granite in reality, had only moments following his baptism to fire up the root ball of a fallen pine. He struck a match with his last effort and, the upraised roots fiercely blazing beside him, he dried his clothes, warmed himself, and saved his own life.

Patterson's elegantly reserved prose had given Kemper more than a pause for thought. He wondered at the tenuous threads that bind a human life to consciousness. His own life, he understood quite clearly and undramatically, was tethered to this earth by few dreams and very little hope, as though he were playing out the denouement in some Sophoclean delight. He didn't feel particularly tragic—he'd lived too long for that—but he was bewildered by his loss of energy.

The winter sun had moved in its bleary course across this northern sky. His room had darkened. He had memories enough. But he was, he realized, more alone than he had ever been in his life. And Patterson's description of a life lived on the edge had given Kemper relief in his aloneness.

He was alone; he was alive. And being alive was the whole ball of wax.

Patterson had taken short steps by lighting flimsy roots to save his life. Kemper's task was not to walk a hundred miles through snow. His task was to take the first step: to strike the match. Beyond that first step lay the remainder of the journey.

He needed a telephone.

"I thought this day would never end," Hannah whispered as she snuggled against his shoulder. She had slept for a few minutes after eating the sandwiches he'd carried to her bed. "The cold will be here—after Christmas."

He had held her against his skin, listening to the few cars splash through the new slush on the road. The afternoon rain had turned to snow in the evening and was layering his bakery truck with mush; he'd push it aside in the morning as he left for the last time. If Berlin had even a hint that Streicher was in this bed in this room, he would be yanked back to Germany by his neck, he thought, and shipped on to Poland or, worse, Rumania.

"January frightens me so," Hannah said into his ear. "When it goes to thirty below. The cold is lethal. Even the animals are threatened."

"I shall miss you," he said.

"And I you. Will you call me?"

"I'll try."

"You'll be gone," she said. "Just gone."

Hannah had been ravenous, as always; he wondered what she ate when he wasn't with her. Did she eat at all? She didn't seem to care enough to care for herself.

She ran her fingernails across her chest to her crystal pendant and wrapped its chain around her thumb. "I'll open the shop on Friday, the day after Christmas. And Saturday. I wouldn't, if you were here. I gave Mr. Burgoyne *Eyeless In Gaza* as a Christmas present."

"He must have been very pleased."

"He was," she said quietly. "I'm so afraid you won't come back."

"I will," he said rubbing her arm. Hannah's breasts were pendulous and perfect when she stood out of her bath or turned at her bed to pull her nightgown over her head. Never had he thought that beautiful breasts would be perfectly his to hold and to feel soft with the hard points of her nipples against his chest.

"You are very beautiful," he whispered.

Hannah reached to the table for the mirror. "Would you show me?" she asked.

He did. She lay with her arms above her on the pillows while he moved the mirror from her knees to her breasts to her thighs. She rolled over and looked over her shoulder to watch as the lamplight shadowed her spine. "Let me see my ass," she said. "I've never seen my ass—not like this." Her mirrored perspective of herself was new, so acutely familiar yet so curious, as though she had lived as a blind child all her life in a gracious garden and was only now stricken with sight.

Hannah raised her bottom, inching up her knees gradually as her Blue rubbed the skin on the backs of her thighs.

"Will you show me?" she asked. She felt the cool night air when his fingers opened her like a shy orchid. "Touch me there," she said. "I want to see you touch me there."

She reached to adjust the mirror. "Just up a little," she said. "Yes . . . yes, that's it. I can see you. I can see your thumb. Put it into me. Slowly, Blue."

She watched all that he did to her with a fiery stare, until she had to close her eyes to invite the spasms.

"Incredible," she said at last when the final flutters quieted and he entered her quickly and hard. "I want to hold all of you in me."

He was an alchemist in midnight blue robes behind her and above her, patiently folding her with his hands and fi-

103

nally pushing her out among the blossoms with his liquid gold. And as she lifted her wings, her eyes stung and blurred the pink shell pathways below until the warm air was all and everything.

"Get him on the horn," Kemper barked. Assorted clicks and thuds in New York let Kemper know that someone— the college kid, probably—was hustling.

Moffet was yelling before he picked up the receiver. "Where the hell are you, Frank? I ordered you to call me!"

The Jesse Welden desk clerk went back to work counting dining room receipts. "Your ordering days are over," Kemper said. "Hear this, Moffet. I'll call you from now on. Then again, I might not."

"Where are you?"

"Vermont."

"Why didn't you call me?"

"You weren't worth the nickel, Moffet. You aren't now. Doubt you ever will be."

"You goddamn guys—I've had it up to here with all of you. This was a very simple job, Frank. And when I say I want you to call, take that as an order."

"There are no more orders. Shoot at somebody else's feet. I'll finish here and move on to Ottawa in a day or two. Don't bother calling. Naval Intelligence will let you know what happens. If anything does happen."

"I'm going to have your ass, Frank."

"Not anymore, you're not. You're all done, Moffet."

"No—you're all done, Frank. Pack it in and come back here."

"Go to hell," Kemper said, dropping the receiver.

The kid at the desk started to smile.

"It's okay, kid." Kemper smiled. "You little pukes haven't got all the fire. Must surprise the hell out of you. I need another long distance line for Richmond."

Ball said Baskins was beginning to grow on him.

"Fond of him, are you?" Kemper asked.

"I'm not fond of any of 'em," Ball said. "I mean he's been here too long."

Kemper wanted to tell Ball to take Baskins out back and incinerate him, but he knew he'd really be in the soup if he destroyed evidence. "Let's hear it, friend," Kemper said.

"Except for an itty-bitty skeetie bite on his neck, this one's a good-looking dead man. Kinda' hard to tell, he's so smashed up."

"Describe the bite."

"Small. Very small—a skeetie bite!"

"In December?" Kemper asked.

"It's on his neck. Right side, under the ear. Could be a spider bite."

"Swollen?"

"Not now. He's *all* swollen. Say, you going to be around on Christmas?"

"I might," Kemper said. "I hope not."

"Thought we might have some turkey together."

"Got the bird in your crematory now?"

"Not yet," Ball laughed. "Barely have to get the thing hot. Only takes a few hours."

Kemper knew better than to continue. "Everything else all right?" he asked.

"Someone has to get this fella out of here."

Kemper suggested Ball get on to the coroner's office.

Ball laughed. "Merry Christmas," he said.

The kid looked over once more. "Another one," Kemper said. "Winter Park, Florida. The Coral Hotel. You get me a line and I'll get the number from the operator."

The kid leapt off his stool and lunged for the telephone on the wall.

Sylvie's voice came through the lines wrapped in childish defensiveness. "Hi, Daddy," she said as though she were nine. "Where are you?"

"I'm in Vermont, sweetheart."

"I tried you in New York."

"I'm not in New York," he said crossly. "But your Christmas gifts are."

"We're coming back a week from today," she said. "Could I see you then? Will you be there?"

"I don't know. You and I are very far away just now."

"How is Vermont?"

"I'm not talking about miles, Sylvie. I want you to have a good Christmas under the palms—humor your mother. She loves you very much." Kemper had no idea what he should say next. "I'm going to stop working. I may even buy a place up here. If I do—and even if I don't—I'd like you to have Christmas with me next year. I'm making my reservation now."

This was very difficult, he thought. She was further away than he had imagined.

"Are you all right, Daddy?" she asked, sounding frightened.

"I'm going to be," he said.

"Where will you be on Christmas Day?"

He said he didn't know. That it didn't matter. She would be with him next Christmas. "I can't make up for those we've lost," he said. "And neither can you. But I do want you next year."

"I miss you," she said.

"We've spent our lives saying good-bye to each other," he said. "You're my daughter—"

"And you're my dad," she said softly.

"I am," he smiled. The kid at the desk had heard enough and walked past Kemper into the kitchen. "Enjoy your Christmas. I'll enjoy mine." And when he said "I love you"—something he rarely said to her now—Sylvie's "And I love you" broke like hot glass.

Kemper felt better; his resolution was tentative and fragile when he climbed the stairs to his room. He knew he'd make it.

FOURTEEN

WHEN PAUL STREICHER LEFT HANNAH at her door, he wondered if she had guessed; did she know with a disturbed and mysteriously feminine sensitivity that her lover was not coming back? He had no way to judge. He did know that he hadn't the courage to tell her that she had become a weight for him. His experiences with women had all been brief and unrewarding, coming as they did for the most part in beer-drenched attic flats with women from the Augsburg cafés.

He could feel the jaws of the vise close against his capacity for clear thinking. Hannah had stalled his mission—he ought to have been more productive, and his Berlin masters would impatiently demand evidence of his efforts soon. He knew he wouldn't be alone in Ottawa. Other SS agents, including that wise-ass Diekhoff, who lived in Ottawa, would hover around Churchill's conference with Canadian officials in the same way crows will congregate near a fast highway when the field mice are pulling up stakes for greener pastures.

And because he was thirty-one, Streicher believed he could select his path by willfully driving away from her. He hadn't lived long enough to know that each man is his only vise.

The roads to St. Albans were rutted with slush and muck, and Streicher drove slowly for more than an hour around the city and toward the lake. There was a dead-end road

107

circling a narrow inlet of the lake, a road Streicher had come to loathe, because this was where he lived for the present. Early on, Hannah had come to believe that he lived in New York State north of Plattsburgh. To protect her and to maintain his own independence, he'd never corrected her.

The hedge came along after the curve, the lake lapping up to the road for a quarter-mile. The cottages along this stretch were boarded for the winter and gave the road under the maples a secluded look, with their empty porches and covered windows like bandaged eyes. The cottages gave Streicher ominous pause—it was as if he were being watched.

He ran his Cushman's truck into a driveway through the hedge, bouncing slowly over holes in the drive, which was close-bordered on both sides. Every time he drove it, this stretch seemed like a fenced trap for wild ponies because the house was immediately there at the end. Streicher had known from the start that, had he needed to, he could simply smash through the cedar hedge and get back to the road through the old garden. He was always unconvinced by the silence of the house and grounds when he shut off his motor in the garage.

The morning clouds were low into the trees and heavy. He went quickly into the house and came out again, pulling a thick wool sweater over his head. He had eight minutes to go by his watch.

The antenna lead hung inside the garage wall next to the bakery truck. He'd strung a receptive pattern of wires in the maples surrounding the garage months before. This was his only permanent antenna. When he was on the move, he had to stop the truck and fashion a temporary arrangement however he could.

He pulled the antenna lead with him in through the back door of the truck. Streicher's radio was not the standard German intelligence Afu, the small suitcase radio with a limited range. Telefunken had constructed for the

Sicherheitsdienst a new relatively portable but immensely powerful radio set capable of transmitting almost anywhere in the northern hemisphere.

He snapped the radio's green glass dials awake; their needles rose. The set needed a minute or two for its vacuum tubes to warm.

He felt better away from Hannah. More certain that he was vital and alive. Streicher cupped his hands over the earphones. There they were! He tapped his response code, a variation on the day's date with the proper rotating number sequence following. Then the air was silent. "What are you doing?" he said quietly. "Come on . . . talk to me."

He knew they were verifying his response code. "Come on . . . it's right," he said. His pencil stub waited over his pad. Where were they?

Berlin's signal came with such speed, Streicher fumbled his pencil. S-S-D for *sehr sehr dringend* . . . very, very urgent. They paused. He stared at the eight numbers sent in patterns of four each. What the hell is that? he thought. Their signal began again, and this time the number sequences came like lightning. He scratched as fast as he could, the pencil fluttering across his pad, and he realized Berlin had changed the code.

Most Abwehr radio codes were simple substitution codes for which both operators needed the exact edition of the same book. Page numbers depended on the transmission date to further obscure listening enemies. But once received, the Abwehr agent had only to begin at the right page of the right book, substitute letters for numbers, and the message would come clear. The *Sicherheitsdienst* had much the same system, but their agents were more highly trained and their keys for each book were more complex than the Abwehr's keys.

The signal paused, then chattered the old response sequence. They wanted him to answer and would wait while he dug out the new book—one of Scott's Waverly novels,

Redgauntlet. In training this moment had invariably been Streicher's worst. For routine transmissions, his acknowledgment was all Berlin listened for before they went off the air. Rarely would they engage a working agent in conversation.

He got the book from the house. He worked it all out. They were waiting—he knew they were. They would smile amongst themselves in a moment and Holm, his radio instructor, if he were with them—"Oh god," Streicher groaned—Holm's right temple should twitch any second now:

POSSIBLE CHURCHILL TO OTTAWA 28. FIRST REPORTS TO FLY. LILY CLAIMS FLYING FALSE. CHURCHILL BY DELAWARE AND HUDSON NIGHT OF 28/29. POSSIBLE KATZ TO INTERCEPT AND DISPATCH?

Streicher counted the days. Four—the twenty-eighth was Sunday. Sunday night. Lily was the *Sicherheitsdienst* agent in Baltimore. The Delaware & Hudson tracks ran up the west shore of Lake Champlain after Albany, and then on into Montreal. "Dispatch" is a strange word for it, he thought.

He worked out his answer, "Possible," and tapped it back to them quickly.

Berlin's acknowledgment must have been perched on the tip of their operator's finger. Streicher wondered about the sureness, the speed of their response. The German operator sounded like Holm himself.

Berlin signaled for the last time and shut down. They would transmit again in twenty-four hours.

Streicher drew in his breath slowly as he read the message again. The SS wasn't at all interested in intelligence about Churchill's Ottawa visit. "They want me to kill him," he whispered. His pencil stub quivered in his fingers.

The war had come to him.

FIFTEEN

KEMPER HAD A SLOW DAY in mind for himself, but not after hearing Quenneville's voice from Montreal.

"I told you," Quenneville had shouted through the receiver. "But did you listen to me? Of course you didn't. I have another dead man."

He went on to tell Kemper that Mouton had been found dead by a fishing friend at Black Lake. Kemper felt the gears click inside his clockwork mechanism as Quenneville's voice wound his spring.

"The coroner's report says it looks like a heart attack, but I've ordered an autopsy by an RCMP pathologist."

Kemper watched a loud woman and her husband check in at the hotel desk. She wanted a room facing the park . . . they were here from Cleveland to visit her sister, Myrna. Kemper wanted to offer them his room.

"You there?" Quenneville asked.

Kemper said "Yup."

"I don't know why I do this to myself," Quenneville said. "You don't give a damn."

"Baskins is only corpse number one," Kemper said.

"You make me so angry. There is more," Quenneville said slowly. "Those high-speed transmissions have increased. Your Naval Intelligence guys in Virginia say the strong signal is coming from Mexico City. And they think they know who it is. An SS agent—not Abwehr—in Baltimore, code named 'Lily,' is using the Abwehr radio in

111

Mexico City to relay messages through to Berlin. But the other radio is not as powerful. And it is—they are certain of it—this radio is up here with us somewhere. My Mounties say it's in Ottawa, but they like everything near enough to them so they can walk. Remember? I told you SS?"

Kemper shifted his feet: Baskins and Mouton could be links in the same chain, he thought. "You want me to look for the radio," he said.

"Two things. There is a boathouse near you. Those guys in St. Albans have used it to hide agents. I have never been there. Would you look for me? And number two—" Quenneville said before Kemper could answer, "—would you see Hannah Doll in Sutton for me? She lives alone." The Montreal cop explained that he hadn't seen Hannah Doll for some time and that he was concerned. "I told you she is innocent. Please tell her to be careful—from me."

Quenneville explained that he'd been ordered to Ottawa for a Christmas Day meeting. He couldn't see Hannah Doll himself. "You will know how much to tell her," he said. "She is not truly one of them, so be easy with her. She has helped me a lot."

The boathouse belonged to an abandoned hotel on the lake called the Cedars, Quenneville added. He did not know where it was. "And be careful yourself, my friend. Menard wanted to meet Hannah at the boathouse tonight. So he, at least, will be around. I told Hannah not to meet him."

"I'll be okay as soon as I get out of here," Kemper said.

"*If* you get out of there," Quenneville said. "I don't want you hurt—a man in your delicate condition. Hannah's bookstore is across from the post office in Sutton."

Quenneville railed against the idiocies of his life: his wife had baked pork pies for weeks, his kids were tearing the house down. Kemper wished him a Merry Christmas.

"That is not funny, my friend. I should be at home. I am too old for this."

Kemper hung up the telephone and filled his lungs with Jesse Welden air, the aroma of breakfast and coffee and cigars. They are pushing hard, he thought.

SIXTEEN

STREICHER MADE HIMSELF COFFEE and took the mug into the cellar. In a dark, wet corner there was a tottering bench. He kept his chemicals under the bench in a wooden chest. If Churchill were killed, England would suffer greatly and might, he thought, yield to Germany in the confused aftermath.

At the very least, an unsuccessful assassination would rain British recriminations on the bumbling Americans, and this, coming at the inception of the Grand Alliance between the two countries, would in itself lead to confusion, mistrust, and vilification. Either way, Streicher realized that his Berlin mentors would be elated. And he would be a hero.

But how? The hero must escape to enjoy his rewards. No suicide mission this, he thought.

How, he wondered, do I stand close enough to Churchill to use the injector? Pistols and violence were out; Churchill was closely guarded. Streicher had been to Ottawa twice. The city was easily maneuvered. The border was no problem at all because Streicher never used official border crossings, but drove instead through the woods and fields over dirt tracks the farmers used to transport pigs and cattle without paying import duties either way.

He needed to think this out. The urge to compile extravagant plans was strong. He'd been selected to represent the best of the SS. "INTERCEPT AND DISPATCH."

113

"Where the hell have you been?" Alex Jaeger said, aiming a pistol from the stairs.

Streicher laughed at him. "I might ask you the same," he said.

"You know where I've been," Jaeger said heatedly. "It's you I worry about. You scare the shit out of me."

"Not for much longer," Streicher answered, turning away to unsnap his chest. Alex Jaeger was a man sinking under a burden of hate.

"You come and go as you please—" Jaeger began.

"Shut up," Streicher said quietly. "I pay you enough. I'm almost finished here."

"I hope so. You've been saying that for weeks. I don't like doing this. I come home—I've worked three trains in twenty-four hours—I need to sleep."

Streicher stared at Jaeger as the man approached him in his conductor's uniform. "Sleep," Streicher said. "Go have some soup and sleep." Jaeger kept a simmering pot of potato soup on top of his kerosene stove.

"I'm tired of this!" Jaeger shouted, shaking his pistol in the air.

"You worry too much."

"Bullshit, I worry too much! A man asked me about Baskins. I told you that wouldn't be easy."

"Who was he?"

"I'm getting to it, dammit. He's Baskins's brother."

"What did he want? How did he find you?"

"He was with my superintendent. He wanted to know who shut the car door after Baskins bailed out."

Streicher returned to his chest and the corked flasks that gleamed when he sprung the lid. "So what?"

"I shut the door!" Jaeger bellowed. "He's obviously asking questions because he doesn't believe his half-wit brother fell off the train. I told you, didn't I? Drop the bastard, I said. But what did you do? You threw him!"

"I didn't know there was a station there, did I? I didn't

114

know *because*—" Streicher narrowed his eyes "—you didn't tell me."

Jaeger swore. "I've talked to Ben Sykes and he says the guy is peculiar. Sykes doesn't think he's anybody's brother. But Sykes is so scared after Baskins—they all are—they're so scared right now they can't shit straight."

Streicher told Jaeger to go up to bed, he'd wake him in the afternoon.

"I've got a train tonight," he said, stumbling up the stairs.

"Wait a minute." Streicher stared at Jaeger. "I need to know about the Delaware & Hudson tracks in New York. Where are they?"

Jaeger said there was only one main line along the lake shore to Montreal.

The message had said "Intercept and dispatch." Streicher wondered what Berlin meant. Should he meet Churchill in the Ottawa rail station with the injector? He'd be damned if he'd get caught. "Where do trains usually stop over there?"

"Everywhere," Jaeger said. "It's a busy railroad."

Streicher told Jaeger he wanted a Delaware & Hudson timetable right away. And a map of the railroad.

"Shit," Jaeger said. "This before or after I sleep?"

Streicher looked up at him slowly. "Afterwards is fine."

Streicher got out his chemicals. Jaeger stomped through the house and up to his bedroom. Only Hannah and Jaeger knew Streicher was in North America. If Streicher wanted to get out after the Churchill blitz, Jaeger would have to be silenced. Permanently would be okay, Streicher thought.

How the hell am I going to get near Churchill? he wondered as he took the injector from his coat pocket. If he used hydrogen sulphide again, Churchill's eyes would bug out and the old man would drop dead where he stood between his bodyguards.

115

Can't have that, he thought—dead heroes never know they're heroes. He'd have to signal Mexico City for help in getting home.

Streicher twisted his chemical flasks so that he could see their labels and grew very quiet.

And Baskins's brother? he wondered.

SEVENTEEN

THE HARPY WHO WAS THE COUNTY CLERK in the courthouse told Kemper the Cedars was not in the city at all, but part of the town of St. Albans.

"I'm looking to buy a place," he said.

She was put out that Kemper wanted anything at a little past noon on the day before Christmas. "Are you?" she responded acidly. She told him to go to the town hall. "They have the deeds down at the Bay."

She pointed like the stygian queen she was and said, "Look, just drive down. Honest to god, you men are a sorry sight. But they won't be open. Not today."

Kemper drove to St. Albans Bay and found the brick town hall. A separate village of some sort, he thought as he left his car and knocked on the locked door. The janitor answered.

Kemper asked about the Cedars, who owned it, how much land went with it.

"Why don't you look for yourself," the old man said, letting Kemper into the town hall. "Vault's open. All the deeds are there. Cassey Halloway ran the place for years, 'til her husband ran off with that Frosty woman."

"That her name—Frosty?" Kemper asked as he went behind the town clerk's desk and into the vault.

"Hell no. She made ice cream. We called her Frosty because of that. There's snakes out there, you know."

117

"Out where?" Kemper said, searching the leather-bound town records above him.

"The Cedars. Place is full of snakes. Big ones."

"What year do I want?" Kemper asked.

The janitor had a very small head impaled on a long neck of wrinkled skin. His mid-section was fatter inside bagged overalls than his head and neck might suggest. Kemper thought he looked somehow diseased. The janitor said to try 1938. "That's about when it all happened."

The search took Kemper some time. The janitor said he had to make up the furnace. "Christmas, you know," he'd said, leaving Kemper in the vault.

The Cedars was owned by Roland Sykes, based on a deed recorded in 1939. Kemper copied the information about land and buildings and the former owners, the Halloways, on stationery from the town clerk's desk.

He slapped the book shut. The janitor was back, leaning in the doorway. "The sheriff got a brother named Roland?" Kemper asked.

"Rolly," the janitor said. "Those bastards." He cleared his throat as if he were going to spit.

Kemper put the book away in the vault.

"Think Rolly Sykes would be hard to deal with if I wanted to buy the Cedars?"

"You'd be a damn fool to buy that. You'll be killing snakes the whole of the first year. There's no water there, either. The wells run dry before Cassey sold it."

"Rolly Sykes is a tough man to deal with, is he?"

"He ain't tough, but he's shifty. He and his brother have bought up land all over."

"Real busy, aren't they?" Kemper said, stepping past the janitor into the lobby. The wood on the walls was smoke-mellowed oak. The glass in the windows was old enough to have bubbles in it.

"Rolly Sykes is the mayor, yes?"

"He's the mayor of St. Albans. And St. Albans is wel-

118

come to him. He's as big a snake as any he's got living out at the Cedars."

Kemper got directions and drove along the edge of a wide bay in Lake Champlain. When he finally stopped on a hill, the main house was a grey hulk across mangy fields that Kemper guessed were once lawns.

He eased the car over the track through the grass. The downstairs windows inside the enormous porch of the main house were boarded up. There were cottages, like doll-houses, in a row under the trees at the shore.

Kemper left the car and buttoned his overcoat over his sweater. The south wind off the lake raked this barren point of land with a constant bitter breeze that smelled of winter stagnation.

The main house had been grand at one time, he thought, mounting the steps to its porch. The columns supporting the roof had ornately carved capitals.

Its doors were locked. Kemper turned to look out over ruination and neglect. The snakes are happy here, he thought, imagining that the Cedars must have had moments of pride and laughter. Tennis courts had gone to meadow. A flagpole base, with the splintered beam still in its grasp, stuck up out of the grass near lilac bushes. A gazebo had been blown to bits on a distant rock that overlooked the lake. There were sheds and a small cottage hidden in the woods near the road.

Then he saw the boathouse. And the man walking toward him.

Kemper stumped off the porch and met the man on the road.

"You wanna buy odor control products? They're little pads you put in your shoes?"

Kemper saw the hollow spaces of mental retardation in the man's gaze. Kemper said he didn't. He was thinking of buying the Cedars.

"What's that?" the man asked. About Kemper's age, he

119

wore a checkered wool hunter's cap and a long, dirty twill service overcoat buttoned to his neck.

"You sell little pads?" Kemper asked.

"I do," the man said.

"You can't have much business out here."

"Don't have any. I take care of this hotel."

What hotel? Kemper thought. "I thought I might buy this place," he said.

The man looked stunned, as though he'd just heard that the king had died. "What for?" he said.

"I like to fish."

"Me too," the man said. He kept his hands deep in his coat pockets. "Only I don't hook 'em, I shoot 'em."

"I'll bet you do," Kemper said. The boathouse was at the base of the hill, down the road and under the trees. It looked deserted. The man asked again if Kemper wanted to buy odor control products.

"I might," Kemper answered. "People still use the boathouse, do they?"

The man grinned, looked around as though he were in a crowd and not in the middle of an empty field. "They take their clothes off," he said, grinning even more until he laughed and shook his head.

"Not all of them," Kemper said.

The man appeared stunned again.

"Some of 'em. The girls," the man said, lowering his voice to an excited whisper, "have big titties. I've seen 'em. Big titties."

"Are they here now?"

"'Course they ain't here now. Why would they be here now?"

"This is a hotel," Kemper said, pointing with his cigar to the main house.

"Not that," the man said. And looking toward the boathouse, "That's the hotel. God, you're slow."

Kemper said he was slow. "But the mayor says I can look around if I want."

"Sure," the man grinned. "Sure, you can."

The side entrance to the boathouse had been padlocked; the man took Kemper along the side to the water and from a rock foundation scampered up onto the narrow porch of the boathouse. Kemper climbed up after him.

The boathouse was built on two levels. Kemper went into the upper half, where there were tables, iron cots, and lamps with ducks painted on their shades. There was a larger bed in the back and a stairway down along the wall to the lower level. Kemper looked down and saw the black water. He shuddered, moving down a step or two. There was a wooden duckboard in the shape of a square U and then the doors that opened onto the lake. There were no boats.

Kemper looked up at the man on the iron cot. "How big are their titties?" he asked, cracking open an electrical fuse box. The power was on in here. The boathouse was not deserted at all.

The man had laughed and held his hands out. "Big ones," he said, shaking his head.

"Do all the girls have big titties?"

"Nope. Just one."

"They don't show you their titties, do they?"

"'Course they don't. I peek through the walls." The man got up and went from knothole to knothole, pointing and shouting, "Here! Here! Here! Over here!"

Kemper sat on the double bed and tried to imagine what this man knew but didn't know he knew. "These people are your friends," Kemper said. "Aren't they?"

"Yup," his friend said, tripping over a stool and smoothly continuing his fall into a cushioned chair.

"Except some of the men," Kemper said. "Sometimes, you don't know some of the men."

121

"That's right."

"And they only stay in this hotel for a little while."

"'Bout a week. One man gave me a turtle."

"And they have parties here."

"Not those guys. Well, sometimes they do. Mostly they just stay by themselves. Rolly has parties here."

"Does he?" Kemper smiled.

"He even asks me if I want a beer. 'Course I do. I want all the beer!" He shrieked with laughter so loudly that Kemper jumped.

"Did you ever know Leonard?"

"Sure, I know Leonard," the man said, his eyes drifting in visions. Kemper waited, then tossed his cigar into the water at the bottom of the stairs. "Leonard's my friend," the man said.

"I'd love to see Leonard's girlfriend," Kemper said. "I'd love to see her take off her clothes."

The man grinned. "Them's big titties," he laughed.

"They are," Kemper said. "Now, let's see . . . Mr. Menard comes here . . ."

"Morison," the man corrected him.

"Morison. And the sheriff—that's Ben."

The man nodded his head slowly. He was listening carefully.

"And Rolly—he comes a lot," Kemper said.

"Yup," the man said. "He cooks the fish. He makes the best perch."

"And let's see, who else comes here?"

Kemper felt a shudder run up his back. The boathouse was very cold and damp. His friend's eyes were hung in the tops of their sockets, deep in thought. "There's Minor . . . and Raymond—he's got cancer—and Alex and Rene . . . and—"

"Wait! Wait a minute," Kemper said. "Is Minor a big guy or a little guy?"

"Little guy." The man had become intent.

122

Kemper felt the pull on his clockwork gearing click another cog. "And Alex is the guy with the black hair?"

"That's right," the man smiled. He looked puzzled again.

"Alex is the trainman, right? The conductor?"

"That's right," the man smiled. "You got all of 'em. Good for you."

There was no radio here. The boathouse was sparsely furnished, its beams open and its roof exposed. I'll be damned, Kemper thought. It's not much. But Alex, the trainman, does love to slam doors.

Kemper gave his friend a ride back to St. Albans Bay and left him standing by the side of the road, waving as Kemper turned for the city.

Simple festivities marked our Christmas. The traditional Christmas Tree was set up in the White House garden, and the President and I made brief speeches from the balcony to enormous crowds gathered in the gloom. . . .

This is a strange Christmas Eve. Almost the whole world is locked in deadly struggle, and, with the most terrible weapons which science can devise, the nations advance upon each other. Ill would be for us this Christmastide if we were not sure that no greed for the land or wealth of any other people, no vulgar ambition, no morbid lust for material gain at the expense of others, had led us to the field. Here, in the midst of war, raging and roaring over all the lands and seas, creeping nearer to our hearths and homes, here, amid all the tumult, we have tonight the peace of the spirit in each cottage home and in every generous heart. Therefore, we may cast aside for this night at least the cares and dangers which beset us, and make for the children an evening of happiness in a world of storm. Here, then, for one night only, each home throughout the English-speaking world should be a brightly lighted island of happiness and peace.

Let the children have their night of fun and laughter. Let the gifts of Father Christmas delight their play. Let us grownups share to the full in

123

their unstinted pleasures before we turn again to the stern task and the formidable years that lie before us, resolved that, by our sacrifice and daring, these same children shall not be robbed of their inheritance or denied their right to live in a free and decent world.

And so, in God's mercy, a happy Christmas to you all.

EIGHTEEN

WHEN KEMPER SAW HANNAH DOLL standing alone in the yellowy light of her hallway, he knew she was a woman like few other women in all his fifty-eight years. Aware as he was—as we all are to some extent—that the myths of love at first sight have been tattered with misuse and abuse, Kemper at first sight blustered on about who he was and why Marcel Quenneville had sent him to her.

He had switched off his car in front of the Sutton post office and crossed the empty street feeling rankled and weak that others should observe the holiday and this night together with glistening red and green Christmas lights in their windows. The houses and farms had been there after every curve as he drove north from St. Albans.

But after Hannah's first frightened suspicions had settled, she invited him in, unwillingly, he knew. She had to make concessions to what she was no matter what night it was, while he, hunched in the dark of her porch, he was a consequence of her life to this point. She didn't want him there; he felt like an intruder and apologized again as she took him to her Christmas tree and the fireplace.

She was tall, and not at all thin or emaciated: her arms and breasts had heft and resiliance. He thought her face young. That she had let him in at all on this night gave Kemper reason to believe she could handle herself.

She asked him to leave his coat on the chair by the window and to sit down near the fire. He nervously patted his

125

pockets to feel for his cigars and went to the chair opposite the couch. He knew when he watched her shift her dressing gown—she wore a gold chain—before she curled onto the couch that no matter what time lay in front of him, he would remember Hannah Doll with a wistful hesitancy.

Strong emotions, he realized. He wondered about having been more or less alone for years and dismissed his loneliness as self-serving and demeaning.

Hannah Doll was a good deal more than any man's dream. She had been brusque with him at the door when he tried to convince her he was harmless—she had courage. Hannah Doll, he decided, was a woman with spit.

She listened as he explained more of who he was and why he was in her house. He told her what he knew about Leonard Baskins and about the collapsing Abwehr network she was a part of. He explained Quenneville's suspicion that some deadly anomaly had disrupted the relatively unimportant mechanics of her particular group of agents and couriers. He also told her of Quenneville's fear for her safety.

"How did you come to lose your leg?" she asked.

Kemper twisted his face toward the fire and its lively sputtering. He told her about the French sentry, the *poilu,* who had smashed his knee, femur, and muscles with a single errant shot in the glare of a flare near Albert in 1918.

She considered his story, weighing all the parts consecutively. Her eyes were very dark and persistent. Few people ever said anything to Kemper's face about his missing leg and the prosthetic log that he dragged after him every day of his life. He knew, as all the obviously handicapped know, that he was a target for the perfectly formed. People had in the past, for instance, wondered that he could think straight with a vacant limb. In much the same way, crazed aunts addicted to parakeets and Bromo-Seltzer believe their deaf nieces are additionally cretinous.

"Do you smoke?" he asked, seeing that there were unburned matches at the edge of the fireplace ashes.

126

"I don't," she said. "But you may if you like."

She asked him to explain why he was here on this night, nodding her brown hair toward her Christmas tree. Hadn't he any family?

Sylvie was in Winter Park, he said. His son, David, in Amsterdam. He spoke of his years in London and Germany, and finally of the steel-hooped duties of Naval Intelligence.

Incredibly, he thought, he told her everything that mattered in him, as though she were the last messenger for redemption in the last circle of hell. He apologized, again, for sitting in her living room on a night like this.

Hannah's smile went to her eyes, but not to her mouth. "I can't think of a better night," she said firmly. "For either of us."

She told him about Margaret and the medical magicians who lied to increase their profits, of her five years with Margaret, and about sheep and the awful returns on their wool.

When he asked her if she lived alone, she said she did, but let her gaze fall to her lap, as though she knew he'd seen her wish for more.

"We're all a little lonely," he said.

Hannah didn't answer, but traced her knee with her thumbnail.

Except for the crackle of the fire, the room was intensely silent. Kemper felt that he had at last arrived home after an odyssey notable only for its witlessness. And also that she had arrived in this room after her own trials.

"I grew up in Tubenthal, Switzerland," she said suddenly. "My father was a poet. He tried to edit a literary quarterly, but he was so crushed by his lack of talent—he couldn't judge anything written by anyone. He died in 1932. I miss him still. He sent me away to live with a family in Zurich so that I could go to school. My mother died when I was twelve."

She stopped speaking to rub her temple.

"I was married for seven years. I don't know where he is. I came to Montreal as a translator—German, Dutch, French, and English. And I divorced him in 1931. He was a waiter in Antwerp when I last heard from him.

"Margaret was an active socialist in Montreal, and I liked her right away. But she died in April of last year."

Hannah stared into the fire. Kemper waited for her to go on, but she was frozen in remembrance.

He asked her about her bookstore.

"He was so small," she said. "We lived in Brussels. I left our house every afternoon before one o'clock to visit him.

"I never thought he'd die. I never did. I don't know why," she said, resolved to press on. "I got on a bus in hot pouring rain near our house and rode through all those trees to the hospital outside the city. The trees were so green . . . and wet. It was raining and I ran up through the hospital gates. I didn't know.

"When I went into his ward, the sister at the desk wouldn't speak to me at all. I went to his bed. He wasn't there."

Kemper moved in the chair; he wanted to cross the civil distance between them and collect her in his arms. Her face had lost all its life; her gaze was hard and connected to the fire. "He wasn't there," she whispered, drawing a long breath.

"Where was he?" Kemper finally asked.

"Dead," she said. "The sisters had taken his body down to the cellar. He was so small. His arms and legs. And his fingers were so tiny. And he never cried—they said he never cried."

Her eyes pooled with tears.

"You miss him so much," Kemper said softly.

"It was so hot—muggy—at the end of the summer, and I rode back on the bus in the rain through those awful green trees."

Kemper felt his heart pulsing in his neck.

"He was all I ever had. So small. He never cried. And I don't know why he never cried," she said, her voice gathering power. She looked hard at him as if he were responsible.

"He was my son," she said finally, looking away. "I know we're meant to go on past these things. Something in me didn't, though. I remember thinking on the bus in the rain that whatever happened to me, I'd never heal. I've tried, but . . . I can't."

You damn fool, he said to himself as he fished for a cigar. How could this happen to you at fifty-eight? He let his shoulders relax against the chair. He knew he had to wait for her to gather herself back into this room. He also knew he'd wait for her forever.

She told him about Baskins's and Margaret's routine as a German courier. Margaret, she said, wasn't really convinced of anything political, but Margaret did loathe capitalism's demands on the little people who had to scramble after a living. Margaret had thought Germany an anodyne for the painful iniquity of the capitalists' moral insolvency. He believed everything she said.

"I don't know anything about Leonard. He was a tiresome man. He wasn't up to it."

Kemper asked her what Baskins wasn't up to.

"And those others—Menard and that bunch in St. Albans," she answered. "If they've broken any of your laws, you should arrest them and relieve the good people in this world. They shout always about the Jews—how the Jews have caused all the wars, how the Jews have caused this war, and how we should spit on a Jew whenever we see one. Of course they never see any Jews, living where they do."

Kemper watched her hands; her fingers punctuating her thoughts with soft taps on her thigh. "Do you know Alex Jaeger?" he asked.

129

"No," Hannah said. "Is he one of them?"

"He's a railroad conductor."

"And Marcel believes Leonard wasn't drunk, didn't fall off the train. Do you?"

"He may have been drunk," Kemper said. "But he didn't fall."

She said she didn't want to hear any more on Christmas Eve.

Kemper knew that his sitting by her fire was an act of volition . . . and he had no one but himself to blame for what followed.

He remembered his boyhood swing in the elm behind his father's house in Newton, Massachusetts. So long ago. Swinging idly from side to side as he read the treasures of Robert Louis Stevenson, he had wanted someone in his life who would love him.

Stranger things have happened than this, he thought; our existence is crammed with moments of incredulity. But here he was, alone in the Quebec Townships on Christmas Eve in 1941. Hannah was here, and Kemper thought in another flash of incredulity, that this wasn't possible, that he wasn't—couldn't be—drawn to a woman as he was to Hannah Doll. "I'm too old," he said clearly to himself.

But he wasn't, and he knew he wasn't, because he was a man trapped in the vagaries of his spirit. And his spirit had, on this night, been released.

He imagined a man escaping through the smashed window of his sunken automobile; this same man pawing through yards of water and, miraculously, bobbing into brisk starlit air and safety.

She brought them steaming bowls of pea soup, soft rolls, and tea. Her bookstore was barely an enterprise at all, she told him, but she was able to support her house, leaving a slender bit of cash for her essentials. After Hannah described Margaret's illness, he spoke of Norfolk and the other hospi-

130

tals, but especially of Norfolk where, one morning, he'd had his exquisite presentiment of immediate death.

Hannah seemed to listen while he spoke. She handled her soup spoon gracefully, carefully, and the heat of the fire colored her face.

The roads to St. Albans that night shimmered with rain as Kemper took himself back to the coagulated emptiness of the Jesse Welden. He understood why Marcel Quenneville did not want her hurt. The thought came to him as he clomped up the hotel stairway that she might not have told him the truth—possibly, about anything; his next thought was that he didn't care.

NINETEEN

DORCAS BALDWIN AND MORISON MENARD got to the
boathouse just before seven on Christmas Eve. Menard
backed his car into the field and shut off his lights to wait
for Hannah Doll. Menard was nothing if not careful, careful
in all that he ever did. He was not an officer of the Union
Bank for nothing. Menard's enduring advice—to his two
sons and daughter, to his wife and mother, to his executive
assistant, and to nearly all the friends and patrons who
glided by his desk just inside the bank entrance—was that
they must be vigilant; that vigilance bred great care.

Morison Menard grew up in the house he still lived in on
Berkeley Terrace at the summit of the city. The mayor lived
across the street, the mayor's brother two streets down.

He was careful enough tonight to have Dorcas meet him
after dark in her car behind the Catholic church in St. Albans Bay. And careful enough to wait for Hannah with his
lights off in the vigilant darkness.

Menard kept his heater fan on low until seven-thirty.
Then he cranked his window down. "I thought so," he
said.

"You were right, Morison," Dorcas said in a hush.

"She hasn't got the money. I knew she didn't. They've
had too many extensions already. They must think we've
got cowshit for brains."

"What will you do?" she asked solemnly.

Morison Menard knew to be careful; his options would

be his alone. "I don't know," he said, shutting off the car. "But this is the last time I'll wait for these bums."

"Are you sure she knew it was tonight?"

Dorcas was herself vigilant, and in this instance said that the French woman was "taking advantage," as she put it, of Menard's prime business sense of equity.

"We sign agreements at the bank," he said, "because most people aren't good for it. But my word's good on my handshake."

"And these people would never sign an agreement," she offered. "This French woman lied to you."

"She's German," Menard said.

Dorcas had a certain pride in what she knew and said, "She's foreign—that's my point."

Menard cast a long gaze over the blackened clearing before him, to the main house to his left, to the lights across the inlet behind him.

They got out of the car and went inside the boathouse, where Menard lighted a lamp. Dorcas was cold in the damp winter chill and stamped her feet. "How could they ask you to meet them here," she said, "and not show up?"

"It's the way they are," he said, lowering the lamp wick.

"Cold in here, Morison. They've got their nerve."

But Menard had already sunk into his famous fury—the fury she knew he used on bank customers who lied and said they had no money, while everyone knew very well that their wives had new coats or that they'd been to the Jesse Welden dining room the night before for a birthday celebration, as though they had money to burn!

Dorcas Baldwin smoked cigarettes in private and did so now while Morison watched her from a wicker chair by the table. She butted her cigarette and said, "Not tonight, Morison. Too cold."

He sighed and stared off into the darkness under the roof.

"We have to go," she said.

"I'll be busy for a few days," he answered.

133

"Not tonight."

Inevitably, she finally crossed to the cot next to him. Morison, Dorcas knew, was a man of unspoken quandaries; he carried the burden of his banking vocation as a silent responsibility to hold his tongue. She slipped off her underpants and lay on the woolly mattress with her knees together. "Be quick, Morison. It's cold in here. I swear, if you don't get a steady diet of sex, you are a terror."

Morison took his time; he was being careful. "Not if you don't want to," he said.

"Of course I want to. You know I do. Are you sure it's all right here? Tonight, I mean?"

"I am," he said, pulling himself out of the chair like the weary man he was. Commerce had its unique stresses, and Morison was prey to all of them.

He opened his pants, swept his overcoat behind him, and knelt on the bed. "Open your legs," he said with the heavy husk in his voice that she loved to hear.

"Be careful of me," she said. "I'm dry tonight. It's too cold in here."

He said he would.

Dorcas opened her coat and gathered her dress up to her waist. "If you get any bigger . . ." she said, raising her eyebrows, smiling.

She lay perfectly still, letting Morison balance himself on his elbows and knees, and whistled as she drew in her breath when he went into her. She had carefully turned her head so that he wouldn't muss her hair, and had caught a whiff of the wonderful cologne she'd given him at Halloween—when a man's face came up out of the stairwell into the room's dull light.

"What do you want?" she yelled. "Get out! Get out!"

She threw Morison against the wall. "Get out of here, you filthy beast!" she said to the man.

Streicher stood at the top of the stairs. He wore his heavy canvas pants and his hunting coat.

Dorcas leapt off the bed. "Get out of here!" she screamed. "You filthy backwoods pig!" But she knew as she said it that this man was not from the back woods. He had strong eyes and his hair was smooth, soft, and neatly combed. He looked like a movie star.

Morison had collected his careful wits and said, "Get out of here."

"Are you Menard?" Streicher asked.

Dorcas stared straight at Streicher but spoke to Morison, who climbed off the bed. "He must be one of them. *You* said no one was coming."

"He's late," Menard answered. "Get out, you!"

"Hannah couldn't be here," Streicher said. "I've come instead."

"You're late!" Menard spat, pushing in front of Dorcas. "Where do you get off just walking in here like that?"

"You wanted to see Hannah tonight," Streicher said. His hands were in his coat pockets.

"You're damn right I did. Who are you?" Menard said, zipping his pants.

"Doesn't matter. I've come to tell you that all our plans have changed. We won't be using your services anymore."

"Where's the money? You people owe us money," Menard said threateningly. "You're months behind and we've waited too long!"

Streicher looked around the room. "There isn't any money. There won't be any more money. We are finished here."

"The hell you say!" Menard stalked toward Streicher. "I told that stupid woman that we would protect ourselves. We've taken risks, you know. Great risks."

"And there are many of you," Streicher said quietly. "Who are *you*?" he asked, glancing toward Dorcas Baldwin, who, after buttoning her coat and stashing her undies in her handbag, had lifted her chin and braced her shoulders.

"Never you mind," she said.

"You are Leonard Baskins's girlfriend, aren't you?" Streicher said.

"I was not his girlfriend, Mister Whoever-You-Are. He was a drunken bum. He lied to me. Morison, tell him to get out of here."

"Not yet," Menard said. He reached into his suit pocket and brought out a folded piece of yellow paper. "I've got all their names, every German agent who ever went through here. And the woman," he said to Streicher. "All the installment payments are listed. I've made copies and hidden them in the bank. Either we get our money, or we telephone J. Edgar Hoover in Washington."

"Are you threatening me?" Streicher asked.

"Call it what you like. If you don't pay us what you owe us—to the penny—we'll nail your asses to the wall. The choice is yours, pal. Who are you, by the way?"

Streicher looked once again around the room. "You are a difficult man to do business with," he said.

"You bet your ass, I am," Menard said.

"There isn't any way you might cancel everything now?" Streicher asked. "Everybody stops?"

"Can't," Menard said. "We've taken risks—you owe us money. We want our money and we want it now. Our patience has run out."

Streicher hesitated, settling his eyes on theirs.

Dorcas Baldwin was the first to see the man's disdain for them. She reached to warn Menard.

"My patience has run out as well," the man breathed.

TWENTY

The President and I went to church together on Christmas Day, and I found peace in the simple service and enjoyed singing the well-known hymns, and one, 'O little town of Bethlehem,' I had never heard before. Certainly there was much to fortify the faith of all who believe in the moral governance of the universe.

HANNAH DOLL PASSED CHRISTMAS DAY ALONE, locked in her house. She made up a fire in the morning, wrapped herself in a thick quilt from her bed, and tried to read. She didn't go to mass because she understood that energy is finite and that for good or bad—and probably for the worst—she had bled her endurance at the crossroads and must now choose.

As much as she loved her Blue, he was not the resourceful man she needed at the moment. She couldn't imagine herself settled with him. He was too young and still felt the drive to remake the world according to his wants. His promises of escape to South America and Europe were hopelessly tinged with bravado. Words were to him only vagrant, shortsighted responses to the demands of the moment. He lied, and he didn't know that our greatest untruths are those we reserve for ourselves.

She knew that she and her bed had only momentarily

deflected him from his responsibilities to the war and to Germany. He might abandon intelligence work, he might cash it all in and stay with her wherever they went, but she also knew he would eventually lie about his dissatisfactions with her and probably leave her, saying she'd changed for the worst.

The strange man with her in this room last night—his white hair and his obvious power of concentration, his body and personality—had artlessly demonstrated his own dissipation, and she had liked being the younger of the two. She had had no need to explain to him how tired she was; he had known that instantly. Kemper had been through a few crossroads himself and wore his scars gently and without pride. But more than anything else, he had listened more closely to her secrets than she did herself, as if he expected them.

He wore his age like a shot-shredded uniform. She thought of the English hero, Chinese Gordon, in beleaguered Khartoum. Surrounded for ten months in 1885, General Gordon and his few British troops had held off thousands of the Mahdi's frenzied zealots, only to be killed before the British relieved the garrison.

She thought Kemper's tranquil resignation must resemble what the Mahdi saw in Gordon when his forces smashed into British headquarters to silently confront Gordon alone on his grand marble staircase. The General had brushed what filth he could from his dress tunic to stand before the Mahdi as the extraordinary man he was. The Mahdi bowed deeply to the equally ferocious Gordon; much later, after his antagonist had been executed, the Mahdi swore that Gordon's death troubled him to the brink of madness.

The world was a terrible place, Hannah thought. Life was, itself, a great war on the spirit, one that exacted the most terrible costs.

These were idle thoughts, she decided. Heroes were in short supply just now. She would have to fend for herself.

★ ★ ★

Kemper got through Christmas morning by finishing Patterson's tale of survival in the frost-cracked North; it gave him the sense that all men are ultimately alone.

Farley Ball telephoned before noon to say he was on his way, despite Kemper's reticent objections. Kemper stood out on the porch of the hotel to watch for him and smiled when he saw Ball ease the grey hearse up to the curb.

The expansive Ball bewildered the dining room staff with his mortician's dress and cast a genuine pall over the Christmas dinners being eaten by many of the city's better families.

Baskins's body had been taken from his Poughkeepsie by the coroner's office, he told Kemper. And glad he was to be rid of the man. "No, they didn't say a word about the autopsy," Ball said. "'Course they wouldn't—not to me, they wouldn't."

But Ball was more interested in Kemper. Ball asked him about his heart—his "condition," he called it. Kemper told him about Hannah Doll and her Christmas tree. Ball said nothing, but seemed to understand when Kemper said he felt almost like a lovesick kid. He was going back up to Sutton to see her.

They talked after dinner in the sitting room of the Jesse Welden with a decanter of brandy and a bottle of seltzer on the table between them.

Ball said he wouldn't retire until he died. But generally, they entertained each other with comforting dreams of fishing Vermont's rivers for the largest trout. Ball seemed to know his fishing. "I don't kill 'em, though," Ball admitted sheepishly. "Can't stand to kill fish."

Ball said he knew of a farm for sale near him that Kemper should look at. "Sits up on a hill," he said. "River runs through the trees at the bottom of the fields. You could just saunter on down to some damn fine fishing. I think you ought to do it. I could swing over in the evenings and we could have a brew or two."

Kemper heard about the burned boathouse the next morning.

TWENTY-ONE

STREICHER LEANED BACK in Alex Jaeger's kitchen and spooned the last of some of Jaeger's potato soup from the bottom of his cup. Jaeger's black Chevrolet had just come bouncing down the drive, and the railroad conductor was at his door, his uniform matted and creased from hours of work. Streicher saw Jaeger spot him, saw that persistent sneer Jaeger had whenever he realized Streicher was living with him still.

"Merry Christmas, you sonofabitch," Jaeger said.

Streicher dropped his spoon into the cup. "And to you, you friendly bastard." Jaeger was a man who got out to kick his Chevrolet whenever the automobile had the nerve not to start straight away. "You've been gone a long time."

Jaeger hung up his coat and took off his shoes. "Any soup left or did you eat it all? You never cook."

"I couldn't make soup like this."

Jaeger took this admission as fact and looked around the kitchen.

"I made coffee," Streicher said.

Jaeger rubbed his eyes and yawned. That Streicher would do anything other than exist was too much to expect.

"Goddam town's in a froth this morning," Jaeger said.

Streicher was filling his pipe with more of Jaeger's tobacco from the Prince Albert can on the kitchen table. "That guy, Menard, and Dorcas Baldwin were burned to death in the boathouse."

140

Streicher struck a match on his heel and touched his pipe. "That the banker?"

Jaeger looked at him with blood-red, tired eyes. "The boathouse burned into the water sometime Christmas Eve," Jaeger said. "They were in it when it went."

"What were they doing?"

Jaeger pushed his hands through his hair and said, "Fucking, probably. God knows she was a banshee for it. Old Leonard couldn't take it with her. Old Leonard couldn't take anything."

"What happened?"

"Nobody knows. Sykes thinks they fell asleep with a kerosene lamp burning. The lamp must have gone over. Menard's wife tried to kill herself when she heard about it." Jaeger stared at Streicher. "You wouldn't know anything about it, would you?"

"I don't even know where this boathouse is."

"Shit, you don't. I told you months ago. You think I'm an idiot?"

Streicher put his hands behind his head and rocked back in the ancient, creaking chair. Jaeger had obviously had enough. I'll get Churchill—I need this man for the train, Streicher thought. And then I'll be gone. He smiled at Jaeger and said, "You don't trust me at all, do you?"

"Goddam right I don't trust you."

"I've paid you."

"Hasn't got a damn thing to do with money. I think you'd kill your own mother if you had to."

"I'd like to," Streicher grinned.

"This is all news to you, is it?"

Streicher shrugged. He'd have to keep close watch on the unreliable Jaeger.

Jaeger had gone to the stove for coffee. "You've let this pot boil! Honest to christ, I told you, you can't let coffee boil! You smug bastard," Jaeger said turning around. "Where were you last night?"

"I was here."

Jaeger stirred sugar into his mug. "I'll bet you were. Do you know they were burned so bad, Sykes says they looked like charred wood when they found their bodies in the water. Fire department had no idea anyone was in there. The whole thing fell into the lake as it burned. Sykes thinks they were asphyxiated in bed. Somehow the lamp leaked or fell over—anyway, they were burned to a crisp. Whole town is shocked into its shit-kicking boots that Menard and a high school teacher were fucking on Christmas Eve."

"They were there a lot, you said."

Jaeger said he had the timetable Streicher wanted and the map of the Delaware & Hudson route through New York. "Menard was such a pig," Jaeger said. "Do you know— Sykes says Menard once fucked a widow for months. He told her he was going to foreclose on her house. She finally threw him out, and that bastard did foreclose on her and chucked her into the road with her three kids. They thought he was their rich uncle or something. And Sykes thinks that's a funny story. Thinks it recommends Menard. These people are awful."

Streicher puffed smoke into the air.

Jaeger looked away. Streicher knew he had been right to add Jaeger's name to Hannah's list before sending it to Quenneville. He'd been warned about the fat Montreal cop's curiosity before he left Germany, but now Quenneville would help him suck all of these yokels, including Jaeger, into the vortex around Churchill's death. Streicher had mailed a copy of the list of all their names and cash transfers to Montreal yesterday, along with four bank account numbers he got from Hannah's desk drawer.

Streicher would snatch Hannah from Sutton after Churchill and head west toward Chicago. He had the means to do it. And Hannah would go with him. They could drive on to the safety of Mexico and Central America before anyone knew a Paul Streicher existed at all. These local Bund

142

people have a mess closing in on them, but nothing like the mess they'll have in forty-eight hours, he thought.

"How can I get on a train in New York?" he said.

"You climb on," Jaeger said.

"If there are no stops?"

Jaeger stopped stirring his coffee. "What train are you talking about?"

"A special."

"What special?" Jaeger was suddenly intent. "The Delaware and Hudson doesn't run nonstop to Montreal."

"This one will."

"You can't get on if it doesn't stop," Jaeger said. "Why do you want to get on a special? Where's it going?"

Streicher hesitated, then said the train would go to Montreal.

"If it's a special, they won't stop it unless they have orders," Jaeger said suspiciously. "Why do you want to get on the thing? Why not drive to Montreal?"

Streicher said it would be easier if he got on before Montreal.

"Okay, I'll tell you what," Jaeger said, resting at the sink. "This is going to cost you something. I took a wicked chance with that Baskins bullshit, but I'm not doing that again."

"You're leaving anyway," Streicher said.

"You bastard. If you need me enough, you'll pay. I want the money up front this time."

"You'll get it," Streicher said. He had counterfeit American currency in the cellar, as well as a few thousand in real cash. Berlin wouldn't care if Streicher lost it all if Churchill were dead. He said, "I need a Canadian National conductor's uniform that fits."

Jaeger asked how much money.

"Enough," Streicher said. "I'm leaving after this. You'll get five hundred if you decide to help. Nothing, if you act like an asshole. I need to get on a train."

Streicher knew that if he offered the conductor too much money, Jaeger's suspicions would become a real danger. Streicher did not want Jaeger to so much as hear the name Churchill. He thought he had enough money to satisfy Jaeger, but timing was important. Jaeger was a man given to indecision and plagued with regret; money might not be enough to control him if the man had too much time to consider what was at risk. Jaeger had not enjoyed Baskins's departure from the train at seventy miles an hour. He'd like this even less.

It was midafternoon and Jaeger was asleep upstairs when Streicher sat bolt upright on the stool at the cellar bench. Something about Jaeger's description of the boathouse turmoil had troubled him all day. He blew out his alcohol stove and stood up. Now, he knew: the sheriff was probably aware that Hannah was to meet Menard at the boathouse. "Damn," he muttered. Sykes was in this courier business with them all and would probably support the story of a Christmas Eve assignation between Menard and Hannah. Sykes would cheerfully keep his mouth shut and allow the town to believe Menard was up to hanky-panky with the dead woman—better that than have their efforts for the Germans exposed. Before the war was one thing; with a war on, they'd all be finished and probably jailed.

But if the sheriff knew Hannah was to see Menard on Christmas Eve, then he might decide to cut his losses now. Sykes had no jurisdiction in Sutton, and obviously wouldn't tell Canadian authorities, but he could get to Hannah. And Sykes would hurt her.

Who would know? Streicher thought. Quenneville will have their names in a day or so, and he'll probably tell the FBI about Sykes and his friends. But that would take time—more than enough time for the sheriff to awaken Hannah in her bed.

Hannah thought her Blue was off and gone.

Streicher ran up the stairs to the kitchen.

TWENTY-TWO

FRIDAY
DECEMBER
26
1941

*IT WAS WITH HEART-STIRRINGS that I fulfilled the invitation to
address the Congress of the United States. The occasion was important
for what I was sure was the all-conquering alliance of the English-
speaking peoples. I had never addressed a foreign Parliament before . . . I
must confess that I felt quite at home, and more sure of myself than I had
sometimes been in the House of Commons. What I said was received
with the utmost kindness and attention. I got my laughter and applause
just where I expected them. The loudest response was when, speaking of
the Japanese outrage, I asked, 'What sort of people do they think we
are?' The sense of the might and will-power of the American nation
steamed up to me from the august assembly. Who could doubt that all
would be well? . . .*

*Afterwards the leaders came along with me close up to the crowds
which surrounded the building, so that I could give them an intimate
greeting; and then the Secret Service men and their cars closed round and
took me back to the White House, where the President, who had listened
in, told me I had done quite well.*

Kemper felt good as he crossed Main Street and went into
the drugstore. He needed a few supplies, toothpaste and
shaving soap. A rack of brown combs attracted him as he
waited to pay behind a young woman, obviously a secretary
on a morning ritual errand for coffee. The cashier had on a

gray smock, her hair was piled in knots, and she wore eye-glasses shaped like butterfly wings.

He realized they were talking about a boathouse. The cashier reached for Kemper's things and returned her attention to the secretary. "What a tragedy for his wife," the cashier said, examining Kemper's toothpaste for its price. "I hear she's poorly."

"How could she do that?" the young woman asked.

Kemper leaned carefully on the glass counter.

"How could *he* do what he did?" the cashier said.

"But to shoot herself like that—or try to, at least. How awful. She shot his picture first, you know."

Kemper watched as the cashier cranked his total up. He held out a five.

"That's what I hear," the cashier said, snapping bills from her cash drawer.

As she counted his change, Kemper waited for her eyes to lift to him. And when they did, he asked what had happened.

The secretary backed away from him in fine xenophobic style—he wanted to tell her to forget her mother's warnings about strange men and candy on automobile seats. "I'm staying at the Jesse Welden," he said, to clarify his curiosity for the cashier.

"A man and a woman died in a fire over Christmas," she said.

Kemper pocketed his change. "Isn't that terrible," he said.

"Worst thing we've had around here in years." The cashier smiled to him.

"Tree ornaments?" he asked.

The woman shook her head. Kemper sensed a finely brewed animus from the secretary beside him, but he didn't look at her.

"An old boathouse—on the lake," the cashier said. She

gave him his things in a brown bag. "They don't know how it started."

Kemper's clockwork gears tripped another cog. He didn't want to ask for more; he wanted to walk to the hotel. He could drive to Ottawa in three hours from here. "Is this the boathouse at the Cedars?" he asked, leaving.

The cashier flashed a look of consternation to the secretary. "It is," she answered. Her morning smile, such as it was, had fled. "How did you know?" she asked with some trepidation in her voice.

"I thought I might buy the place."

She hesitated. "You wouldn't want it now. Not after this," she said.

Kemper thanked her and left the drugstore slowly. That little chat, he thought, will be repeated word-for-word through this city by the end of the day.

The local paper on the hotel desk carried a frustratingly cold account of the incident: Morison Menard and Dorcas Baldwin, both long-time St. Albans residents, were found dead in the burned ruins of Hollaway's boathouse on Christmas morning. A fire of undetermined origin . . . investigators at work now to discover its cause . . . the boathouse destroyed before the fire department got there. In a related incident, Sarah Menard . . . wife of . . . was wounded by a gunshot at her home . . . is in stable condition in the St. Albans Hospital.

"Goddam," Kemper muttered.

The room clerk wanted to know if he was leaving today. Kemper said he didn't know and crossed into the sitting room to think. What the hell is going on? he thought, sitting by a window. An ornately framed portrait of one of the state's governors—the old gent lean, a Calvinist's delight—leered at him from across the room.

Menard was supposed to meet Hannah on Christmas Eve at the boathouse—that from Quenneville. But Quenneville

147

told her not to go. Did Hannah drive to the boathouse after Kemper left her that night? Unlikely, but possible, he thought. The sheriff had lied about Dorcas Baldwin. Changed his story and said she was upset, that Dorcas and Baskins had had difficulties, that Baskins had been serious about her. Sykes obviously suspected Kemper of something. But what? "Official curiosity," Kemper hissed. "Bullshit."

An ancient woman teetered across the hotel carpet to a leather couch.

The coroner's office had removed Baskins from Ball's Poughkeepsie; Moffet must have done that after my telephone call, he thought.

Quenneville had said to be careful. Of what?

Kemper lighted a cigar, to the disgust of the old lady on the couch, who tapped her cane as though she might be forced to escape for fresh air.

Possibly Menard and that Dorcas woman were just having a Christmas celebration at the boathouse—an accident. Quenneville wouldn't think so, though. When they were in Alsace, the fat cop had believed so furiously in the powers of Fate that he wouldn't even consider random selection and coincidence. He'll howl when he hears this, Kemper thought.

The events in the town whirred through his head. He was confused, irritated, and anxious. Dr. Wally had said Kemper's anxiety could kill him. I should care, but I don't, he thought. I'm responsible for an assignment that means nothing to me. And the fetid gruesomeness of Baskins in that drawer, and now two charred bodies slung out of the lake, and Quenneville's dead man on another lake—they were pictures of death and disfigurement that frightened him and triggered thoughts of his own death.

Just finish and go home, he thought. He decided to talk to the train conductor.

He walked to Cody's office. Vera Lynn's voice on a radio

soothed the morning routine. Cody was in Montpelier, but his secretary had a crew roster and said Jaeger would be running a train late in the afternoon. She said Jaeger lived on the lake and told him how to get there. How close to the boathouse? he wondered. As Kemper left the warm office an announcer in Plattsburgh was droning his morning weather forecast. The day would bring snow.

The green sedan drew up beside him as he walked back to the hotel. A man threw open the passenger door. "You Baskins?" The man leaned across his front seat.

"Who are you?" Kemper asked, picking tobacco off his tongue.

"Sheriff wants to see you. Get in."

"I asked you who you are."

"My name's Corliss. I'm one of his deputies."

"You don't look like a deputy. Where is Sykes?"

"At the jail," the man said. "He said I was to bring you in."

"I'll walk," Kemper said. He saw the park ahead of him, the courthouse in the distance. "Where's the jail?"

"I'm supposed to bring you in for questioning."

"Tell Sykes you found me. I'll be along," Kemper said.

The man jerked on the parking brake and got out with his arm on the roof. "Get in this car, mister."

Kemper flicked the ash from his cigar. "Show me a badge," he said.

"I haven't got it with me."

"Then you haven't got a passenger. I'll walk over. Why don't you just follow along?"

Kemper turned and walked up the sidewalk. He saw a man with a refrigerator on a loading dock ahead of him point at him. Kemper turned around just as the man from the sedan hit him in the head with his fist. Kemper collapsed. Hands lifted him off the sidewalk and into the back seat of the sedan. The refrigerator clod sat on Kemper's legs while the other one circled the park and drove behind the

149

courthouse. The red-brick jail was there. Kemper had lost his cigar. His hands were wet with sidewalk slush. His head had felt like this when he'd been hit squarely with a baseball bat as a kid. He tried to slow his breathing.

They had him across the porch and into the jail's steam heat in seconds. Sykes was in a huge red chair in a sitting room.

"Ah, Mr. Baskins. Good of you to come. What happened?" Sykes asked Corliss.

While Corliss talked, Kemper reached down to twist his prosthetic log into place. He thought one of its leather straps felt torn. Kemper shut his eyes to focus.

"I've been looking for you," Sykes said.

When Kemper reached for his wallet, he thought Corliss would hit him again. "My wallet," Kemper explained.

"Take it out," Sykes said.

Kemper flipped Sykes his Naval Intelligence ID and the FBI ID and his British security ID. "Let me know when you've had enough," Kemper said.

"Do I call you Frank?" Sykes asked.

Kemper didn't answer, but turned to Corliss. "Get me a hot towel," he said.

"Get it!" Sykes said when Corliss grinned. "You were at a boathouse day before yesterday," Sykes said. The odor control salesman knew his stuff, Kemper thought. "You left there just before dark. When did you go back?"

"You've had your fun, Sykes," Kemper said. "Don't so much as think of leaving this town unless you tell me first." Kemper felt his heart throb, but thought he was all right. He had to quiet down.

A door opened and two men in overcoats stepped into the room.

Pointing to Kemper, Sykes asked them, "He one of yours?"

They nodded and introduced themselves, but kept their hands in their pockets. Both midtwenties, thin, and as FBI as the FBI got. They couldn't be anything else. Their shoes were new. The dark one spoke first: "Answer the sheriff's question."

Corliss was back and handed Kemper a cold wet towel. Kemper stared at them, at Sykes, while he wiped his hands.

The FBI college kids didn't believe a word Kemper said when he explained his boathouse visit. And with Sykes right there, he wasn't about to say much.

The redheaded college kid said, "You went to see a Dorcas Baldwin. Why?"

Kemper said she knew Baskins.

"He the guy on the train?"

Kemper said he was.

"He's been trying to make something out of this train stuff since he got here," Sykes said. "Says the guy was killed." And to Kemper: "I knew you weren't you. I knew you were lying. You been to Canady?" Sykes asked.

"I went to Winnipeg in 1913," Kemper answered.

"You smart-ass bastard," Sykes hissed. "Have you been to Canada in the last two days?"

"Did Dorcas Baldwin tell you herself that I visited her the day she died?"

Sykes said "Shit."

"Or did she tell your brother and he told you?"

Sykes stared at him with undiluted hatred. If he could, Kemper thought, he'd kick the hell out of me right here.

"Or did she tell Menard, who told Jaeger, who told your brother, and your brother told you?"

When Sykes didn't answer, Kemper said to the college kids, "Gets thick right about now—they're like rats in a maze up here."

The dark one motioned Kemper into the other room. "Close it," he said to his partner when they were inside.

Kemper threw the wet towel over Sykes's marble nameplate onto his desk blotter.

151

"Jack Moffet wants you out of here," the dark one said.

Kemper said he had to be in Ottawa anyway. His indignation began to rise with the mention of Moffet. He raised his hand to explain.

"No," the dark one said. "Moffet wants you out *now*."

Kemper watched the redhead go to the window and stare at the courthouse wall. "I haven't finished yet."

"Moffet says you have. He wants you back in New York."

"Leonard Baskins was not a suicide," Kemper said.

The dark one rubbed his nose. "We know that. The coroner's report says he was poisoned and probably was dead before he left the train."

They were chucking him. Kemper breathed slowly. He pointed to the door. "Sykes—that clown," he said, "is in this up to his ass. They've been running German agents and couriers through here for years. They like money. But now their little sideline has become treason. They killed Baskins when this country went to war because he was the only outsider who knew."

"Not likely," the dark one said. "Baskins was killed with hydrogen sulphide. I guess it isn't all that hard to make, but hydrogen sulphide isn't anything these folks would know about. Must be Abwehr."

Kemper noticed his boots had been stomped and scratched.

"Sykes asked you if you went to Canada in the last two days. There's supposed to be a German contact in a town called Sutton. Do you know him?"

Kemper said he did not. He breathed deeply and patted his coat. His cigar tubes had been crushed, the cigars would be shredded. Bastards, he thought.

"Have you still got the car?" the redhead said from the window.

Kemper said he did.

"Leave it with us," the redhead said. "Take the train back."

"I don't think so," Kemper said slowly.

"Moffet wants us to put you on a train. Go back to the hotel and pack."

Hydrogen sulphide *was* too neat, too clean for Sykes and his boobs. Kemper had had a taste of what they did to anyone they didn't care for.

"How about the fire in the boathouse?" Kemper asked.

"Just pack your stuff."

Sykes and his deputy had abandoned the outer room when Kemper left the jail to walk across the park to the Jesse Welden. Large wet snowflakes spun through the maples like white leaves. "I'll be damned," he said, watching the snow. Moffet would have his revenge.

Quenneville had telephoned and left a message at the hotel desk for Kemper to call him. Kemper balled up the slip of paper and tossed it into the trash.

The snowstorm began as Kemper wound out of Richford, Vermont, following the narrow highway up the northern slope of the Missisquoi River Valley. He slid going into the Canadian customs outpost and got out to clear, thick, wet snow off his windshield. Afternoon rain had slicked the roads to make his journey to Sutton that much longer. Now, on the flat open fields and mounds of Quebec, the road was white like its surroundings, and driving on pavement was a matter of perilous luck. Kemper kept a string of telephone poles to his right. His headlights irritated the snow so that it flew at him; this was late afternoon, early nightfall. Kemper thought of the settlers, who must have wondered why they had ever sailed with anything like hope for this lost existence. Their separation from Europe and home must have been paralyzing, the distance between their rock-edged farms must have taunted them with dreams of

153

resurrection and deliverance, because even the delicate yellows of their neighbors' windows were consumed by the darkling snow to render any living thing on these flats a bewildered lonely breath.

He knew he could die out here. If his heavy Buick buried itself in a ditch, he'd try to walk. He hadn't passed or seen another set of headlights since Vermont. He'd never survive the fifteen-mile trek to Sutton, the only settlement nearby. He imagined his hard corpse, just another one found face down in the drift, another someone wholly relieved of his fears. He thought of Patterson struggling in the Nahanni River. Patterson must have been quite ordinary when he poled into the Northwest Territories on the Nahanni, but he was a man with deep reserves of confidence when he paddled madly back down the spring rapids to the Hudson Bay fort at Great Slave Lake.

Kemper kept the car at a steady crawl, certain that once stopped, the Buick would founder, exhausted.

The lights of a gas station surprised him; he strained to see them again through the snow. He remembered there was a garage at Sutton's southern edge. Then someone walked into the road ahead of him with a kerosene lantern. Kemper guided the Buick around the being—an old man, Kemper guessed from his pottering stride.

Kemper shut off the engine and released the steering wheel. The bright lights were on in her shop, and her windows patterned the snow across the road.

"In a minute there is time for decisions and revisions," he said quietly, his breath rising like smoke through the open car window. Was he to announce himself, announce his intentions, that he wanted nothing so much as to step into her house as though he were home? She could so easily laugh at him. That's not it at all! he thought. And was he to stand there, naked with her, diminished, an old man with an inflamed heart?

He rolled the window tight, opened the door, and stood up in deep, wet snow.

She wasn't in her shop, but called from the kitchen when he shouted.

She was confused for a moment when she met him in the hall, warming suddenly. She smiled quickly. "What are you doing here? Hello." She asked him into the kitchen. She had a large white procelain teapot on the counter and poured scalding water from a kettle. "You've come out in a bad night," she said from the stove. "Take off your coat."

Hannah offered him tea. "It's very strong," she said. "How are the roads?"

He told her about the fierce, open flats south of Sutton as she gathered cups and saucers, placing everything on a silver tray lined with a pink napkin. "You look exhausted," she said, resting against the sink with her arms crossed. She wore grey slacks and a white sweater.

He told her about Sykes and Corliss and falling on the sidewalk.

"I'm not surprised," she said gently. "You're not all right, are you?"

He dropped into a chair. The torn leather strap on his prosthetic log snapped free and the leg loosened as he pushed it under the table. He'd have to fix it.

And then he told her about the boathouse fire—that both Menard and Dorcas Baldwin had died in the flames.

Hannah raised her face. "Why was that woman there?" she asked quickly.

He told her about the odor control salesman and the others who used the boathouse.

It was at this point that Kemper realized that her immediate warmth for him was dissipating. But he had to tell her, to warn her about Sykes and the FBI. She grew more distracted the more he explained. "Baskins was poisoned before he was tossed from the train. And a man named Mouton up here in Quebec is dead."

She stared away from him, then turned to look out to the snow through the window over the sink. "Don't go on," she said. "I know who Mouton is. I knew him. Oh god . . . how did he die?"

Kemper said he didn't know.

She asked when, softly.

"I don't know," Kemper said. "I spoke to Quenneville the day before Christmas.

"Two days before that . . ." she said mysteriously. "Did Mouton die at Black Lake?"

Kemper said yes. He wondered what she was doing; her body was rigid against the edge of the sink. She kept her face away from him and poured their tea. Her hands were shaking.

She brought the tray to the table and sat down near him. Something had happened to her.

"There are four people dead now . . . I knew them all," she said, trying to hand him his cup. Kemper forced her hand to the table and finished serving their tea. He stirred cream into her cup and dumped sugar in his own. He wanted to take her hand.

She tossed her hair.

He said, "Quenneville knows something is very different here now." He sipped his tea and then told her about the *Sicherheitsdienst* and the SS in Alsace in the thirties, and the coldbloodedness of the men who wore the black uniforms. "Heydrich has recruited only the most obnoxious fanatics," he said. "They like to kill."

"Quenneville told me not to see Menard at the boathouse," Hannah said. "Were they murdered also?"

"Do you think they were?"

"Leonard was poisoned," she said. "Jean Mouton is dead, and now two more."

"The FBI knows you are here—or that someone connected with the network is. Quenneville cannot hold off the RCMP forever. The war has changed everything. But four dead people tell me that something has changed here and very fast. Dead people are the only trail the SS ever leaves. Have you seen them?"

She brought her teacup to her lips and looked at him over the rim.

I'll be damned, he thought. There is someone.

"There isn't anyone new," she said. "I don't understand all of this business—Margaret did."

"She's dead," Kemper said.

Hannah's shoulders sagged like a puppet's.

"This life is drenched with sadness," she said.

He lowered his teacup to its saucer. Nothing gained, all lost, he thought. "I won't insult you with bullshit," he said. "I couldn't even if I had to. My own people want me out . . . too old for them. I drove here to get you. Not for them . . . for me."

"*You're* the FBI. What are you talking about? Why don't you arrest me?"

"I want to help you."

"You can't," she said, whispering. And then, stronger, "It's too late. I love someone else—is that terrible to hear?"

Kemper felt his chest heave. "I didn't say love."

"You didn't have to say it."

"Will you come back with me?" he asked in panic. He knew she was lost to him.

"This world is a sewer," she said.

"I'll leave," he said and got up out of the chair.

"I was happy here, for a while," she said, looking around her kitchen. "I love this house." Tears began to track down her cheeks. She raised her eyes to him. "You've been good to me."

Kemper jerked his coat from the chair by the wall and poked his arms through its sleeves.

157

"My name is Hannah Doll," she said. "Please remember me and this house."

He said his name. "I'd be pleased if you remembered me at all."

"Lift your chin. You are a very handsome man, Frank Kemper. Be careful as you drive. I wouldn't want you hurt."

"Nor I you," he said. "Will you come with me?"

Hannah smiled. Her hair had its red brilliants amongst its browns. "Always seems to be a matter of timing, doesn't it?"

She looked away from him.

He left her house feeling collapsed within, as though he were carrying internal wounds out into the white of the abating storm. He stepped behind the bakery truck and crossed the desolate main road through Sutton. As the engine idled before he turned back for Vermont, he wondered if he shouldn't go back in, hoist her onto his shoulders, and carry her off into the darkness. "You're an old man," he said to himself. The clouds of breath as he said it rose against the windshield where the wipers slashed under the snow and dropped the stuff into the road.

He looked once more at her lights—he knew this was the last time he'd be able to see her—then he spun the wheel and turned the car for St. Albans and the Jesse Welden.

He wasn't at all frightened of the snow or the flats or of the Buick in a ditch. He'd drive until he got somewhere. And somewhere was just fine. Anywhere, he thought, imagining Hannah sitting quietly in her kitchen with only the heavy teapot to warm her. The car skidded on the curve out of town, but he caught it and pointed the thing south.

Hannah lifted the teapot off the table and added more water from the kettle. She'd pack and be gone. But where? No matter what she did, the costs would be severe. She couldn't just throw up her hands and say I didn't mean to

158

do what I've done. The RCMP wouldn't be easy; Quenneville's avuncular concern wouldn't be there. She had let herself be trapped.

Gradually, she realized there had been a series of faint scuffs and thumps—some part of her brain had been hearing the sounds for a minute or two.

Where? Hannah stopped breathing to listen. Had Kemper come back for her?

In the cellar!

The back door was unlatched. Someone was on the cellar stairs, behind the white door there—the refrigerator humming quietly beside it.

Again—behind the door.

"Dear god," she said, lowering the teapot to the stove.

The front door, her coat and scarf were far away. He'd be on her before she got out.

She took a step toward the back door.

Kemper must be in his car by now, she thought.

She lifted her other foot—

The cellar door burst open—Blue!—and shuddered as it bounced off the refrigerator.

"You!" she cried.

Streicher held out his hands, moving slowly around the table. His eyes darted toward the hallway and the front door.

"No more," she said. "Don't come near me."

"Hannah, you must listen to me."

"Not to your lies," she said.

His face was hard in a way she'd never seen. "Leave me alone," she said, backing away from him. He saw her glance at the back door and moved stealthily to block her, his hands out like a sleepwalker.

"Leave me here," she said. "I'll say nothing. Just leave."

"Not without you," he said. "We'll go away."

She shook her head. He was close to her, coiled to catch

her in his arms. "I believed you. I believed everything," she said, her voice choking.

"I won't hurt you," he said.

She sobbed, knowing instantly when she heard him say it that he could hurt her, would hurt her.

"Mouton!" she screamed. He'd be on her back before she got into the hallway. "You killed Leonard—I know you did. Don't lie. You killed Menard and that woman in the boathouse. You burned *them* alive! You used me. All along you used me. You have killed me!"

Streicher's face muscles twitched, his eyes blinked into hatred and fear. "Not now," he said.

His hand got her left wrist. She twisted, pulling, screaming "I hate you!" Then she cried out the name—"Kemper!"

With that, Streicher threw her to the floor. Her head hit the table. He knelt on her shoulders. She spun out from under him, reaching for the stove, and her hand caught the teapot as his fingers clutched her hair. She jerked hard away from him and tried to swing the pot, screaming. He caught her wrist. She jerked again—he had her sweater.

She hit him in the eyes with a crash of white porcelain and steam. He staggered, his head turning slightly in disbelief, then went down at her feet.

She watched his hands tremble up to his head where the blood gushed to cover his face. She watched until he stopped shaking. His hands were limp; his eyes, grown grisly huge, stared at the light over her head.

Hannah's body vibrated. She felt nausea convulse her stomach. The house was suddenly still as she bent over the table. "Oh god . . ." But she hesitated for only a moment before she was running through her hall. Somehow, she ripped her coat off its hook . . .

. . . and was clawing at the bolt and knob on the front door. She could hear herself whimpering; she couldn't control her hands. She screamed in desperation and, with a final wrenching jerk, the door flew open . . .

. . . just as the wet hands covered her face, pulling her back into the house.

TWENTY-THREE

SATURDAY
DECEMBER
2 7
1 9 4 1

"GET UP!"

Kemper rolled over into early morning darkness. The redheaded college kid pulled the chain on the bedside lamp. Kemper rubbed his eyes.

"Get up!" the dark one said again.

Kemper sat up. The FBI agents in their shiny gabardine suits hustled him out of bed, the dark one perplexed when Kemper swung his stump from under the blankets. "You've got to come downstairs."

Kemper asked for the time. He was cold; he couldn't think what to do next. The redhead carried his prosthetic log from the chair. "It won't hurt you, kid," Kemper said, angered that the agent handled the thing and its dangling leather straps as though he were picking up real meat.

They tossed his clothes at him. "Moffet wants you on the phone. He's waiting. Hurry up. It's almost six."

Kemper struggled to get dressed—they told him to forget his bow tie. He stretched his braces over his shoulders. "You can come back and shave," the redhead said. "Jack Moffet is waiting."

Kemper wondered if he weren't enjoying another nightmare.

They pushed him into the hushed corridor and led him downstairs to the hotel manager's office, where the lights glared.

The redhead handed Kemper the telephone, saying, "He's on."

Kemper tried to listen—the voice rasped like steel shot in a barrel. "Wait a minute," Kemper said, trying to clear his mind.

"I'll go through it one more time, goddam it," Moffet said. "You better write this down—*You are fired!*"

Kemper looked at the college kids.

Moffet asked him if he understood what being fired meant. "Are you there, Frank?"

Kemper said he was.

"You don't work for us anymore. And you don't work for Naval Intelligence. Is that clear? You're a private citizen." Moffet told him to get on a morning train to New York.

"I'm going to Ottawa," Kemper said.

"The hell you are!" Moffet wanted Kemper on the train. "And if you don't get on that train," Moffet added, "I've told Rowell and Masterson to arrest you and bring you back to New York. Is that clear? Either get on the train yourself, or take the consequences. I've talked to Andrews at ONI—they want you in your office by nine tomorrow morning."

Sheriff Sykes and Corliss let themselves into the office on tiptoes. Kemper saw the mayor's face out at the desk before the door closed. Sykes had raised his eyebrows when he came in, and the dark college kid had nodded affirmatively. Corliss glanced around the office like a trapped cat.

Kemper gave the telephone to Masterson, the dark one. Adrenaline had fired into his gut when he was knocked out of sleep and continued even now to roil his insides. He shut his eyes to stop the dizziness. Masterson dropped the telephone finally and stared straight at him. "I don't like doing this," Masterson said.

Kemper drew in his breath. "I'll bet you don't."

The redhead told Kemper to go upstairs and pack; Corliss would go with him.

"He will not," Kemper said. Sykes suppressed a grin. The sheriff was tripping the light fantastic on a high wire to safety, and Kemper knew that his own cause was bankrupt. These people, he thought, Sykes and the others, will do anything they can to stay cuddled up to two FBI agents who act like FBI agents.

"Did you kill Menard?" Kemper asked Sykes.

Sykes laughed. "You're crazy," he said. "It's either you . . . or that woman in Sutton. She was there."

"The woman in Sutton was with me," Kemper said to Masterson. "She didn't go near the boathouse."

"Someone did," Sykes said.

Masterson nodded solemnly. "They were dead before the fire," he said. "If the floor hadn't caved into the lake, their bodies would have been burned worse than they were."

"They was bad enough," Sykes said.

Masterson didn't like being interrupted and regarded the sheriff intently. "They were both pretty well messed up," he continued. "The guy's arm was broken."

"And you think a woman did that?" Kemper asked him.

"You were there that afternoon," Masterson said. "We have a witness. Our problem is that we don't know what you've been doing up here."

"He *has* been to Canady," Sykes said. "He said he was Leonard's brother. And he bothered Dorcas Baldwin the same day she died. I think he was a friend of Leonard's or worked with him as one of those double agents or something. He came in here all mister big man with his cigars and his fancy clothes."

Masterson told Sykes to shut up.

"I think he killed Dorcas because she jilted Leonard. Leonard couldn't take it—being told to move along. And this fella killed Morison Menard because he knew Morison and Dorcas was sort of sweet on each other. We don't like it that those two were carrying on—happens here like any-

163

where else. This guy found out about the three of them and came here to make trouble."

Masterson told the redhead to clear them all out of the office.

"I don't know what's going on," he said quietly to Kemper, "but you've stirred up a swamp."

"The swamp was here."

"So were you. And you made it worse." Masterson sat on the desk, looking at his hands. "Look. You lost it. The thing blew up on you. Get on the train and forget about all of them. We'll straighten it out. I'd hate to do it, but Moffet means business and I'll lock you up and take you back to New York myself if I have to."

Kemper stared at his boots. He'd been too long without bearings. Enough was enough. Dr. Beam had said to stop dancing. Have the good sense to let it go, he thought. Masterson is being gentle when he says the thing blew up on me. The fact is, I haven't done a damn thing right. He hadn't even gone to the railroad station in Richmond, violating one of the principal rules of investigation by not examining the evidence for himself. Instead, he'd been scared to death in the Ball Brothers' Memorial Funeral Parlor and Crematory.

His shoulders sagged. He rubbed his stump for compassion, holding at bay the realization that he was, at fifty-eight, a vibrating, tired man; too tired and too frightened by conflicting imperatives to operate as an agent. Moffet said he was a private citizen; so be it, he thought. None of it matters. Time for me to gracefully leave the dance floor.

He hobbled upstairs and shaved while the redhead leafed through a *National Geographic* in the chair by the window. Kemper could eat on the train to quiet his indigestion. He'd like to see Ball before he left. Ball had none of this trash in his life.

The redhead carried his suitcase down to the lobby behind Kemper. They were all there: the mayor appeared

164

ready to detonate with nervousness; Sykes and Corliss were out on the porch. Masterson shook Kemper's hand and muttered that he was sorry. "We can't take you to the station," Masterson explained. "You'll have to go with Corliss. Don't give him any trouble. The guy's a bucket of loose change and he'd hurt you."

Kemper said, "He already has."

Kemper rode in silence next to Corliss down to the rail station. The morning train wasn't due for a half-hour. Corliss had Kemper sit in the waiting room. He hadn't had a chocolate bar for days—that should please Beam, he thought. Women and children crowded the waiting room. Various men paced; most of them wore the creases of traveling salesmen. Everyone talked about time and the early hour. Kemper leaned against the bench and closed his eyes to shut them out.

The minutes dragged like lead. There were train whistles from the yards; at each one the waiting room stirred. Then the doors opened and a man in greasy overalls with grimy hands said the train was here.

Corliss reached for Kemper's arm as they rose from the bench, clutched Kemper's arm while they stepped with the others onto the platform, steadied him amid the jabbering salesmen and children, up the stairs and into the coach until Kemper chose a seat and sank into the soft grey plush. The deputy shoved Kemper's suitcase into a luggage rack, then came back and patted Kemper's shoulder. Saying nothing intelligible, distracted, but grunting fluently, almost boarlike, Corliss satisfied himself that Kemper was settled— much as a hospital orderly might hesitate before abandoning a ravished octogenarian to his wheelchair in the bleaching sun.

Kemper saw the deputy's head bobbing toward the waiting room entrance to vanish into the station dark.

He sat alone with his burning heart, exhausted and fumbling with his watch chain. They had shoved him aside, as they had propelled Baskins into the night air. The grasping claws and beaks had vented their animus against the one man left awake.

They're coarse; everything is black and white; ready to knock your block off. These people live in a barroom, he thought. One must either act with conviction according to their expectations, or face their consequences. And there were always consequences—always the claws at a man's back.

Had Corliss any wits at all, had he experienced life outside the barroom, he might have thought it wise to complete his chore; he might have paused long enough to see the last coach rumble safely out of the train shed. If he had waited, he'd have seen the man standing beside a brown suitcase on the far platform. After the train left, Corliss would have seen the man hunch his shoulders to protect the match, then puff a blue wreath of fine Panamanian tobacco essence over his head.

TWENTY-FOUR

KEMPER HEAVED HIS SUITCASE across the tracks and went up to the Central Vermont superintendent's office. Cody was deferential when Kemper said he needed to borrow a railroad automobile. The superintendent sniffed and said Kemper could have one; Cody would bill the FBI for wear and tear. When Kemper explained that he wanted to ask Jaeger about the drunken Baskins for a background report and ran through the directions the secretary had given him, Cody sighed and drew a map on railroad stationery.

When Kemper asked to use his telephone, Cody said Kemper should run the railroad. "I'll be back," Cody said, leaving the room. Kemper waited while the RCMP office in Montreal hunted for Quenneville.

Kemper felt the fatigue of Ulysses, the queasiness in the gut that comes when anyone takes that first step into the cave. The odds were against him.

Quenneville answered in French and continued in English to treat Kemper's call with embarrassed futility. "Naval Intelligence in Washington told me to cut you off," Quenneville said coldly. "Moffet has men coming for you."

Kemper explained that he hadn't finished the Baskins business yet—that he knew the locals were implicated up to their necks in Baskins's death, and that Menard and Dorcas Baldwin had been killed, then left to burn in the boathouse.

"Go home," Quenneville said. And then, as though to

167

convince Kemper, he said, "Mouton was murdered with hydrogen sulphide."

Kemper said he had been with Hannah on the night of the boathouse murders.

"It's not Hannah," Quenneville said. "Whoever killed Jean Mouton was strong enough to drag a boat into Black Lake. Hannah couldn't do that."

Kemper said that Sykes and his local loonies could have.

"Go home," Quenneville said. "You're worn out. You said you didn't want any part of this. From the beginning! You told me so yourself. We can handle it. Save yourself some embarrassment, Frank; Moffet doesn't give a damn about your honor. They don't want you and, damn it friend, I'm just too busy right now to be your nurse. God knows we are in some shit. Just go back to New York and take care of yourself . . . leave Hannah Doll to me."

The Montreal cop's chilly distance was mitigated by his loyalty to his old friend, and Kemper knew he was bleeding that reserve to its last.

Kemper asked about Jaeger. Quenneville launched into a monologue about being overworked and too old. "I will retire right behind you," Quenneville said. "I've got Jaeger—I have a list of those Vermont creeps, and he's on it. Hannah sent me everything, including their bank account numbers. Moffet will nail all of them. Sykes and his brother are finished. I've sent a copy of the lists to Moffet. He'll take care of those guys."

Kemper asked about the boathouse fire. Quenneville said he didn't care about any of them, that Churchill was traveling through New York on the train to Ottawa tomorrow, that he had enough to do. "I am very sorry," Quenneville said. "You have done so much in your life that is good. Please go home. I like you."

Quenneville's farewell had the bitter curl of remorse.

The Montreal cop believed the worst, and the worst was Kemper himself. A man was only as good as the information he produced, only worth his last hopeful signal. Kemper pushed the telephone to the dustless rectangle on Cody's desk and left the office.

The worm had turned. Farley Ball said his Poughkeepsie got them all. Kemper had been horrified with his own mortality. And more shamed than he could easily admit that his own connivance had been a prerequisite to his predicament. He hadn't, of course, believed that he deserved anything like peace.

How cruel that the victim, the man condemned most by his self-pity, so unwittingly extends his neck to the axe.

He'd been feigning recovery. He'd wanted only to survive, to never again experience the blinding grip in his chest. But surviving wasn't enough. Dr. Beam had said, "You *are* alive. Act like it."

Nothing was clear to him except his exhilarating fury that he should be judged by the likes of a Moffet, or worse, by someone like Sykes and his smarmy minions; but there was a new courage with him as he shut off the '37 Chevrolet Cody had lent him. His courage came with his remembrance of Hannah. Her bookshop windows were dark, empty.

A sign on the front door in both English and French said that the bookshop was closed.

He shaded his eyes to peer inside. The glass doors to the shop were shut. Her living room was to the right. He moved down the porch to see the empty fireplace, her Christmas tree stark and alone standing by the couch.

He went around back to the grape trellis and the bulkhead to the cellar. He knocked on her door, peeking into her kitchen. Had she gone completely? Was she out buying groceries?

He looked in again and saw the black stain on the floor, the scattered white shards of something smashed.

Reaching to steady himself against a post, Kemper kicked

169

her door. He raised his leg again and kicked hard beside the doorknob. Wood ripped, the door cracked. Once more, with the awful knowledge that he was about to encounter all the evil this world has for us, Kemper crashed the door open and went in.

Dried black swipes and spatters of blood were on the stove. Something bleeding heavily had left a long dark scar of blood across the tabletop and upset the sugar bowl. His teacup was there still from the night before.

Pieces of the teapot were everywhere, the handle at his feet where the blood had seeped into the wooden floor and hardened like gelatin. Kemper pushed at it with his finger.

The blood went out of the kitchen. He followed the spots down the hall rug. Blood again on the front door, its knob waxed with blood.

More on the stairs and along the wall, as though someone had staggered there going up. There were two bedrooms, one of them an ascetic cell with an iron bedstead and a chest of drawers. But the other room must be hers, he thought. The bed was unopened, the walls a dull lonesome pink in the hideous winter light. A sudden vision of the pulpy Baskins sliding out of the Poughkeepsie caused Kemper to grip her bedpost. He was breathing too fast. "Slow down," he said to himself.

He went into the small bathroom with its round porcelain sink. Blood everywhere. Someone had washed there—or tried to. Towels had been dumped in bloody piles in the bathtub. The oval mirror over the sink had been sprayed with a fine jet of blood.

Had she cut herself somehow when the teapot broke? Kemper knew better. He was seeing the aftermath of some terrible violence.

Back downstairs, he went into the kitchen after examining the bookshop and living room, both of which were undisturbed. The blood begins in here, he thought. This door was locked, as was the front door. Had she run from the

170

house? Her car was gone. But if she were bleeding, why would she stop to lock doors and put the shop sign in the window? There is too much blood here. Panic was here. Fright, panic, and death.

The cellar door.

He flipped on the light—the dirt floor was black and moist. The thin, narrow stairs wobbled with his weight. And immediately he saw the bootprints in the dirt under the stairs, more of them from the black bulkhead in the wall. He pushed the bulkhead door up. It wasn't locked. The same bootprints in the snow next to her driveway. Confused now, Kemper stumbled through the snow following many prints close to the house to the front porch. There was blood in the snow. A lot of blood.

The bootprints were deep corrugated tracks. The others—Hannah's, he knew—were smaller and lighter.

He went back in through the cellar to search the house for the corpse. Into the closets and the storeroom behind the bookshop. The bathroom again.

Then he sat on her stairs, the Christmas tree tinsel flickering with a draft from the fireplace. The house was cold. She hadn't been here for hours. Someone had waited in the cellar—had he waited for me to leave last night? he wondered. He drew in his breath and fought back the terrifying image of Hannah, dead and battered. Had the menace been under him while he spoke to her for the last time? The smashed teapot. Had the man come up out of the cellar at her?

He tried to remember each movement, each sound from the night before. He doubted she had known the man was there. She had seemed self-contained and quiet. Had she told Quenneville about the someone else, the someone else Kemper had sensed when he asked her about an SS agent?

The bootprints in the cellar—Sykes wore galoshes that jingled and flapped when he walked. Kemper got off the stairs, feeling exposed, as though someone might appear above him from somewhere in the upper reaches of the house.

He found the same bootprints, bloody on the kitchen floor. Mouton and Baskins were killed with hydrogen sulphide. No blood, just instantaneous death. Baskins had been flung off the train with great strength. The bootprints had been made by a heavy man.

Sykes was heavy. And Sykes would leave blood, couldn't help but leave blood. Menard's arm had been broken in the boathouse.

Mouton was the odd man out for Sykes to have done all of this. Sykes and his crew knew little of Mouton, he thought. Not so much the distance to Black Lake; the greater barrier to the Vermont yahoos would come with the language and strangeness of Quebec. Sykes had arrived at Ball's in Richmond to see Baskins's corpse. Why? To be certain Baskins was dead? Kemper doubted Sykes would show himself like that if he were involved in Baskins's death.

Hydrogen sulphide was lethal. Someone had to know what he was doing with it. And the injections suggested training beyond the powers of a crowd of small-town bigots motivated only by greed. The poison was too clean, too deliberate.

But the boathouse murders? And now this, he thought, glancing at the silent debris on the kitchen floor. Both acts of unpremeditated violence.

He went outside, slamming the remains of the kitchen door behind him. The bootprints didn't follow Hannah's to the driveway, where hers vanished. She'd been alive when she got into her car. But the snow had lightly filled her tire marks where she'd backed out and turned for the main street.

Kemper stood on the front porch and watched two elderly women pass. Their arms were linked, their heads bowed in conversation and concentration as they stepped

172

gingerly over the frozen sidewalk and over the corrugated bootprints that Kemper saw went from the porch to the street.

A deep, incisive tire mark in the snow at the curb made Kemper look up from where he knelt. The railroad's brown Chevrolet was across the road. He'd left Moffet's car over there last night. He had left her at her door and crossed in the snow. Her lights had been yellow as he turned. Had she gone back into the kitchen to bleed? A knife? he wondered, getting to his feet.

But he had surely left her to it last night, blithely absorbed in his own demise as he drove back to St. Albans. What a fool you are, he thought.

You've been dancing so hard you couldn't hear your heart. Moffet and Naval Intelligence had given him his freedom. The music had stopped. I'll find her, he thought. And this one is for me.

TWENTY-FIVE

THE GLOSSY CORRIDORS inside the Cowansville hospital were painted the color of pea soup, and the red exit globes were the chunks of ham. Kemper stared at one of the red globes. The duty nurse huffed into the emergency room. He could hear the woman's nasal French inquiring—he heard Hannah's name repeatedly. Finally, he left the steel desk and went into the empty emergency room himself, where a tiny black-haired doctor seemed not to believe his story. Kemper explained again what he knew—that the woman may have been bleeding.

But the doctor was more interested in Kemper and reached across the white examining table to shake his hand. They were both curious, Kemper knew; the plump duty nurse clasped her hands at her waist. Kemper saw the frustration in her face as he again said that he was looking for a woman from Sutton.

The doctor asked him if he'd like to sit down. There was a round steel stool by the table. The room reeked of iodine and ether.

Kemper tried again in his miserable French. They nodded; Kemper felt like the patient suddenly. He nervously scratched his face—a line of sweat had wet his upper lip.

The doctor asked Kemper to sit while he made other inquiries, but Kemper knew very well the man was on his way to get help with this incoherent American. Kemper thought he'd explained everything correctly, although his

174

rising panic may have been more medically interesting to these two than the whereabouts of a bleeding woman, if indeed that was what they'd understood him to ask.

"I'm not staying," Kemper said to her in English. The grey sheets would be here as well. The sheets and the needling drugs that reduced him to a chattering mess. He tried to say it again in French, tried to laugh, but the woman only stiffened.

I may look like hell. I probably do, he thought. But I'm not ill. I'm not anywhere close to seizing up right now. I might look like it, though.

When he left the room, the duty nurse trailed along behind him, as though he weren't sane and could effortlessly stride into an open hole if he weren't watched closely. As he turned for the lobby and the reception desk, she lumbered ahead of him to block the exit.

"I'm all right," he said. "Could you check your admissions records?"

She had hair on her cheeks like a balding Airedale.

Kemper pushed past her and asked the receptionist to flip her little cards for the name Hannah Doll. "She is not here," the woman said, shaking her head and staring beyond Kemper to the duty nurse, who was circling him to stand at the heavy wooden doors.

"Get out of my way," he said in French, and left the Cowansville hospital.

If Hannah were hurt, she would go for the familiar, and no matter how much she hated these people and this hospital, Hannah would come here if she were bleeding. There were no other hospitals.

He slalomed out of the parking lot in the railroad's Chevrolet, glad for his escape from whatever trap these medical malcontents had in mind.

His performance in there had not been convincing.

Kemper tried to collect his thoughts as he drove south toward Vermont. Where was she?

He wanted Alex Jaeger. The conductor had been on the train with Baskins. Alex Jaeger could have worn corrugated boots.

I leave tomorrow afternoon for Ottawa, staying two clear days and addressing Canadian Parliament on Tuesday; then back here for another three or four days, as there is so much to settle. We are making great exertions to find shipping necessary for the various troop movements required.

TWENTY-SIX

PLATTSBURGH WAS THE ONLY CITY in upper New York State to light the great darkness of the Adirondacks and their countless hidden lakes and locked tourist cabins. Built on the lakeshore across from Vermont, Plattsburgh had no major industry nor any cultural magnet, but was merely a collective of human gregariousness against the lonely clefts in the mountains where the bobcats scowled at winter snows.

The Delaware & Hudson main line tracks skirted the lake front north of Albany to rifle overnight passenger expresses through vague settlements like Port Henry and Crown Point. Still on the lake shore, the rail line squeezed past Plattsburgh and went off north to Montreal. There were warehouses and factories, once busily crowded by their proximity to the early lake traffic; but with the Depression the echoing brick buildings had decayed dismally, shoulder to shoulder, their steel window panels clanging through the winter nights, their brick flanks wheezing with the steady northwest wind that skirted the Adirondacks to plunder Plattsburgh of its timid warmth.

One of the longest of these abandoned factories, its dusty sides only feet from Montreal-bound Delaware & Hudson trains, had found new purpose as a chicken ranch. Sealed against the snows and cold with boarded windows, the old building housed thousands of chickens. An aroma of ammonia left the building in pungent waves so that the snow-covered street near it was always empty, always hopelessly bereft of any activity.

On December 27, 1941, the open lake took on the cast of old tin as the short day collapsed in gelid apprehension. Late-afternoon dreariness had chased a few rusted trucks out of the cobbled streets to leave the empty warehouses and factories unlighted and still. The loading docks, the rattling steel fences, and the dim courtyards were, on Saturday, the kingdom of the rat.

Because everything was chained and padlocked, Streicher loosened a board that covered a window of the chicken ranch. The stairways were shadowed and reverberated with his soft scuff as he made his way up through the four floors. Sliding a metal barrier, he looked into a bright stadium of light bulbs and white chickens. The birds nearest the barrier shrivelled and pushed the others away when they saw him standing there. There were so many chickens, as if some glibly heroic genetic experiment had gone sadly wrong.

Streicher slammed the barrier shut and went back down the stairways, slowly down under the main floor and beneath the silent offices above. Here was the boiler room, its torn pipes gashed and split.

Although faced with brick, the chicken ranch was built entirely of oil-soaked timbers.

Streicher listened for a moment, his breath coming in short stabs. This had to work. As the last pearl on the SS string from Berlin, he alone had the task. He alone knew what the task was.

Slithering, ticking claws made him freeze. The rats were here: two of them had sauntered gaily into the boiler room to pause, mesmerized, at this man who cared enough to be with them this evening. The rats were the size of small dogs, their bellies rotund—with choice chicken parts, he guessed.

He swore at them in German. Then smiled to think he would terrify even the rats.

Streicher poured the kerosene the length of a wooden barricade behind the boiler. He listened again, holding the box of matches at his side.

He was alone—the rats had left.

Streicher loosened splinters of wood from the wall, laid them in a pyramid at his feet, and left the boiler room to climb quickly up out of the cellar, through the twisting narrow corridors until he found the loose board at his window.

Slowly, he went back down. The rats were behind him on their ticking toes, following him below.

The match sputtered; the pyramid flushed into life. The smoke was instantly black from the oil. Then the wall caught, the flames fluttering quietly, but nonetheless eager for their meal.

Streicher wanted to be certain the wall was alight, and when the flames fanned across the ceiling above the steam pipes, he walked carefully out of the boiler room, his steady kick on the stairs echoing high into the building. He walked past the offices, his hands carefully balancing his steps over broken glass. He found the loosened board.

He had been frightened on the stairs, but felt better now. So long as the board swung out into the night, he was all right.

Smoke came along the corridor in a moment—nothing so much that he could see, but he caught the smell, the thick muskiness of hot oil and tarred wood. He thought he could sense a vibration through his feet—had the inferno gathered that much power?

From the loading dock, Streicher climbed over the chain-link fence to the sidewalk and hurried along beneath the smashed streetlights to the alley where he'd left the truck in a narrow courtyard.

The thing started quickly; Streicher kept his lights off and eased the truck along the alley. The chicken ranch was the

179

looming wall to his left at the end of the street. Should he wait? This *had* to work.

But then he noticed a tiny orange light at the base of the black wall a hundred yards away—one of the barred cellar windows. And with that, he threw on his headlights and turned out of the alley. He could watch the fire from the lake road north of the city.

TWENTY-SEVEN

KEMPER REASSURED HIMSELF with memories of Hannah and Christmas Eve as the Chevrolet dipped with the roads through the sparse fields of the Townships. She was not a phantasmic wish fulfillment, and their Christmas Eve had indeed been rare for both of them, a rare but sombre awakening to the knowledge that each was not alone.

Had he been fitfully foolish? Had he been taken in by the artful female adorning her nest with yet another male carapace? He hadn't any gifts for her, he didn't bring her the delightful promise of better days. This '37 Chevy was not a white horse. Nothing like that, he thought. He was fifty-eight and damaged. No bargain.

And Hannah, while physically tempting to a man with ardent fantasies, was more than a woman trapped in carnal mysteries; she was not coldly degrading or bemused by intuitive tugs from within. She seemed self-contained, but not absorbed with it all. She had warmed to him and loved his company—possibly for the chance to speak without trepidation.

Had he got it wrong? He thought not.

Kemper pushed through the smashed door and into her kitchen. He satisfied himself that she was not there by dashing up the stairs to her room.

His breath came in long clouds of vapor as he stood in the lamplight at her bookshop desk. She had an address book: unordered columns of names, addresses, and telephone numbers in a black school composition notebook tucked in the desk drawer.

Kemper pushed at the pages to discover where she was. Quenneville's telephone number was there, but written alone in green ink with no name. Another green number below that. He dialed.

A child answered. Kemper asked for Marcel Quenneville. In rapid, loud French, the kid said his father was not at home and clapped the line dead.

He dialed every number in the book. A few were answered in English, many rang desperately until he hung up. Nothing.

Where was she?

He brought out a cigar to quiet his hands, absently looking for matches in her desk. Store records and publishers' invoices were neatly collected and filed according to date. In the middle drawer, bound in flannel, there was a pistol. A loaded, ancient Colt with a great octagonal barrel. An unlikely weapon for any woman, he thought.

She must have been surprised in the kitchen, must have used the teapot because she hadn't had time to run for the Colt. Or, he wondered, had she known the man in the cellar and not been frightened until it was too late?

He found a Catholic missal in the hall table. The house was dark and ominously steeped in silence as he moved back into the bookshop to open the missal's pages. Prayerful bookmarks, some fragile from use, were placed at odd moments of the mass. Her name was inscribed on the flyleaf with "May—1939" in the lower corner. And beside that, in the same blue ink, "Sister A. M. Philippa."

This was Saturday evening; any nun worth her habit would be close to home.

Kemper scrambled through the telephone book looking for churches, found them, and dialed everything on the page. The first five didn't answer, the sixth gave him an elderly lisp.

He said he was trying to find Sister A. M. Philippa.

The woman told him his French was very bad and hung up.

The Catholic church in Sutton had not answered. Did Catholics have services on Saturday evening? Probably, he thought.

He replaced the pistol, but took the telephone book and her missal, left the light burning in the bookshop, and hurried out to her driveway. A jet-black sky with gleaming pins of light. Farley Ball should see this, he thought, staring for a moment at the penetrating immensity overhead.

There was something going on in the church when Kemper stumped over the rope rugs into the foyer. Lighted candles and the murmur of unison prayer pressed against him when he entered the church. Mostly women. They were reciting the stations of the cross. Kemper waited for the priest, attended by three altar boys in white, to cross the back of the church for the other wall where the stations continued.

Kemper held out his hand. The priest stopped, bewildered. Kemper said he was looking for Hannah Doll. The priest shook his head no, glanced at the kid at his elbow, then began to move on. He doesn't understand, Kemper thought.

He touched the priest's sleeve and asked again.

"She is not here," the priest said.

"Does she usually come here—to church?"

The priest shook his head no and pulled away from Kemper.

"Where does she go to church? I'm looking for Sister Philippa."

The priest said he did not know. "Hannah Doll is not one of us. She should be."

"Then where?"

The priest was irritated.

"Sister Philippa?" Kemper asked.

"I don't know Sister Philippa," the priest whispered. "Be good enough to be quiet. We are in prayer. Are you Catholic?"

Kemper let the man go. The last kid in the line of four carried a crucifix on a staff. When he got to Kemper, this kid backed against the last pew and, having escaped the wild man with the heavy eyes, scurried after the others.

"Damn!" Kemper said, and left the church.

He telephoned Quenneville's office from a general store. Quenneville was not in, he was told.

"Where is he?"

"He's not available."

Kemper spelled his name for the man. "Find Quenneville," Kemper said. "Tell him Hannah Doll may be dead. She has disappeared. Tell him I will use Cody's office in St. Albans."

The store owner wanted to close up for the night and didn't want to talk. He waved Kemper down the center aisle, shooing him toward the door.

TWENTY-EIGHT

STREICHER HUGGED THE LAKE SHORE as he drove north out of Plattsburgh, rattling past hollow-eyed tourist camps and hamburger stands closed for the winter. When the road swung to the east, he strained to see back to Plattsburgh on the cusp of its harbor, and there, as he dipped off the road apron into a boatyard, the cloud underparts were washed in crimson.

My northern lights, he thought, slamming the door to walk out onto a narrow pier. Miles in the distance across the black water the city lights blinked against the empty wall of the Adirondacks. The chicken ranch blazed beautifully amid the lights, dazzling the empty night with a carpeted path of water-borne flame to his feet.

His head ached so terribly. Streicher went to the lake to dip a cloth into the liquid cold, and pressing it against his throbbing left eye, he let his right eye memorize the sight. The day would come when he'd describe this triumph.

He could think, now that the factory had been fired. There was so little time. Churchill will climb up into the coach sometime tomorrow, he thought. His security people should breathe a bit easier because dear Winston would be safely on the move. He tried to smile for himself, but his head and now his face throbbed under the cold rag. They do not know I'm here, he thought. They have no idea the SS can reach this far from home. With a single stroke of mind and determination, a lone SS captain will alter the lives of

185

millions by ending the life of a fat little man who is the British Prime Minister. Streicher knew he could do it.

There was fresh blood on the rag.

He got the truck over the bridge across Lake Champlain and into the islands that crowded the northern border of the United States. He had sutured his eyelid and temple with waxed fishing line at Jaeger's cottage, but the gash bled easily now. He'd have to fix that and get something for the pain as well.

After miles of slippery macadam through swamps, his headlights swept across a broad, black river on his left, and next a small town with houses built to face onto a circular park. He slowed the truck long enough to read a clock in a grocery window. Eight o'clock. There must be a doctor here, he thought.

Beyond the park on the main road south to St. Albans, Streicher braked carefully and turned into a side street. There was a house across the pavement and a white sign with a name lettered in black. Streicher cared only about the initials M.D. after the name. He pushed the switch and killed his lights. The house was dark. He reached for his flashlight.

Saturday night. Where is he? he wondered. Christmas celebrations? Was the doctor out on a call? How far out? Was he asleep inside? Did he have a family? The house was very wide and very white.

A separate entrance with an arrow in the snow led Streicher up the walk to the dispensary that adjoined the house.

Streicher went quickly along the side of the building under the windows. A garage behind, but no automobile in the flat drive.

He'd take his chances. The house is too quiet—all of these houses are too quiet, he thought. The back door was unlocked, incredibly enough. Streicher smiled as he went in.

The odor of camphor reassured him as he snapped on the flashlight.

Twenty-four hours were all he needed; after tomorrow night he'd be away and could rest. He found the morphine, opened a towel on a side table, and reached into the cabinet for all the codeine as well, which would deaden most of his pain without knocking him out. Dextroamphetamine, packed in white boxes, would keep him awake for the train. He dumped a fistful of sulphur vials on the towel, split one, and salted his eye with the yellow powder. He scooped bandages and syringes, a scalpel—he was certain some of his eye muscles had been severed. He might never use the eye again. No matter, he thought. They'd fix him up when he got home, where wounds of war were medals of honor.

He rolled the towel, turned for the door, and froze. Where was it?

A click in the office.

Streicher shut off the flashlight.

The door into the house!

Streicher pulled the pistol out, flicked the safety off. Go for the outside! he thought, hugging the towel.

He raised the gun as the door swung open with a screech . . . light flooded the dispensary.

The child's body was outlined in light through its nightgown, its hair like a red halo. Thumb in its mouth, trailing a blanket, the little one regarded Streicher calmly.

Streicher swore in whispered German, said "Good night, little one," and tore into the cold, across the lawn, and into his truck.

Anyone else would have blown those curls into the wall, he thought. His hands were still shaking as he thumped over the iron bridge and turned for St. Albans and Jaeger's.

TWENTY-NINE

CODY'S MAP WAS ACCURATE. Kemper left the Chevrolet behind another cottage and walked between Jaeger's hedges. The house was dark in front of him as he stepped near the garage. No dog, Kemper realized with relief. Jaeger could be asleep, although there were no cars in the yard or garage.

Kemper wished he'd brought Hannah's Colt. Still, she might return home and need the thing.

Jaeger could be Quenneville's deadly anomaly.

His discomfort, his nervousness as he crept to Jaeger's house were his to bear. Always the consequences; we're entitled to them, he thought. He opened the storm door and beat on the glass with the sense that he was heckling something odious.

The silence thickened around him.

He went in through a window off the porch. This has to be quick, he thought. The cottage smelled of kerosene and dust.

Jaeger's railroad uniforms were in a bedroom closet. A Big Ben alarm clock under the lamp. But there was another bedroom, a weak iron bed, and more clothes. And in that closet, Kemper found the Canadian National uniforms. Jaeger was a small man; the CN uniforms were 48 longs, too large. Someone other than Jaeger lived here. Another trainman. Delaware & Hudson timetables and a map of that railroad's New York routes were on the bedside table. Kemper lifted a towel and saw in the ashtray the same matches he'd seen in Hannah's fireplace. Two crusty pipes and a pouch of tobacco in the narrow drawer. A black cowhide suitcase with clothes.

There were bloody towels in the bathtub and a spool of fishing line on the sink with a sailmaker's curved needle in a dish of alcohol. A small leather bag with shaving gear—all of it American. A bottle of Mennen Afta-Shave on the shelf next to the bag.

He thought for a moment before shutting off the light and went back into Jaeger's bedroom. Kemper looked for the boots with the corrugated treads. They aren't here, he thought. Nothing like them.

The kitchen had a pot of potato soup on the kerosene stove. The house had a cellar.

Kemper hit the switch in the kitchen to light the cellar floor. He shut off the kitchen light and hurried down the stairs. Rapidly considering all that he saw, he knew the cellar was a waste bin for disused cottage life. There were three pairs of oars on ceiling hooks. A canoe on sawhorses. The dampness here was fetid.

He found the box under the bench—the cleared area with nail jars and rusted tools pushed away to provide a work space had sent him looking. The bench was the only disturbed spot in the cellar.

He opened the box, then looked up again at the junk on the bench. Five boxes of insecticide—Pearl's Insect-Go— had been opened, emptied, and tossed onto the pile of tools and coffee cans.

"What do you know?" he said to himself. He opened a glass flask from the box. The smell of rotten eggs. Hydrogen sulphide. No label on this bottle. A miniature chemistry laboratory, he thought, lifting the box onto the bench under the light bulb. Graduated cylinders, a burner, various paraphernalia, strips of what seemed to be green copper.

He reached for an empty Pearl's Insect-Go box. Its ingredients made no sense to him. Something called dinitrophenol made up most of the powder. The instructions said Pearl's Insect-Go was water-soluble and could be absorbed through the skin; that the user should lather with strong soap and rinse hands well after handling.

He packed everything away, replaced the Pearl's, and got upstairs quickly to rinse his right hand in Jaeger's kitchen sink.

He'd seen enough. If Jaeger wasn't Quenneville's SS agent, the other man who lived here could be. One of them played with poisons. Either Jaeger or his roommate had tossed his matches into Hannah Doll's fireplace. Hannah had said she didn't know Alex Jaeger. Had she lied? Quenneville had a list, sent from Hannah, he'd said, with Jaeger's name among the locals. Curious, Kemper thought. She's either lying, or she didn't send the list. If not Hannah . . . Jaeger would not have typed his own name on a list of German agents and couriers for Quenneville or anyone else.

Kemper glanced around instinctively. Had he replaced everything he'd touched?

He let himself out, headed quickly for the lake road but halted suddenly and went back to the garage. There was a light bulb on a cord, and the odor of oil drippings in the wooden floor. And tire marks. He remembered seeing the same tire mark in front of Hannah's in the snow. And half a corrugated bootprint stamped in the layers of old oil on the floor. The same man had been in both places. "Damn."

Had he come here at the start—he'd asked Cody about Jaeger and the train door, but had he done all of this in the beginning—Hannah wouldn't have faced the man in her cellar. The panic gripped Kemper's chest, freezing his arms. Where was their radio?

If the SS were here, then Hannah was probably already dead.

Kemper pelted along the road, slowing only for the complicated fork where the road to St. Albans went right, over the narrow metal bridge.

Headlights flashed in his mirror and then turned off behind him as he skidded over the bridge.

If Kemper had been fifteen seconds slower, he would have met the Cushman's bakery truck as it turned into the intersection from the north.

Cody's office was locked, but the railroad dispatcher was at his desk in front of four telegraph keys. He threw his *Life* magazine on his desk when Kemper blew into the room. The dispatcher said it was late, Cody was at home and most likely asleep by now, as he checked the clock. "It's past ten. Cody's in bed."

The dispatcher said he knew who Kemper was when Kemper reached his identification out of his coat. "Somethin' wrong?" the dispatcher asked.

"Where's Alex Jaeger?"

"How the hell do I know? He's off sick. Try his house."

Kemper said he had. "Did Jaeger ever work for the Canadian National?"

The dispatcher shook his head. "Don't think so. Grand Trunk."

"Do CN conductors ever lay over here?"

"Sometimes. What's wrong?"

"Does Jaeger have a friend who works for the CN?"

"Beats me," the man said. "What is this?"

"I need to find Jaeger."

"Well, he ain't here," the man said.

One of the telegraph keys ticked. The dispatcher listened to it, holding his hand up to quiet Kemper. After he'd tapped a response, the dispatcher penciled something on a clipboard on the wall, then said, "Jaeger's a real sonofabitch. You better talk to the Buffalo in the morning."

"Who's the Buffalo?"

"Cody. I wouldn't wake him up now. He'll take your head off."

Kemper felt weak; his stomach was empty and sore, as

191

though his abdominal muscles had tightened to girdle his strength.

He got a cigar burning nicely while he put in a call to the RCMP in Ottawa—if the FBI were looking for Kemper, Quenneville would keep his mouth shut and might know where Hannah was. The young RCMP voice said it didn't know Quenneville. Kemper left Cody's number.

The dispatcher wanted to know what was going on.

Kemper stared at the man who wore the green eyeshade. "If you had to find a nun, where would you look?"

"Don't ask me," the dispatcher said, listening to his telegraph keys. "I wouldn't get within ten feet of one of them RCs. They're all mumbojumbo."

"How about a nun in Quebec?"

"Oh, shit," the dispatcher said. "Frogs have got nuns all over the place."

Kemper woke up the local priest. "Who is this?" the old priest barked.

Kemper asked about Hannah Doll and Sister A. M. Philippa.

"Who are you?" the priest asked. "Is this Stanley?"

Kemper let the man go back to whatever revelations old priests conjure up.

The dispatcher was busy with clipboards and telegraph keys. He said Kemper could go across to the kitchen in the bunkhouse for something to eat.

A switching engine idled on the tracks near the brick dormitory. Kemper climbed the stairs and went into a long, barren room that smelled of dirty feet and cigarettes. Five men played cards at a wooden table. Kemper used Cody's name to explain himself. The poker game ignored him as he rummaged through a refrigerator for cold cuts and cheese. Their coffee was like hot oil.

He had to slow down, he had to think clearly. St. Albans had a hospital; he'd ask there. All of this might be for nothing because Quenneville might have Hannah by now. Or was she a cold mound of flesh in a Quebec field? Jaeger had a friend. Who had been in Hannah's cellar? Why would the SS, or anyone for that matter, want to harm her? Or Baskins? Baskins was such a small fish. Sykes was eager to throw the blame for the boathouse fire on me, Kemper thought. How the hell does it all fit? Or maybe it doesn't. But all his instincts and fifty-eight years of being alive told him it did.

Churchill! he thought.

Trains. Quenneville had said Churchill would go by train to Ottawa. When? Tomorrow night?

"Is this Saturday?" he asked the poker game.

Some of them grunted.

He finished his sandwich as he walked back to the dispatcher's office. The St. Albans hospital said they had no Hannah Doll; no one with any wounds of any sort had been brought in.

Kemper asked the dispatcher if there was a convent—nuns should know other nuns.

"Not that again," the dispatcher whined. "Why don't you sleep on it? Cody will be here about seven in the morning. There's a convent in Farnham. Nuns always change trains for Farnham."

Kemper called information in Quebec. The dispatcher put a plug of tobacco in his cheek. Kemper got the number and, finally, a timid voice in French. Kemper asked for Sister A. M. Philippa.

The voice said Sister Philippa had passed away last year.

He struggled to control the excitement in his voice. "Could I speak to Hannah Doll, please?"

The voice said the convent would be in complete silence until Monday morning.

"But is Hannah Doll there?"

The voice didn't answer straight away. Kemper let the woman wrestle with her conscience. Then the voice said, "There is no one with that name here."

Not quite a lie, but near enough, he thought. "If a woman named Hannah Doll does come to your convent, would you please tell her Frank Kemper will come for her?" He gave the voice Cody's telephone number, but the woman protested and repeated that there was no Hannah Doll in the convent.

After he hung up, he asked the dispatcher how to get to Farnham.

"Take the train in the morning," the dispatcher said. "It's thirty miles or so over the border. You're not going tonight, are you?"

Kemper headed for the door.

"We've got ice on the tracks north of St. Johns!" the dispatcher called out as Kemper hobbled down the stairs. "Roads will be slick," he chirped.

"Go to hell," Kemper shouted up to him.

THIRTY

Streicher smiled when he saw his face. He got close to the mirror. The stitches seemed tight enough, but the laceration through his eyebrow and eyelid, deep into his left eye, and across his temple leaked a watery pink juice that had stained the bandage as he drove the last few miles to Jaeger's.

He prepared the syringes and injected the codeine and dextroamphetamine into his arm. His nose was not broken, but yellow and blue discolorations had hollowed his eye sockets. He'd cut an eye patch from something. There was time for that. If she hadn't hit him, if he hadn't gone back for her, all of what lay ahead would be so much easier, he thought.

The FBI agent had been in the house with her. Shit, he wondered, had she been talking to the FBI all along? Was she with them now?

He flattened the swollen skin—the sutures were pulling.

A motor!

He cocked his pistol and twisted the light off in the bathroom.

Jaeger yelled when he came in the back door. The conductor had met the cocked pistol too many times to simply walk in on Streicher.

"Where the hell have you been?" Jaeger said as he came into the bathroom.

Streicher thumbed the safety back on before lowering the

195

pistol to the sink. He hit the light and watched the conductor's face empty. Jaeger had eyes like wet fur.

"Good christ," Jaeger said. "You should see a doctor."

"I have," Streicher said.

"You can't get on a train like that. Not dressed as a CN conductor, you can't. No railroad would let a conductor show up for work with a face that bad. You've sewed your goddam eye shut. Jeezus! Is that fishing line?"

"I want you to leave in the morning," Streicher said. "Take the early train."

"Not for five hundred dollars I won't."

"Okay. How's five thousand?"

"When do I get it?"

Streicher let his right eye settle on Jaeger.

"Monday morning. When I leave."

"For good?"

"You'll never see me again. I'll meet you tomorrow night. Bring my Canadian uniform in your bag. Tell me again about the water."

Jaeger shook his head, muttering, "Shit," then turned to leave.

"Tell me!" Streicher demanded. "Now!"

Jaeger came back, angry. "I don't know why you'd want to do a thing like this. I don't like it."

Jaeger was undergoing another moment of irresolution. "I'm not asking you to like it," Streicher said. "Tell me about the water."

Jaeger raised his head. "What do I say to the train crew on the special?"

"You get us on the train. How you do that is up to you. Now, about the water."

"You *are* a prick, aren't you?"

"Tell me about the tanks."

"There are two forty-gallon tanks under each Pullman. Once they're filled by the original yard crew, they'll be sealed if this special is as big a deal as you say it is."

"And the little closets?"

"One on each side of the car—near the exit doors. The siphon pipes are in the far corner of each closet—one pipe for each tank."

"Go on. The plugs."

"The plugs unscrew clockwise. You will need a wrench. They're about two feet off the deck. They might have a chain to secure them to the siphon pipes."

"And the water pressure?"

"Nothing to it," Jaeger said. "The tanks will lose pressure for only two or three minutes. But they'll come back up when the plugs are tight. Make sure they're tight when you put them back."

"As easy as that." Streicher smiled.

"How can you poison a whole goddam Pullman full of innocent people?"

"They're not all innocent."

Jaeger turned to leave. Streicher's smile sagged with his pain.

"God, you give me the creeps," Jaeger said.

Streicher wasn't finished. "Why won't the yard crews seal the siphon plugs when they seal the tanks?"

"No one ever touches those plugs. Damn things are hidden anyway. Yard crews only seal the outside tanks."

"The Pennsylvania yard crews in Washington. And those cars will not be changed, but the locomotives will change with each railroad?"

"They have to. I told you—each railroad on the special's route will have their own loco and crew on board. They have to change—only the home crew knows the track. They don't want anything to go wrong. And they'll lock all their switches."

"And the crew from White River will be Central Vermont." The Americans are truly as clumsy as advertised, Streicher thought. "When I get to California," he said, "I'll send you a postcard."

"Don't bother," Jaeger said sadly.

"How many FBI now?"

"None," Jaeger said. "Sykes says they all left. There were three of them."

"One of them has not gone. The old one."

"Bullshit! Sykes says Corliss put the old fart on a train this morning. When did you see him?"

Streicher's imagination returned again to the sound of those two voices—Hannah's and that man's. "His name is Kemper," he said. He'd thought Hannah would run for the FBI in St. Albans. "That agent, the one with the white hair, he left this morning?"

Jaeger said he had.

"When did the other FBI leave?"

Jaeger shrugged. "The mayor says they went to Canada."

To get Hannah? Streicher wondered. She must have run for them—she had time. "And the woman from Sutton?" he asked.

"I don't know," Jaeger said. "I don't think anyone has seen her. The sheriff would have said something if she had been around. He likes that bitch. Says he'd like to get her in one of his cells on a dark night."

"Does he?" Streicher asked. "He has done this before? With this woman?"

Jaeger shrugged again.

Where was she? he wondered. If she hadn't gone to the FBI or the RCMP yet . . .

"Things have quieted down," Jaeger said. "Except Sykes knows damn well Menard and that god-awful woman didn't just fuck and fall asleep with a candle burning in the boathouse." He glanced quickly at Streicher, then looked away nervously, saying, "I don't want to know about that one."

If the next twenty-four hours went well, Streicher would vanish, leaving Sykes and his brother, the mayor—leaving all of them to explain Churchill's murder. Jaeger would be on the train. Only Jaeger and Hannah could identify Streicher. And Jaeger would be dead.

Streicher turned back to the mirror. His pain was subsiding and the dextroamphetamine was beginning to flush his weariness with exuberance.

I'll find her, he thought, switching off the light.

THIRTY-ONE

SUNDAY
DECEMBER
2 8
1941

HANNAH OPENED HER EYES to see light from the corridor silhouetting the nun's habit.

"You must wake up," Sister André said, rubbing Hannah's forehead. "Someone has telephoned for you. I should not have let you sleep."

Hannah sat up to greet a violent headache. "I'm awake," she said. "What did he say?"

"He left a telephone number. He will come for you. I didn't tell him you were with us."

"I left word for him that I was here," Hannah said. "What did he say?"

"Just that. To tell you he will come for you."

She asked for her clothes.

Hannah dressed in the white light from the corridor. The convent was eerily still. When Sister André bustled back into her room, Hannah asked if Quenneville had said where he was calling from.

"But his name was Kemper—Frank Kemper."

"Him?" she said. How had he found her? She wasn't safe after all.

"We are so worried about you," Sister André said. "You are not well. Stay with us, please."

Hannah said she couldn't. "This man on the telephone was not a deep voice? Not Marcel Quenneville?"

Sister André was certain she'd done it all wrong. She said Kemper's name again and started to chatter.

"Hush," Hannah said. Dear god, she thought, how had he done it? Had Quenneville told Kemper to come here?

Madame Chapdelaine, the housekeeper, came into the room wearing her dressing gown. "There's a man here to see you," she said to Hannah.

"I asked you," Sister André whispered to the house-keeper, "I asked you to let no one in!"

"He was ringing the bell."

Hannah grabbed her coat from the bed. She reached for Sister André. "When did Mr. Kemper call?"

"Hours ago. But I told him you weren't here."

Hannah looked quickly at the housekeeper. "What does the man downstairs look like?"

Before Madame Chapdelaine could answer, the room darkened. When she saw him in the doorway, Hannah's neck tingled. She touched Sister André's arm, "It's all right," she said to the nun to still the woman's fright.

Madame Chapdelaine went for him. "All our callers must remain in the living room. Shoo! She'll be right down. You can't be up here."

"It's all right," Hannah said evenly. "How are you?" she asked the man.

He didn't move.

His open eye glinted like a badge and pierced her with fear. She couldn't let these women be hurt. "I'm ready, Madame Chapdelaine. Everything is all right."

Streicher backed away, but then took her arm when she met him in the corridor. She let him lead her to the stairs. "I'll go with you," she whispered. "Don't touch them."

He was occupied with keeping his balance as they went down the stairs.

"They don't know a thing," she said to him softly. The women were behind her.

She stopped on the rug to embrace Sister André and Madame Chapdelaine. They couldn't take their eyes from Streicher's ruined face.

"Everything will be all right," she said, reassuring the women. "Thank you for being so good to me."

Streicher led Hannah outside. There was a courtyard with high surrounding walls and a stone path to the plank door in the wall. She knew the women were torn by suspicion as they watched her leave with this thing at her side. She waved to them from the courtyard and said once again for comfort, as much for herself as for them, "Everything will be all right."

Streicher lifted the latch, and she was outside the wall with him in the harrowing stillness of night.

"Please. Let me go," she said, stopping him as he closed the door. His bakery truck was at the end of the walkway in the parking area.

"You must listen to me," he said.

"Let me go," she said.

"No," he shook his head, his one fierce eye like a laboratory specimen in a jar. "I cannot let you go. Get in the truck. We can talk."

He tried to pull her; she resisted.

"I won't tell anyone."

"You think I am horrible. I'm not. I have a job to do. Nothing more. I won't hurt you. I love you. You love me."

"No," she said. "You killed those people."

"Listen, please. You must understand."

The darkness beside the wall was pulsing, but he was there with her—his familiar smell of whiskey and pipe smoke.

"We will go away. I've come back for you. We will go to Mexico. We can stay there, or we could even go home to Germany."

"Your Germany isn't my home," she said.

"You love me," he said.

She pulled against his grip, gently, testing him. "I will not love a killer."

202

"I had to do those things. I don't like to hurt people. I had no choice. This is a war, Hannah."

"You have a choice now," she said. "Let me go. I'll say nothing."

"We love each other."

"We did," she said softly.

"And now? That is all gone?"

Hannah wiped at her eyes. She didn't want to cry, wouldn't cry. But his voice was there and soothing. This was the same man who had held a Christmas mirror for her. How far away that night was. How far away you are, she thought, transfixed by the damage she had done to this man she loved.

"I have hurt you very badly." She touched his face. "I'm sorry for that.

He took her hand from his cheek. "I want you to come with me."

"You must go alone. I won't say a word to anyone. You know I won't."

"You would if you thought you could save me," he said.

"I would," she said. "Yes, I would. I'd like to save you now."

She let him lead her to the bakery truck. "No," she said. "I can't go with you."

"I won't leave you," he said.

"You already have. You know you have."

"I promise," he said, "we'll be fine. We'll be safe in Mexico. I can get us there."

She slowly shook her head.

"Please?" he said.

Hannah said no. She took his hand from her arm and walked away from him. Her car was behind the convent. She felt him watching her as she walked around the edge of the building.

Her car started with a roar—too much gas. She threw her

arm over the seat to see behind her. The bakery truck slammed into her bumper, blocking her in. She turned to lock the door, but too late—he dragged her out onto the snow and back toward the truck.

"Let me go, Blue!" she screamed through her teeth.

He had the truck doors open. She tried to stand up. He was too strong. She fought him, ridiculously trying not to hit his covered eye.

Streicher lifted her off her feet and jumped into the truck with her.

"You won't listen to me," he said, holding her shoulders down.

She kicked at him, but he lay on her chest.

Very quickly, in a haze of fear and fury, he taped her wrists with surgical tape. She tried to scream as he held her cheeks while he wrapped her mouth with wide, sticky bands.

Where were the nuns? How could they let this happen?

When he released her, she was bound with tape and sash cord so tightly she couldn't breathe without deliberately filling her lungs against the cords.

"You *will* listen to me," he said, clambering over her into the driver's seat.

She thought her bladder would burst.

"You will listen to me, Hannah."

She felt the truck lurch backward.

As Streicher left the parking lot, he caught a glimpse of a woman's braid and a dressing gown running alongside the courtyard wall.

THIRTY-TWO

WHEN KEMPER ARRIVED at the convent minutes later, Sister André had tales to tell. She had called the police; they said they would come as soon as they could. Her description of Streicher was tinged with ghoulishness. She kept saying, "He was frightful! He was frightful!"

When Kemper asked her how she and Madame Chapdelaine could have let Streicher in and how they could have allowed Hannah to simply walk out of the convent, Sister André admitted to having been uncertain. "But it all happened so quickly," she added.

He dashed for the courtyard and the door through the wall.

He slammed the Chevrolet into reverse, backed out of the parking lot, then shifted, whining and skidding away from the convent, sliding across Farnham's main street and spinning the wheel to recover. The truck had at least ten minutes on him. He'd be going for Jaeger's with Hannah.

The road ahead was empty and white with ice and light snow.

Madame Chapdelaine had described Streicher's bakery truck; Kemper had instantly remembered stepping behind a black and white bakery truck in Sutton.

Cody's Chevrolet was horrible on the ice, but once into the countryside, Kemper leaned on it and blew down the road at an unstable fifty miles an hour.

He doesn't know I'm on his ass, Kemper thought.

The Chevrolet flew over the roads through the desolate distances from farm to farm. No one, not one car, was on the road with him. He thought he glimpsed a red spark of taillight up ahead, but the road straightened and after a mile or so there was nothing there.

Kemper saw the field, the fence ahead, the telephone poles, and the barn off in the dark. He nudged the steering wheel, thought about the brakes, but the Chevy was airborne before he could stomp the pedal.

With a terrific whistling, the fence came at the headlights. Kemper hung on, but felt the car begin to slue and slam into something as hard as rock.

When he regained consciousness, he pushed the lights off. He was in a field—where was the barn? His head ached so much he thought he'd vomit in his lap.

When he woke up again, there was a man reaching through the open door; the sky had changed to a grey hush of early dawn.

The farmer was gentle and knelt in the snow as he spoke to Kemper in French.

Then the farmer was gone. There was a chorus line of faceless Rockettes high-kicking into infinity. There were planets and moons and a woman's voice who said his stump had been cut. He felt hot, then icily strange and floating in a yellow sea with laughing clams and a lobster named Prufrock who smoked opium.

Then the silence of death as he opened his eyes to a dull shell-shaped wall light. He knew that green paint and moved his head away.

Then nothing again, but he knew he was not sleeping.

When the woman's voice came to him once more, he told her to get away from him. "Tell it to the lobster," he said.

He knew he didn't want to open his eyes. She was there, whispering French in his left ear. He groaned when he recognized the odor of alcohol and starch.

His chest exploded the pain into his arms. He swallowed

with difficulty and tried to raise his head. He couldn't breathe. He couldn't raise his shoulders. He knew his hands were trembling at his throat. His chest rocked him with barrages of crushing pain.

Never this bad, he thought. I'm going to die. And I don't even know where the hell I am.

He got his eyes open.

A woman's face almost touching his.

"Help," he said. He tapped his chest with his right index finger.

Another wave of pain bulged the woman out of focus.

His nose was flooded with an indescribably vicious sweetness.

"I don't want to die" came into his consciousness on a beam of flashing light. Then the great silence swallowed it all.

THIRTY-THREE

STREICHER CIRCLED THE RAIL STATION in St. Johns, Quebec. Sensing that his priorities had become confused again, he had abruptly turned back from the Vermont border, cut across the Townships, and swung northwest across the Richelieu River to St. Johns, the main line of the Canadian National and Central Vermont railroads. According to Jaeger, St. Johns was where the American train crew would hand over Churchill's train to the Canadian National crew.

Hannah had fought her bonds. He'd pleaded with her to listen to him, but quickly realized he couldn't jeopardize the next twenty-four hours by taking her to Jaeger's. He'd told her all that their future promised—the safety of South America and the roistering welcome he'd have when they arrived in Berlin. Never again would he have another operation assigned to him like this one. He said nothing of Churchill, but pleaded with her to be still as he backed the truck against a wooden barrier behind the St. Johns station.

She twisted and groaned when he knelt beside her; she refused to listen. He hadn't the time. He injected morphine into her thigh, rubbing the red pinprick with his handkerchief. "You will sleep," he told her. Her eyes were frozen and tortured. "When you wake up, I will be back for you. I'll cover you with blankets and a tarpaulin. And I'll lock the truck. It's Sunday. I'll be back soon."

He kissed her cheek below her left eye and smoothed her

208

hair. "I love you, Hannah. You'll be warm," he said, as if to convince himself that she would live.

The weather isn't cold enough for her to die, he thought.

He moved her nearer the truck wall and bound her snugly to the wooden frame under the shelves.

"You'll be all right," he said to her.

Hannah's eyes were closed.

Streicher wrapped blankets around her, then covered her with the heavy, oily tarpaulin. He got out, locked the truck, and, leather bag in his left hand, he walked over to the station platform. He had only moments to wait before the train for St. Albans steamed in from Montreal.

He was tempting the fates mightily: he'd have to hide the black bag on the train before the border inspection.

THIRTY-FOUR

KEMPER COULD NOT MOVE. His arms and legs had been restrained with green webbed straps. The shell-shaped wall light was there above him in a bright room with three other beds. Another patient slept with his mouth open in the bed next to the window.

He closed his eyes to feel his chest. He hadn't died, but this was a hospital; Cowansville, he thought, concentrating again on the pea-green paint. Where was the pain, the vise in his chest? He raised his fingers.

What day was this? How long had he slept? Cody's Chevrolet spinning into the field—but that memory came to him like something borrowed from another life. He looked at the bed table, at the oxygen tank and black rubber mask beside his bed. Is that for me? he wondered.

The pain shot through him when he tried to raise his hips. He lay very still, waiting for the crush to come again. There was something wrong with him, something sensitive enough to register even slight muscular pressures. His mind wandered easily. He found that the naming of parts— sheets, straps, white beds, that horrid open mouth in the corner—helped to center his consciousness.

They've got my wallet, my identification. They'll have contacted the RCMP. Quenneville will get me out of here. Someone must.

He focused on events. A black and white truck. The convent and the anxious nun awake in the middle of the night.

Someone had come for Hannah. Someone who frightened her. The man who forced her into the truck had been badly mauled. Who was he?

The railroad dispatcher said Jaeger was out sick. Had Jaeger called in because his face was ruined? Jaeger was a sonofabitch. It has to be Jaeger, he thought. Then he remembered the frightful man. Sister André had said he was taller than Hannah and had light hair! That's not Jaeger. Jaeger has dark hair and Jaeger's small.

A nurse stuck her head into the room, seemed delighted to see him awake, and approached his bed. She clucked and said he'd been asleep for a long time. "Do you want me to call a priest for you?" she stammered in French.

He asked her again for the time. "Never mind the time," she said. "You've got to rest."

He asked her again, coldly.

She clicked her tongue and touched his hair. "You've had quite a time," she said.

Kemper told her to take off the straps.

"Will you be good?" she asked.

Bitches, he thought. Why were they all so insufferably puerile?

"I'll be good," he said. I'll be gone, he thought.

"I'll get doctor," she said. "He's gone home, but he wanted to know the moment you woke up. You've had a concussion."

His head didn't hurt.

She loosened the straps and freed his legs, his arms.

When he asked her about his heart, the woman clicked her tongue again. "So many questions," she said, patting his shoulder. "Doctor will talk to you."

Kemper said he just wanted to know if he'd had a heart attack.

"Be good," she said. "I'll be back with something for your pain. Doctor has left medicine for you. The police are here—they'd like to talk to you as well."

211

"I don't have any pain," he said, testing his hips once more. Still there, but he didn't think it was his heart.

He had a tender bump near his left ear.

After she left, he sat up to an ovation in his head. Edging off the bed, his foot touched the cold floor. He took a deep breath and thought he'd faint. He looked toward the grey locker across the room. Gingerly, he hobbled to the empty bed opposite his own. His chest ached.

He got his clothes out of the locker; his prosthetic log. His money, wallet, and car keys were in a Whitman's Sampler candy box. Dressing quickly, he tried to figure the time. Still night outside. What night? He didn't know.

Once he had everything, he looked again at his empty bed, yanked the door open, and walked down a short corridor. The nursing station was around the corner where the laughter came from. A twenty-year-old kid backed out of a room ahead of him. Kemper said hello in French when the kid smiled.

Down an internal stairway to the lobby. This *is* Cowansville, he realized when he saw the receptionist's desk and the furniture. There was a clock over the telephone switchboard as Kemper passed, jingling his car keys. He smiled at the receptionist. Six-twenty, he said to himself. Six-twenty when?

He went back to the receptionist. She said the date was the twenty-eighth, but Kemper saw that she was about to push whatever panic buttons they had here. He left quickly, limping down the outside stairs in the invigorating night air.

The parking lot was busy. An old couple approached the stairs. Six-twenty. Visiting hours, he thought. He searched and felt the adrenaline when he didn't see the Chevrolet. This is tight, he thought. How badly had he wrecked the railroad's car?

Not badly. He smiled when he saw the junk parked in the dark at the end of the parking area. A rear fender had been

212

caved in. Only one of its headlights came on when he started the car.

The Cowansville hospital seemed quiet when he pulled out, but they wouldn't be quiet for much longer, he thought. He found the road to Vermont at the end of the street. At least an hour and a half to Jaeger's on these roads. Maybe two.

He had to stop once, just off the road in a farmyard, when his vision darkened. He waited for it to pass, but the howling in his head only got worse as he breathed slowly, listening to the distant ticking of the engine.

She must be dead by now, he thought. He'd spent the last fourteen hours flat on his back with visions. He had abandoned Hannah to blood in Sutton and arrived at the convent too late to do anything other than slide off a road. This time she will be dead.

He gripped the steering wheel. The dashboard instruments were dancing yellow lights.

At the border crossing, the American immigration guard bent over to look at him and at the car's interior. The guard asked a few questions, then said Kemper would have to come inside.

"Pull it over there," he said, pointing to a parking bay at the side of the brick building.

Kemper buried the accelerator, squirming in his seat to stiffen his resolve as he dropped the car into high gear. They'd be on him quickly. He cranked the window down to flush the cold air on his face. The chorus line to infinity, the breathtaking, silent blackness was with him in the car as his wheels chattered over frost heaves and potholes.

He'd had many frights in his fifty-eight years, but he knew he'd never dangled his legs over the edge like this before.

THIRTY-FIVE

I TRAVELLED BY THE NIGHT TRAIN of December 28/29 to Ottawa, to stay with Lord Athlone, the Governor-General.

Streicher met Jaeger in the rail yards in White River Junction, Vermont. Jaeger grinned when he saw Streicher in the CN conductor's uniform. The German had covered his eye with a black patch. In the dull light under the lamp, Jaeger asked him what he'd done to his face.

"What time is it?" Streicher asked.

Jaeger said it was almost seven.

"Where's the train?"

"Massachusetts," Jaeger answered. "The Pennsylvania crew changed in New York with a New York, New Haven & Hartford crew, who took it to Springfield. A Boston and Maine crew will bring the thing in here about eight-thirty. What's on your face?"

Streicher said he'd used makeup to cover his bruised skin.

"You look like a whore," Jaeger said.

Streicher's eye seemed all the more intense because it was alone.

Streicher clutched his black bag in his arms while they talked quietly beside the signal shack. Streicher wanted to know where the assigned Central Vermont conductor was.

Jaeger said the man was eating in the train crew dormitory. He pointed.

"I'll take care of the conductor," Streicher said. "What's his name?"

"You'll have trouble with him. His name is Worthington. He's got his orders. Unless the St. Albans dispatcher says otherwise, he'll take this train."

"I'll talk to him," Streicher said, stepping over the rails.

They agreed to meet later in a greasy spoon near the station. Jaeger went back into the dispatcher's office to read the train orders.

The dormitory was a smoke-encrusted brick box near the roundhouse. Streicher stood at the windows, aware that he was a stranger to the yard men, wearing the greatest threat to his success on his mashed face. But the dextroamphetamine had relieved his fatigue. He was energized and ready.

Two White River Junction policemen sat at the counter with him while Streicher sipped a blistering cup of coffee. The radio over the grill had just finished the evening news with word that Churchill and Roosevelt had successfully completed the Grand Alliance between their two countries. The Americans are jubilant with their entry into this war, Streicher thought. Their joy is about to vanish with one cut of the sabre. The White House communiqué said that the British Prime Minister's address to a joint session of Congress on Friday detailed the harsh conditions Americans would face in the battle against the Axis powers. Members of Congress were certain that victory would be theirs.

Jaeger lowered himself onto the stool beside Streicher. "Pay up and get out of here!" Jaeger said.

Streicher tossed a nickel on the counter and left the diner cautiously, his bag at his side.

Sleet hit him in the face when he raised his head outside. He crossed the road to the Central Vermont station, aware of Jaeger's quick steps behind him.

"I'm not doing it," Jaeger said when he fell in beside Streicher. "Do you know who's on that train?"

Streicher said he knew.

Jaeger led him to a baggage platform. There were dozens of empty baggage carts under a long roof with few lights. Jaeger kept shaking his head.

Streicher let the conductor jabber, then touched Jaeger's shirt. "You have nothing to worry about," he said. "You're leaving in a few days. You just happened to be here—the assigned conductor became ill and you took the train for him. You've done the railroad a favor."

"What do you mean he became ill?"

Streicher's eye didn't blink. "He's not feeling well."

"Good christ!" Jaeger spat. "You're crazy! You're a maniac! Did you kill him?"

"He doesn't feel well," Streicher repeated slowly. "You've got five thousand dollars waiting for you at home. You do nothing tonight but act like a conductor. You simply be what you are. That's very easy."

"You're an asshole," Jaeger sneered. He spat on the platform. "You're going to try to kill Churchill."

"I *will* kill him," Streicher said.

"Who do you think you are? He's the Prime Minister of England—this isn't Czechoslovakia. You're a maniac!"

Streicher reached for his pipe and pouch, resting the bag on the baggage cart behind him. He glanced around to be certain they were alone.

"I'm not doing it," Jaeger said. He spat again. "And don't threaten me."

"You haven't any choice," Streicher said, filling his pipe. "They know you're here. They'll ask you to take the train when they discover Worthington is sick."

"Bullshit," Jaeger said.

"You once said you wanted to get back to Germany. Have you changed your mind?" Streicher looked away from Jaeger. "If you do go back, you'll get much more than

216

five thousand dollars for this night. I can have you out of this country in a week. You'll be free to do whatever you want. And Germany will give you more money—anything—for your part in this."

Jaeger settled his gaze on Streicher's eye. "You're a maniac. Even if you do kill Churchill, you'll never escape the Americans."

"Don't you ever call me a maniac again," Streicher said hoarsely. "I am a soldier. I have orders."

"Bullshit."

Streicher slowly reached his hand toward Jaeger; his finger touched softly on the man's throat.

"Don't touch me," Jaeger whispered.

Streicher pushed on the man's skin, his finger dimpling Jaeger's neck. Jaeger swallowed—once . . . twice.

"Try to be more cheerful," Streicher said softly. "Smile."

Jaeger leaned backwards.

Streicher raised his finger in the man's face. "Smile."

The conductor closed his eyes.

THIRTY-SIX

THE ROAD STOPPED. Kemper hit the brakes; the Chevrolet skidded through the intersection sideways, mounted the curb, and blew up a blue-lighted manger scene. Kemper heard shouts as he regained his senses. Where the hell was the stop sign? He was in a village, on someone's lawn. The house lights came on. People were rushing down their porch stairs toward him.

He gripped the wheel and kicked the accelerator, backed the clumsy Chevy over wise men and lambs, and thumped off the curb and back onto the road.

He straightened himself up in the seat. Another intersection lay ahead of him in the blackness. Route 7 was to the left. Kemper cranked the wheel, drifting onto the main highway to St. Albans.

He couldn't understand why the border patrol hadn't caught him by now. The engine coughed—he smacked the steering wheel and it caught again. A dark stone road bordered by white loomed ahead of him. House lights flashed in his windows.

Another half-hour to Jaeger's.

THIRTY-SEVEN

WORTHINGTON HAD BEEN EASY. Streicher had gone into the dormitory bathroom, where he found the old conductor alone, shaving. Worthington's dentures were in a glass on the shelf below the mirror.

Streicher had slipped into a stall, opened his satchel, gently eased the glass and rubber stopper out of his flask of dinitrophenol, dipped a toothpick into the liquid, and flushed the toilet.

Back at the sink, his bag on the floor, Streicher had nodded to Worthington, who drew a straightedge up his neck. The water was very hot. When Worthington bent over to wash his razor, Streicher swirled the toothpick in the denture glass then tossed the toothpick on the floor.

He finished washing his hands and drew on his overcoat slowly, carefully keeping his face away from the old conductor, who seemed not at all curious about Streicher's eye patch.

At least *that* had been easy, he thought as he watched the train from the shadows.

Their plan had Jaeger giving Streicher a forty-minute warning before the train reached St. Albans. Streicher would drop the dinitrophenol into the water service siphon pipes in Churchill's Pullman before joining Jaeger in a forward car. They'd jump together from the train as it crept through the clacking switch points in the St. Albans yards

219

and be far behind the train when Churchill's jellied corpse was discovered.

But with Hannah in the truck in St. Johns, Streicher knew his original plan to leave Jaeger dead in his cottage must change. Streicher was not getting off at St. Albans.

The rail yards had been dusted with snow, but now a cold rain dripped down the flanks of the long, maroon Pullmans. Streicher saw the yellow shield of the Pennsylvania Railroad painted on the coach side as he walked toward the knot of men further down the track.

Jaeger glanced at him when Streicher came up to the group of five men. Streicher eased his satchel forward and let it rest on his thigh.

One of the train men was furious. Jaeger motioned his head for Streicher to step around the group to stand next to him. Streicher had to resist a wild urge to search the windows above him for Churchill's face as his shoulder rubbed the coach. Streicher took out the railroad watch and opened its case. Five minutes to nine.

Streicher listened. The Central Vermont was running an inspection train comprised of a locomotive and two cars ahead of the special. It had just left the White River yards for the three-hour trip to St. Johns, Quebec. The big man in the overalls was an engineer. "Not enough time," he said to a man with a black hat who seemed to work for the railroad. The black hat had papers rolled in his hand. "Ryerson will be fifteen minutes ahead of you," the black hat said. "Just watch for flares and torpedoes."

Jaeger motioned for Streicher to pull his cap down over his eye. Streicher thought he'd seen Jaeger's lips begin to smile. Jaeger is good for it, he thought.

"Don't like it," the engineer said. "Fifteen minutes isn't time enough to piss. Call Cody and ask for thirty minutes. I'll be damned if I'll run up Ryerson's ass."

"You're pulling twelve cars, Parker!" the black hat

220

snapped. "Damn it, you'll never catch Ryerson over the mountains."

"Give me thirty minutes," the engineer said. "Romeo! Bring up the steam! I'll be right there."

Another man in a grey overcoat raised his hand. "I don't care how you do it, gentlemen. I want those switches set and locked after the inspection train. I don't give a damn about fifteen minutes."

"Okay," the exasperated black hat said. "I'll telephone Cody. But he'll have something to say about this one."

That was a question. The engineer cleared his throat and blew a huge gob of spit under the train. "Fuck 'im. Cody's not driving. I am. And I'm not going to barrel-ass over ice at seventy miles an hour with Ryerson up ahead picking his nose." The engineer turned to the other man in overalls. "Get up the steam, Romeo. Jaeger, if you're in charge of this train now, why don't *you* hold us for thirty minutes?"

"I'll talk to Cody myself," Jaeger said.

Suddenly, the grey overcoat turned to Streicher. "How ya' doin'?" he said; the man's eyes were drawn to the Canadian National emblem on Streicher's cap.

"I've been better," Streicher answered.

"Haven't we all," the man said. Nodding toward the engineer he said, "Guy breathes fire, doesn't he?"

Streicher smiled and said engineers knew what they were doing. He wondered if his CN identification card would convince these men if they ever asked.

Jaeger had left the group when the engineer turned to walk to the locomotive. Streicher swung his bag and hurried after him. The grey overcoat was at his back.

"Where are we?" the grey overcoat asked.

Streicher stopped and looked at him. "White River," he said, frightened.

"Where is White River? I know the name of the place."

"Halfway up the state of Vermont," Streicher said.

221

"Where's the snow?"

"No snow," Streicher answered.

"You goin' to Ottawa with us?" the man asked.

"St. Johns," Streicher said. Jaeger waited at the steps to an open coach door. The rain was colder, almost in pellets of ice on Streicher's black sleeve as he opened his watch again.

The overcoat went by him. "Nice of the Canadian National to send you down here. Very efficient," the man said before he jumped up the steps into the coach.

Jaeger shut his eyes.

He held Streicher's arm until the grey overcoat vanished into the coach above them. "Don't push it," Jaeger whispered. "Your friend is Secret Service."

Streicher sucked in his breath and pulled himself up the steps behind Jaeger.

THIRTY-EIGHT

THE DRIZZLE HAD CEASED only long enough for a polar gust to glaze the fountain nymphs' breasts in ice as St. Albans lay stunned in a late-evening hush before the Monday morning and the coming New Year. Taylor Park and its attendant, the Jesse Welden House, were wedded in nocturnal suspension. The shoe store, the Union Bank, the drugstore, Rolly Sykes's hardware store—all were as blankly vigilant as a movie set after the director has died. The Congregational church tower rang up ten-fifteen and quit, its bell an intrusive, muffled clang that all was not well, that there was no heaven, but only the gradual, frustrating shift in time.

The purl of struck bell-metal floated over the rail yards, over the lights that danced in the wind, and over the rails that gleamed like polished silver wires on black velvet cinder. The roundhouse, the coaling tower, and the water stanchions cut sharp-edged shapes into the drizzle. A jet of steam fluttered near the train shed, as though that enormity might moan and move away from the city like a black-hulled ocean liner.

Men stood outside the train shed, the dispatcher's office windows alight over their heads.

Cody sat with his feet up on the dispatcher's desk. He passed the yellow signal form back to Eugene, the dispatcher, who wore his sleeves tight and his green eyeshade well over his face. The superintendent wanted to know what the hell turbot was.

Beaman, a railroad detective, said turbot was fish.

"For breakfast?" Cody asked the three men with him. "Send it to the CN dispatcher in Montreal—let the Canadians worry about turbot. When you're Winston Churchill you can order turbot for breakfast. You can order a goddam shark if you want to! Tell Whitley Raymond I want to know when Churchill clears Richmond."

"He already has," Eugene said.

Cody butted his cigarette in an empty coffee mug. "We better get used to having the entire road awake in the middle of the night. This is only practice for what this war will do to us, I'll tell you that."

Cody dropped his boots to the floor. "Beaman—I want the yard locked as soon as Ryerson clears the limits. Everything stops until Churchill is out of here. Where is Ryerson?"

Eugene raised his hand—the CN dispatcher in Montreal was signing off. He raised his eyes to Cody. "A mile north of Georgia Station. And Parker is twenty-five minutes behind him. And gaining."

Beaman grinned.

"That's funny, Beams, that is. Goddam Parker is hauling twelve sixty-five-foot Pullmans over mountains and he's gaining on an inspection train. Eugene! Put orders up to Ryerson when he goes through to jack open his throttle a notch or two. Tell him to be damn careful from here to St. Johns. Where's the late freight?"

Eugene said the freight was being held on the passing track just south of St. Albans.

Beaman and the other man had left the office to get out into the yards. They passed Kemper on the stairs. Cody could hear Beaman's shouts below him while the dispatcher's telegraph keys clicked. Cody snapped his lighter shut and puffed another Camel.

224

"Jumped-up dyin' christ!" Cody said when he saw Kemper come through the doorway. He spun the chair around, letting the smoke out of his mouth as he spoke. "D'you wreck that car?"

"Does Alex Jaeger ever drive a bakery truck?"

"How the hell do I know? What happened to you?"

"Shooting a few Indians," Kemper said, reaching to steady himself on one of the grey electrical cabinets. "Where's Jaeger?"

"He's working a train. Sit down."

The dispatcher was looking at Kemper with frustrated glee.

"I want Jaeger," Kemper said.

"What you want is a doctor. What the hell happened to you?"

The dispatcher said Jaeger drove a Dodge coupe.

"Where is he?" Kemper asked, swaying against the cabinet. His right hand had left a bloody palm print on the metal.

Cody explained that Jaeger was in charge of a special, due to pass through St. Albans in forty minutes. "But he's going through to St. Johns," Cody said. "Why do you want Jaeger?"

"If he didn't kill Leonard Baskins, then he knows the guy who did."

When the dispatcher said "Horseshit!" Kemper swore at him, then patiently told them a brief tale of dark roads and hell on ice. He'd been to Jaeger's cottage; he'd punched in the glass in Jaeger's door; his right hand was bleeding through his handkerchief. He told Cody about Hannah, the convent, and the Cowansville hospital. "I'm not as bad as I look," Kemper finished, unwrapping his right hand.

"You looked at yourself in a mirror lately?" Cody asked. "You should have stayed in that hospital. Eugene—get a first-aid kit for this guy. Don't bleed on the goddam

225

wires," he said to Kemper, getting out of the chair. "How do you know Jaeger's involved?"

"Can you get him off that train?"

The dispatcher had tossed his headphones in disgust and left the office, muttering "Jeezus Christ," as he passed Kemper. The telegraph key started to click.

"No, I can't get him off the train," Cody said, stretching his hand to tap the key. He was listening to the clicks.

"Then I want to get on."

Eugene was back with a red metal box. Beaman and two men came into the office behind the dispatcher.

Cody straightened up and took the box from Eugene. "That's Lucien Beebe in Essex—Churchill just went through," Cody said to his dispatcher. He tugged his watch out of his vest.

"The yard's ready," Beaman said. "Signals are set. We've locked all the iron, except for the freight yard sidings. Malone's doing that now."

"Good," Cody said, handing the first-aid box to Kemper. "Parker must be doin' ninety. Eugene, type those orders for Ryerson. Henry will take them." He turned to one of the men behind the railroad detective. "Get on the head end with Ryerson, Henry, and make sure the yard's set. Let Eugene know from the signal shack. Tell Ryerson he can't let up. Parker's coming like hell . . . damn fool."

"Who's he?" Beaman said, nodding toward Kemper, who had stumbled around the electrical cabinets to a wall map of the Central Vermont Railroad.

"Naval Intelligence," Cody said. "Get going, Henry. Make sure the roundhouse sidings are locked."

Beaman was shaking his head. "*He's* with Naval Intelligence . . . you kidding?"

"When was the last time I kidded you, Beams? Move!"

The detective's smile drooped. He said, "Yes, sir," and left the office.

Cody glanced over at Kemper, who was examining the

226

map like a man lost in the Louvre. A locomotive whistle hooted far away.

"That's Ryerson at the grain elevator," Eugene said, tapping his key.

"Tell the CN in St. Johns that Ryerson's here," Cody said. He was watching Kemper. The whistle hooted again.

"What's Churchill doing on this train?" Kemper said from the wall. His white hair over his ear was blotted and wet with blood. He turned to Cody.

"Long story," Cody said.

"Churchill was supposed to go through New York."

"Couldn't," Cody said. "FBI set this up this morning. Some chicken factory burned last night in Plattsburgh. Warped the tracks—dead chickens everywhere. We've been bustin' our asses all day to do this."

"And Jaeger's on the train with Churchill?"

"That's right." Cody realized what connections Kemper had made. "I'll be goddammed," Cody muttered.

Kemper stepped away from the map, sliding the red box onto a table, distracted. "You'll be more than damned. Jaeger may be an SS agent."

"Alex Jaeger?" Cody laughed.

Eugene, his earphones off once more, turned on his high stool to look at the man in the rumpled suit and stained shirt.

"Maybe not," Kemper said quickly. "Why did you put Jaeger on that train?"

The whistle echoed through the city. Cody said, "I had to. Worthington, the conductor I sent to White River this morning, got sick at the last minute."

"Ryerson's in the yard," the dispatcher said quietly.

"I hear him," Cody answered.

"I thought Jaeger was the one who was sick!" Kemper said.

"I thought so too," Cody answered defensively. "I won-

227

dered what he was doing in White River. But he said he'd take the special—I didn't have anyone else that handy."

The man at the convent was not Jaeger, Kemper thought. But Jaeger is on this train with Churchill.

"I can't stop the special. You can't get on," Cody said. "Not without a damn good reason."

"How about a Nazi agent assassinating the Prime Minister of Britain. That reason enough?"

Cody's face darkened, his eyes squinting. He wiped his hand across his mouth. "I don't know whether to believe you or not."

Ryerson's whistle shook the windows. Kemper felt the vibrations from the locomotive's drivers come up through the floor into his foot. Kemper saw boxes of Pearl's Insect-Go on a cellar bench, the chemistry kit, Quenneville and his radio transmissions, and a man frightful enough to enter a convent in the middle of the night.

"There's a whole lot of people on this train," Cody said. "Secret Service, FBI, reporters, photographers, government people from England, Canada, and Washington—Churchill must have bodyguards."

"He does," Kemper said.

A gathering rumble shook the building as Ryerson's 4-8-2 Mountain-type engine blew out of the train shed and roared beneath the dispatcher's windows.

"They sent a signal from Waterbury asking for fish in Canada for breakfast," Cody said. "They wouldn't be talking about fish if there was any trouble."

"They would if they didn't know there was trouble." Dinitrophenol is soluble in water, Kemper thought. No hydrogen sulphide this time. But why, if you are SS, do you take the enormous risk of chasing down a woman the night before you kill Winston Churchill? Doesn't make sense, he thought.

"I'm getting on that train," he said to Cody.

"I'll have to think about this," Cody answered.

"Not up to you," Kemper said.

Cody was a man accustomed to directing other men's lives. He drew up his shoulders. The telegraph key clicked again. "I can't stop that train without—"

"I don't want you to *stop* it. I'm getting on."

"Why not signal from here? I can stop it at Milton."

"No, you can't," the dispatcher said quickly. "There's no one on the key at Milton."

"Georgia Station then," Cody said. "That's the last station before St. Albans."

Kemper shook his head. "Forget it. No stops. If the train stops, Jaeger will know something is wrong."

"Not necessarily," Cody said. "We could get word to the Secret Service. Tell *them* what the trouble is!" Cody spat. "For chrissake."

"Who would take the order to stop the train?"

"The engineer. We can use torpedoes on the tracks. He'll lock the wheels. But he wouldn't know why."

"And Jaeger?"

"I see what you mean," Cody said. "He's in charge. Anything for the Secret Service would go through Jaeger."

"Doesn't sound promising, does it?" Kemper asked. "How long?"

Cody turned for his dispatcher, glancing at the clock.

"Normally, thirty-three minutes on schedule," Eugene said. "But Parker has no schedule."

"Twenty minutes," Cody said. "The engineer will bring it through the train shed at about ten miles an hour. After that, he'll go like hell for St. Johns. If you're wrong, bub, I'm in a helluva pickle."

THIRTY-NINE

"THIS IS CRAZY," CODY SAID. "How the hell are you going to jump a train?"

The two men stood in the shadow of the train shed. Kemper's cigar blossomed orange and huge.

Beaman rushed up to them. "Alex Jaeger's car is parked at the north end of the yard! Henry signaled Eugene that the yard is secure. Henry says Jaeger's car is right next to the shack!"

"What's wrong with that?" Kemper asked.

"Not anywhere near where we park 'em," Cody said quietly. "Hold on, Beaman. Churchill's coach is second to last. I'll get aboard the coach ahead of it. You take Kemper here into the last coach."

The doors on the train would be locked from the inside. Cody and Beaman carried clumsy keys that would release the locks.

"Where will we find Jaeger?" Kemper asked.

The night was dismally still, the frosted drizzle raw on their skin. "He could be anywhere," Cody said, thinking.

"He's going to jump for it here," Kemper said.

"How do you know that?"

"I don't know any of this," Kemper said. "But I've shot a few Indians."

The men huddled silently for a minute or two, then Cody reached for Beaman. "Run up and tell Eugene to locate Malone. Are we going to stop it?" he asked Kemper.

"I don't think so—depends on what we find."

Cody grabbed Beaman's coat. "Tell Eugene to find Malone. If this train doesn't stop, I want to know if anyone gets off. You hear? Anyone! Have Malone set the yard limit signal to yellow if anyone jumps. That all right?" he asked Kemper.

"Get on quietly," Kemper said. "Find Jaeger. And look for a man with a badly cut face. He's bigger than Jaeger. He may be dressed in a CN conductor's uniform." Kemper gazed into the dimly lighted train shed. "Be very careful," he said. "Don't get near Jeager's friend alone—these guys use poison that'll kill you in seconds. Remember Baskins."

Kemper felt the most inexpressible sadness filter through his mind, as though he'd lost everything he ever loved.

Cody stayed with him as they waited in the pattering drizzle.

"That's it," Cody said when the whistle whooped.

Kemper moved his stump inside his prosthetic log; the repaired strap wasn't tight enough to hold him snugly. His chest throbbed on his left side. He looked at his bandaged right hand and wondered what Beam would have to say about the patient now.

The whistle again.

Kemper brought his head up. They heard Beaman's running footsteps coming back on the cinders behind them. The engine chuffed.

The tracks curved before they entered the train shed. Kemper saw the locomotive's headlight spray the rails with silver.

"Don't show yourself," Cody warned Beaman. "Let it pass before you move."

When the light flooded the train shed with its bright beam, Kemper tossed his cigar against the wall in a cascade of sparks.

"I hope you're right," Cody said over the pounding of the engine. Its clanging bell suddenly burst into the train shed. "Let it come out!" Cody shouted to Beaman. Then: "Parker's going too fast, goddam it!"

Kemper watched from the shadows as the engineer's face passed above him . . . then the tender, and two Pennsylvania Railroad baggage cars, followed by the line of coaches. Kemper tried to count them. He couldn't.

Cody pressed Kemper's elbow tightly. Most of the coach windows were dark as the train slid past them out of the train shed.

Kemper was amazed to see Cody take three huge strides and leap for the steps of a coach. He was on.

Where was Beaman?

Kemper saw the last coach enter the train shed at the far end of the platform. He rocked with the throb of his heart.

"Ready?" Beaman shouted.

The man ran toward the train, then leapt, stretching his hand for Kemper, who ran up to the coach and felt the mighty tug as the machine wrenched his chest when he grabbed the handrail.

"I'm on!" Kemper said, more to himself than to Beaman, his face flat against the cold, wet door.

The door fell open; Beaman jerked Kemper onto the car platform.

Kemper went into the dimly lighted coach and hurried down the corridor. Beaman was right behing him.

When Kemper kicked open the door into Churchill's coach, Cody appeared at the far end of the long corridor.

"Nothing!" Cody yelled.

"Shut up!" Kemper shouted back at him.

He yanked the first compartment door. The rail yards were passing outside the windows. It was empty. Beaman was in the next one.

Kemper heard a loud voice yell "Hold it!" but he ran to the next compartment. When he backed out of the blackness, he was met by a shirt-sleeved man with a leveled pistol.

Kemper said who he was. The man with the gun spun around at Cody's racket as the superintendent crashed into another compartment ahead of them. Kemper tossed his wallet at the man and pushed past him for the next door.

"Nothing!" Cody shouted when Kemper looked again.

"Go into the next car," Kemper shouted back.

"SS agents! Dressed as conductors—they're after Churchill!" Kemper explained to the man with the gun.

Security men banged into the coach and held Cody. Beaman was quickly splayed on the floor by one of them.

Kemper explained again, huffing. They listened to him, but seemed more anxious to use their pistols as the coach swayed and skipped over the switch points.

"There *is* a Canadian National conductor on board," one of them said.

"Bloody hell!" the man with Kemper's wallet said, throwing the wallet at Kemper.

"They may try to get off here," Kemper said.

When the two men looked quickly toward the rear, Kemper grabbed one of them. "Take it easy," he said. "Be careful. They use poison." And to the others, "Where's Churchill?"

"Up forward," said the man who knew about CN conductors. "He's playing cards."

Churchill's alive! Kemper thought.

The men hurried forward, lowering their pistols, Kemper following. Despite their attempts at concealment, the parade of armed men panicked the reporters in the next coach. Kemper broke through the crowded aisle, staying with the man who knew CN conductors and who brusquely ordered the others to stick to their seats. Kemper told him to find the railroad superintendent, the big guy. Cody had quickly vanished in the chaos.

Kemper could think only that they were soon to clear the St. Albans yards. The train's speed had increased.

The forward coaches were quieter, the club car nearly si-

233

lent as men in various states of undress, most in a variety of uniforms, watched the security men hurry up the aisle.

There he is! Kemper thought when he saw the round, white head.

He stopped. A black waiter held a tray with a water carafe and glasses, ready to lower them to the table in front of Churchill.

When the Prime Minister turned in his chair, Kemper saw the puffed jowls, the eyes narrowing.

"Don't drink anything," Kemper said, and bowed.

"Good god! Are you here!" Beaverbrook and Pound sat next to Churchill.

"Not for long," Kemper smiled. "You look older, Winston."

"Well, at least *I* dressed for this," Churchill replied, eyes sparkling quickly. "No time for a cigar, I imagine?"

Cody was hurrying toward them from the front. "We got a green light!" he yelled. "No one got off!"

The train had resumed its speed as the consternation among the reporters turned to anger. Neither Jaeger nor the CN conductor had been found.

Kemper asked Cody quietly between two coaches if Jaeger could have jumped before the train shed.

Cody said he could have, but his men in the yards would have seen Jaeger and anyone else if they'd left the train. The signal would have been yellow.

Two men, both named Thompson, were Churchill's closest guards. One of them was a naval officer secretary; the other was a London C.I.D. detective. They spoke precisely, insisting that absolutely nothing had disturbed the journey from Washington.

The FBI men were hotly garrulous, taking Kemper's presence as an embarrassing breach of security while Churchill was under an American umbrella. They said flatly that they didn't believe anything he said.

However, the Secret Service chief, Webster, listened as Kemper detailed what he thought he knew.

"I saw the sonofabitch," Webster finally said. "Shit, I talked to a CN conductor in White River Junction. He had an eyepatch. He was with the other conductor."

Cody took Beaman and two FBI men on another search of the train.

Webster turned to a younger man at his shoulder. He wanted the train held at St. Johns until everything was under control. "You aren't wrong," he said to Kemper. "I saw both of them. But why didn't they try to kill him before they got off?"

"They couldn't shoot him—they couldn't show themselves and get away, not in this mob," Kemper said. "My bet is they've left a surprise behind. And who says they got off?"

"They aren't here."

"We don't know that."

"I've had the food shut up," Webster said, "and the liquor. No one is to drink or eat a thing until we get this straightened out."

"Shut off the water, if you can. Whatever you do, don't let them even wash their hands—nothing!"

"We've got two cars filled with press up forward. I've had them locked in."

When Kemper and Webster went into the next coach, they met a man carrying a black bag, who introduced himself as Wilson. "Now that matters have settled, I'd like a look at you," he said to Kemper. "I'm a doctor."

Then Beaman came up. "Cody says you're to come with me. He's found Jaeger!"

The conductor was on his back in the front baggage car, his eyes wandering, his breath coming in short spurts. There was a horribly jagged scratch dug into his right cheek and down under his jaw.

Cody stood over him. "I found him behind that trunk," he said. Kemper looked at the heavy steamer trunk. "We've searched everything else. I can't find the other one."

Kemper knelt beside Jaeger and turned the conductor's face. "Get the doctor," he said.

"He's alive," Cody said.

"Not for long," Kemper answered as he saw how deeply Jaeger's cheek had been torn. "A needle did this," Kemper said as he watched the conductor's eyes twitch with whatever mysteries they were watching. "Where is she?" Kemper asked.

Jaeger's eyes bulged; his chest rose, then subsided.

"Where is Hannah?" Kemper asked again.

The eyes centered on Kemper's face.

"Where is Hannah Doll?"

"Poor bastard," Cody said. "What's wrong with him?"

"Someone tried to inject him with poison. I can smell it."

Cody said he couldn't. Kemper realized that Cody felt a strong tug for his dying conductor—Jaeger was, after all, one of Cody's men.

"Not enough to kill him quickly, though," Kemper said sadly.

Wilson confirmed that Jaeger was nearly dead, and that the scratch on his cheek seemed to be his only injury.

Kemper sat down near Jaeger while the others covered the conductor with a blanket to keep him warm. When Webster came to sit next to Kemper, the Secret Service chief said, "You were right. We'll be in St. Johns in twenty minutes. We'll take him off there. The other guy must have jumped."

"No," Cody said. "The yard signal was green. We're going to look again. Parker must be doing nearly eighty. He'd be crazy to jump after the yards."

The baggage car was cold. Kemper felt exhausted, spineless. His shoulders ached.

"Come back to the coach where it's warm," Webster said.

Kemper looked up at Webster and Cody and shook his head. "I'll stay here."

As he left, Webster told a boyish FBI agent to sit on the floor next to Jaeger.

What did those eyes know? Kemper wondered. He tried again to talk to Jaeger, but gave it up and got off his knees.

Why was Jaeger in this car? Kemper looked toward both ends of the baggage car, over the valises and suitcases and trunks.

He walked back to the tail end of the car, stepping over broken glass. Had the CN conductor gone out this door? Kemper snapped the handle and stepped between the cars. The rubber curtain covered the shifting plate—the doors out here were shut.

Baskins! Kemper thought.

He turned and went back into the baggage car. Both side doors that slid on tracks along the wall were chained and padlocked.

There had to be a door open. Somewhere!

The FBI agent looked up when Kemper stepped over Jaeger. The head end door was closed. Another chain and a brass railroad padlock. The windows in this door were barred.

Kemper yanked the chain that had been wrapped securely around the latch handle. A loose end of broken chain fell away and swung against the wall.

Kemper slid the loose end through the hasp and cracked the door to the rushing black cold. The rear wall of the tender was there.

Kemper unwound the four-foot length of chain; the padlock dangled like a Christmas ornament in its middle.

He looked back at the FBI agent on the floor of the car. And at Jaeger, dying.

237

Then again out the door—the tender, its black hulk humping with the speed of the train like the ass end of an elephant.

There was a ladder up one side of the tender's bulkhead.

Kemper kept the chain with him as he edged along a narrow metal framing. The rails and ties blurred below him, the dense blackness of a forest rushed by on either side of the tracks. Coal ash from the engine exhaust burned his eyes.

His head hit the tender bulkhead when he caught the ladder. He hung on, the chain like a pendulum over the tracks. He wound the thing around his arm.

Up the ladder. The engine was far ahead, its white plume of power spewing high into the night sky. It was raining again, he realized as he pulled himself onto the top of the tender. The metal decking was wet, slippery. The forward half of the tender was an open coal pit. The locomotive cab ahead was dark.

Kemper slid across the lurching, ash-covered tender and fell. The train heaved—he gripped a hatch cover, its hinges biting into his hands. His right hand seemed to be coming apart. His prosthetic log, he knew, was out over the edge of the tender. Another heave from the train would send him sliding onto the ballast at terrific speed. His chest ached, but when the tender did heave again, the ache became a sharp, incisive string of pain into his back.

He sucked in his breath and pulled himself away from the edge, both his legs sliding on the deck. The CN conductor could have jumped from the edge of the baggage car. He looked back toward the swaying train.

He'd raced through two nights to get to Jaeger's empty cottage because he thought that was where Hannah had been taken in the bakery truck. What if the truck had gone north from the convent? "Sonofabitch!" he muttered, twisiting to see the locomotive. Cody's wall map had St. Johns northwest of Farnham and the convent. Why would

the man wear a CN uniform? Because the other Central
Vermont crew would know he wasn't one of theirs, Kemper thought. But the Canadian National was waiting with
new crews in St. Johns.

The coalpit was bottomless and black. Kemper threw his
legs over its hard lip and hung on his arms, trying to touch
the top of the pile. He couldn't, and dropped, slamming
into a steel hump. He hit so hard he thought his chest had
exploded. He collapsed across the coal, his feet deep in
chipped anthracite. He rolled onto his side and balanced on
all fours before scrambling for the forward bulkhead. There
were steel rungs!

Up the rungs—the open locomotive cab. The engineer to
the right, the fireman to the left, his gloved hand turning a
valve on the boiler backhead. The roar was deafening.

He saw the other man below him—a man in a uniform,
one hand raised to hold on to a ladder railing on the tender.

Kemper unwrapped the chain. He used his arms to inch
along the steel edge of the bulkhead, his prosthetic log
whacking the metal wall somewhere below him.

The train had emerged from the woods into open fields.
Kemper saw houses speed past out of the corner of his eye
as he crept nearer the man in the conductor's cap.

Finding the rungs in the corner of the tender with his feet,
Kemper braced himself. He got the chain in both his hands.

The man's head bobbed.

Kemper tossed a loop of chain out over the head and
pulled as hard as he could.

He heard the head slam into the tender bulkhead.

Kemper wrapped the chain once around the railing and
pulled again. The man's hat was gone!

Kemper saw the pistol come up—he reached for it.

A shot, like a puff of wind, went past Kemper's ear.

He held the chain tight in his left hand, grabbed the man's
hand with his right, and came away with the pistol.

He heard the engineer shout. Kemper looked up as the fireman turned, his black face and white eyes aghast.

Kemper hung over the edge of the tender to get near the man's head, holding the pistol away from the man's hands that grabbed and tore at the chain.

"Where is she?" Kemper bellowed. Again. He screamed into the man's ear. "Where is she!"

"Stay away!" Kemper yelled at the fireman, as Romeo raised his hand. "Stay the hell away!"

The engineer hadn't left his seat, but the fireman had jumped onto the plate between the engine and tender.

There was a river, houses near its bank, car lights waiting at a crossing ahead of the train.

The whistle shattered the night.

"Where is Hannah Doll?" Kemper screamed into the man's ear.

The head twisted upwards—the eye patch!

The man waved his arms wildly. He couldn't breathe.

Kemper released the chain, tumbling the man in a heap on the plate. Kemper swung his prosthetic log over the edge of the tender and fell onto the man's chest. He felt the man's hands push him into the air.

Kemper rolled, then stood, chain dangling, pistol raised, balancing himself on the rattling metal plates.

The man was up, searching for his attacker. When he saw Kemper, his one eye blazed with fury; he hunched like an ape in a cage.

"Where is she?" Kemper yelled in German.

Streicher grinned, his teeth a white scar.

Kemper shot him through the shoulder.

"Stay where you are!" Kemper shouted to the crewmen. "He's a Nazi—he tried to kill Churchill!" He pointed the pistol at the fireman, who threw his hands in the air. And to the engineer: "Don't stop! Get us to St. Johns!"

Streicher had been blown beneath the fireman's seat. He got to his knees, coming for Kemper.

Kemper let off another round into the air. "Where is Hannah Doll?" he screamed in German.

Streicher fell with a crash as the locomotive clattered through switch points. Kemper saw the river ahead, the black luminous width of open water.

"Where is Hannah Doll? You bastard!" he yelled in German.

Streicher was pushing with one arm, his hand on the plate, getting his feet under him. He looked up at Kemper. "You can't have her!" he shouted, standing up, weaving, his hands searching for edges.

Kemper leveled the pistol even with Streicher's battered face. "Tell me where she is."

Streicher reached behind himself; his other arm hung from his ruined shoulder.

"You are a dead man," Kemper smiled.

Streicher swayed, reaching down for the plate to brace himself, then collapsed at Kemper's feet.

"Hannah is alive!" he cried. "She is alive!"

"Where?" Kemper shouted.

"In the truck!" Streicher yelled. "You stupid old man—she's in the truck!"

The locomotive lurched—they were on a wooden trestle, rattling, roaring across the river.

Streicher got slowly to his feet once more. Kemper looked to see where the fireman was.

Streicher hung by one arm from the gangway handrail. His legs were giving way again.

"Stand up!" Kemper shouted at him.

That one eye.

"You can't do it, can you, old man?"

Streicher's eye patch hung around his neck. He raised his head, his teeth bloody, his chin out. Proud.

"Jump!" Kemper ordered.

Streicher looked behind him into the river. He was confused. "What did you say?"

"I said, jump!"

"You are a fool! You're all fools! You will never win because you are not hard!"

"I have won," Kemper said, leveling the pistol at Streicher's face.

Streicher looked back at Kemper only once, then struggled for the edge of the plate. The river below.

He was gone, flapping, screaming into the howl of the night.

Parker hit Kemper and knocked him backwards.

FORTY

"GET THIS ASSHOLE OUT OF MY CAB!" Parker was shouting as Kemper opened his eyes.

Webster and Cody were above him.

"Why did you let him jump?" Webster pleaded.

Kemper realized the train was stopped.

"Had no choice," Kemper said, trying to get up.

"Damn it!" Webster said. "How could you do that?"

"You all right?" That was Cody's voice. Kemper balanced on his legs, reaching to cling to the cold steel edge of the locomotive. He pushed Cody away. "I'm all right," Kemper said.

"The hell you are," Cody said.

Marcel Quenneville was below him at the bottom of the ladder, his great, fat Montreal cop's face staring up at him. Kemper smiled. "We are in some shit, Marcel," he said.

Quenneville was surrounded by shouting uniforms and a crowd of reporters from the train. Quenneville shrugged and reached up his hands.

Kemper lifted his face to the soothing rain, then looked for the bakery truck.

It was there. Alone in a far corner behind the St. Johns station against a wooden fence.

Quenneville had Kemper under the shoulders like a child.

Kemper heard Webster's shrill voice yell, "Get him!" But Kemper pushed them away. Quenneville had his arms.

"See the truck, Marcel?"

243

"I see it," Quenneville said.

"Keep walking."

Quenneville told them all to get away. Kemper heard the Montreal cop say, "I'll stay with him. Leave him alone!" The locomotive whispered somewhere behind him.

Kemper started to run.

Quenneville muttered, "Easy, my friend. You are in some sad shape."

Kemper kicked the handle, releasing the door. He pulled at the tarpaulin, lifting himself into the bakery truck.

Someone yelled, "Get a light!"

"Easy, friend," Quenneville said, helping Kemper unroll the wrapped bundle.

Kemper heard Quenneville swear in French.

Kemper ripped at the tape and cord. He realized he was crying. "Get her out," he choked.

"Easy, friend," Quenneville said, pushing against Kemper's leg with his enormous body. The montreal cop swore again softly in French.

Kemper raised the blanket edge and froze.

Hannah's eyes were open . . . filled with fear, then with the most incredible relief. Someone had a beam of light into the truck.

Kemper unwound her head, gently releasing her chin, then her lips.

Hannah screamed and sobbed and kicked away the cords. She tore a gold chain off her neck.

Quenneville said, "Oh, my god."

Between the cars, the maroon paint like glass, ready to step down from the platform, the stairs shining with rain, Kemper hesitated, and then put out his hand again.

Churchill gripped Kemper's hand.

"He said we won't win because we're not hard," Kemper said.

"He did, did he?" The cigar smoke curled up over the brim of Churchill's cap. "Just before he hit the river."

"I wish you well, Winston."

The grip tightened on Kemper's hand.

"I'm glad you're home, Frank—teach them well. Will you write to me? Just a line or two? Not hard . . . is that it? They don't know, do they?"

"Not yet," Kemper said, releasing his hands.

"I'm awfully fond of you, Frank. Does that make me a softie?"

"Two of us," Kemper said.

"Here," said Quenneville, giving Kemper his handkerchief. "You embarrass me."

The great maroon train was there, basking wet in the lights of St. Johns station. Hannah stood wrapped in Kemper's arms, her head buried against his chest.

"It's time," Quenneville said.

Webster waited next to the baggage cart on the platform, Cody beside him lighting another Camel. One of Webster's men at the riverbank was missing.

The Canadian National locomotive let off a wild squeal of steam into the night. The couplings crashed, the train moved.

Kemper tightened his arms around Hannah's shoulders.

"We can leave now," Quenneville said softly.

Kemper watched the coach windows. The round white face pressed to the glass.

Kemper lifted his hand to Churchill.

Churchill waved his cigar.

Quenneville reached for Kemper's arm, a huge smile on the dark Québécois face.

"How did I do?" Kemper asked his friend, hugging Hannah to him.

The fat Montreal cop shrugged.

FORTY-ONE

WHEN I RETURNED IN THE TRAIN to Washington on New Year's Eve I was asked to go to the carriage filled with many leading pressmen of the United States. It was with no illusions that I wished them all a glorious New Year. "Here's to 1942. Here's to a year of toil—a year of struggle and peril, and a long step towards victory. May we all come through safe and with honour!"